STRANGER IN VENICE

by

ROXANE BEAUFORT

CHIMERA

Stranger in Venice first published in 1998 by
Chimera Publishing Ltd
PO Box 152
Waterlooville
Hants
PO8 9FS

Printed and bound in Great Britain by
Caledonian International Book Manufacturing Ltd
Glasgow

New authors welcome

STRANGER IN VENICE

Roxane Beaufort

Prologue

I'm dreaming, she thought. I must be. I know I'm in bed with my best friend, Emma. At least my body's there, but what about the rest of me?

If I look down with my dream-world eyes, I can see us curled up like two spoons under the quilt and feel her soft breasts pressed against my spine, and this too is strange because the roof of my father's house has become transparent.

I can hear the night sounds of London, the clop of horses' hoofs, the rumble of carriage wheels, the cacophony of a city that never sleeps. The gas-lamp in the street outside casts a yellowish uncertainty through the bedroom window.

This being so, why am I in two places at once? In bed, yet here in this weird landscape of snow-capped mountains and huge ziggurats and outsized staircases rising up into infinity. And that voice calling my name, commanding yet irresistible – even tender.

The dream was so vivid, so enchanting, that she did not want to wake. She moved without conscious motivation, drifting towards the source of the seductive voice. Fragrance swirled in shimmering clouds, incense-sweet as though in church, heady as the waters of Lethé. The indigo sky flickered with rainbow shards, a celestial firework display she could have watched throughout eternity.

Had she died and gone to heaven?

Invisible hands touched her, delicate fingers skimming over her nakedness. The warm lapping of lascivious tongues pressed against her belly, venturing lower, nuzzling among the fronds of her pubic hair, sipping at the juices seeping from her cleft. The fingers circled her breasts, embroidered patterns round her nipples, then settled into mouths, nipping and nibbling.

Other hands kneaded her flesh, prodding and examining her, skittering along her body. They stroked her limbs, running lightly down her spine, hovering over the hollow where her buttocks divided, slipping between, silken caresses in her furrow, ringing her nether hole. She opened her thighs to make their invasion easier, her entire being melting into sheer bliss at this skilful manipulation.

The voice caressed her, its melodious cadences reaching deep into her epicentre as a fingertip folded back the wings of her labia and dipped into her juices. Then, slick wet, it coaxed her clitoris from its hood. Exquisite waves of pleasure rolled over her. She bathed in light as blue as the Mediterranean – in lusty crimsons and the vibrant hues of birds-of-paradise.

The voice. The radiance. As she hovered on the edge of climax so the glow formed into an iridescent column. It gyrated upwards in constant motion, melding into the starry sky that dripped down velvety darkness. It solidified into a figure, shining like basalt – a masculine figure bathed in a golden aura. She closed her eyes against the assault of such unearthly beauty, and the image remained imprinted on her retina.

The ethereal hands and lips vanished.

Now there was only him.

She lifted her lids but dared look no higher than his perfectly formed bare feet. He did not move or speak. She followed the curve of his strong legs, shapely knees, the slender thighs ridged with muscle and sinew. The fiery radiance centred on the bulky outline between his legs. His lightly furred skin shone with a silvery lustre, his flat stomach banded by hard muscle, the pectorals of his broad chest crowned with small wine-brown discs so neatly shaped that she ached to tongue them. He towered over her. Tipping back her head she gazed into his face.

Up-tilting emerald green eyes pierced hers, penetrating

her vitals, spearing the scarlet blossom of her root chakra. His expression was austere. Dark arched brows, high wide cheekbones, an aquiline nose, lips cruel, sensitive and sensual, this extraordinary visage framed in a mane of ebony, shoulder length, serpent writhing curls. Tentatively she reached out to touch him, a tingle running through her fingers to her sex as she encountered a fine substance, firelike and vaporous yet possessing the qualities of flesh.

'Who are you?' she whispered, and her voice echoed across the cosmos. He smiled gravely and shook his head, his gesture accompanied by a rustling sound – leaves in autumn – waves sifting through sand – the brush of great wings. They rose above his head, the feathers of the outer pair of an intense Stygian darkness, the inner ones blazing like a peacock's tail in full display, a hundred eyes flashing before reverting to luminous cobalt blue, to glittering sea green.

His hand rested on her shoulder. The other touched her face. His eyes measured her, even as his hands moved over her skin, one on her cheek, the other slipping down to her breast with so light a touch she was hardly aware of it. They were entirely alone, as if they stood at the top of a mountain with no one else in the universe. After Judgement Day when all souls had been weighed in the Recorder's scales. Thoth or St Michael, it did not matter which as both were one and the same.

Sounds now, music in the distance, barely heard – women's voices high and clear, as alluring as the Lorelei, and an undertone of sonorous chords. She sank into the music, sank into the entity's embrace.

His thumb revolved on her nipple, feather-light, possessive. He was marking her as his own and she wanted nothing but to yield. Pleasure stabbed her, connecting with the ultimate centre of sensation hidden between her secret lips. She heard a whimpering noise, realising it was herself.

'Oh, yes... whoever you are, whatever you are. Angel or demon... don't stop!'

With infinite grace and delicacy his fingers alighted on her other breast. Both nipples resonated in harmony, joined by a third song as her clitoris thrummed. She stared into the mystery of his eyes, seeing worlds within worlds, and he silenced her cries with his mouth, the pleasure-shock making her head spin. Such a mouth, such lips – so sweet. Perfumed breath like a breeze wafting from spice islands, yet with an underlying bitterness – like iron – or blood.

"And he on honeydew hath fed and drunk the milk of paradise", she thought, while thought was still possible.

His tongue glided over the cavern of her mouth, exploring her teeth, her palate, her own tongue coiling round his, a passion dart. His arms tightened, the heaviness of his phallus pressing into her belly. Might and length and thickness, a priapic organ on a scale with his height and power. She wanted to touch it, to close her palm around it, though her puny thumb and fingers would never meet.

They were rising, the scintillating towers shooting away to become no more than a speck of diamond dust. The music grew louder, woven together as many strands of silk in a multihued tissue. Every part of her responded, the great symphony of sound filling her with a sense of expansion, liberation and joy.

Her thighs relaxed and the pressure of his magical phallus increased, icy-cold yet burning white hot, boring into her swollen labia, a brand to sear the damp, sensitive membranes. She opened her legs to give him greater access as their tongues locked, parted, danced, locked again.

He took his mouth away and lifted her body. She was cocooned in a vast feathery wrap, prone across his arms, supported by air as he raised her till her loins were level with his lips. She hung there, suspended in space as his fingers parted her silky-fringed labia and stroked the precious pearl concealed within. Her knees drifted slowly apart like the petals of a flower. His mouth was at her throat: the sharp nip of incisors, a wet trickle of blood, a rasping tongue licking

8

it up, fondling, tracing a pathway down to her breasts, darting from nipple to nipple, sucking each till the tip was rock hard.

His hand left her throbbing clitoris and smoothed her buttocks very lightly, trailing fingers back and forth, and she was alive for him, warm and flowing, filled with strange, thrilling sensations, wildness, wildness – and he descended into her virgin body in stages, dark head bending lower, tongue washing across her navel. The heat of fire, the heat of the music, the freezing heat of his tongue as he spread himself about her like a protective shell.

Tense, she arched her spine, wanting him to feed at her centre again. His lips continued their unhurried exploration, touching the hip bones, twin peaks on either side of her body, washing across the glossy puffed fur of her triangle and the plump mons that swept down to her rampant, pleasure-hungry bud. His tongue became a hard point stabbing at it, but leaving before it could explode, lapping around its stem and each side of the engorged labia.

She whimpered. That deft stroking returned to the gem-hard nub, settling into a steady rhythm matching the music beating in the cavities of her brain. Her moans became a shrill, plaintive cry, begging for completion – a wail, a chant, a strange litany pouring from her heart. His body was her temple. His breath her incense. His eyes her candles. His phallus her altar. She longed for him to become liquid and fill every orifice of her body. Water or blood or fire. Redemption or banishment to the deepest pit of hell – she no longer cared.

Images flashed as his exquisite tongue transported her higher and higher. Hushed now, locked in an awesome silence, seeing nothing, understanding everything, the whole universe opened before her in a blaze of light, all the colours of the spectrum fusing and overlapping. Out of that stillness came the almost invisible movement of water as it formed of dew and mist, of clouds settling and the snows melting, giving life to a myriad drops forming into streams and rivers, swelling torrents and crashing waves – age-defying, inscrutable and symbolic as the Sphinx.

Her body jerked, her head snapped back, racked with pleasure so acute it resembled pain as sensation erupted within her. A bubble of ecstasy broke into a series of mini-explosions, rolling over her one after another in ceaseless, timeless waves. Shuddering from the impact, she felt consciousness slipping away, struggling to remain, failing, drowning in the shining black pupils of his eyes.

Chapter One

Candice came awake slowly. She was aware of Emma's body nestled close to hers, and could feel her warmth through their white cambric nightgowns. Frilled, high-necked and chaste, with full skirts that reached the ankles and ballooning sleeves banded by cuffs at the wrists, these garments were all-enveloping.

Even so, despite what their mothers and chaperons might think, such demure attire did not prevent the exploration of breasts and intimate parts by determined, hungry female fingers.

Now both eighteen years of age, Candice Fortescue and Emma Collingwood had first met at finishing school and there, besides learning skills which would equip them for their expected roles in life – that of marriages to aristocrats – they had experienced their first taste of sexual satisfaction. Rosemary, the senior girl, had ruled the dormitory, and it was she who, after lights out, had initiated them into the wonders and delights of their own bodies.

A close bond had remained between Candice and Emma, even after they had left school, been presented at Court to the elderly Queen Victoria, had their 'coming out balls' and attracted the attentions of several eligible suitors. Candice had become affianced to one of them, Clive, Viscount Kerrick, the son of an Earl, who her parents had decided was an admirable choice for their only daughter.

Waking fully into the dawn of a spring morning, she thought about him and sighed discontentedly, an ember of resentment smouldering within her at having her future mapped out for her. Almost in a spirit of defiance, she slipped a hand into the button opening of Emma's nightgown, finding the swell of voluptuous breasts crested by luscious nipples that hardened at her touch.

Candice worked on these tender targets lovingly, her juices wetting her inner thighs as her own teats tingled in sympathy, while the ardent bud between her legs thrummed.

What could she want more in the world than her beautiful, caring, amorous girl friend? How convenient it was that when she came to stay no one questioned their right to sleep together, even though Emma was given an adjoining bedroom. It was a common enough custom among young girls who liked to giggle and chatter far into the night, and was considered perfectly proper.

But Candice was to be married, promised to one of those strange and alien creatures called men. Always chaperoned by her mother or Miss Gwenda Turner who had been employed to guard her virtue, she had never been alone with Clive – not truly alone – this would not be permitted until the ring was safely on her finger. Then, like a sacrifice to Hymen, god of the nuptial bed, she would be handed over to him.

It would be within the law for him to treat her as he willed – possess her virginity, whether or no she wanted him, and put children in her without a by-your-leave. She would be his chattel, as much his property as his horses, his estate in Ireland, his tin mines in Cornwall and coal-fields in Derbyshire.

The thought of being owned was distinctly repugnant.

It was all very well for the ladies of the sufferage movement to rant on about the rights of women. There had been no reforms as yet, and these were unlikely to happen for years to come – if ever. Not that Candice worried her head over political issues, but it was impossible to avoid hearing her father going on about the shameless exhibition these rebellious harpies made of themselves.

Candice privately thought "bully for them", using one of her brother Fabian's slang terms which she, as a genteel young lady, would never be allowed to voice. It might be fun to join protest marches and be written about in the daily newspapers.

Clive was good looking, personable, approved of by her father, Lord Oliver Fortescue, and admired by her mother, Lady Sarah. Candice had only a vague idea of what took place between a man and his bride on their wedding night. Though her fellow-pupils had whispered about it at school, the act was still shrouded in mystery, and birth even more so. Some believed babies were found under gooseberry bushes, others, more enlightened, imagined they were born from a woman's navel. None of them had the true facts.

Clive stirred Candice's curiosity, but not her budding passions. She felt the same affection for him as she did Fabian. They rode together, played tennis on the wide lawns of her family seat, Hightor Grange in Gloucestershire, entered archery contests, were of the same background and expectations, their betrothal approved of by both sets of parents – and yet – and yet—

Suddenly her dream returned, vivid and powerful.

Her heart thumped and a coil tightened in her womb, making the little pink kernel of flesh that crowned her cleft harden beneath its cowl. So savage and wonderful a lover – so strange a dream!

Though an untried virgin, she had felt, or imagined that she felt, the thickness of his ice-cold phallus boring into her unbreached channel, filling her with pain and bliss, his fingers palpating her sensitive bud, bringing her to ecstasy.

But even as she struggled to keep hold of the vision, so it fragmented, splintering like glass and leaving her bereft. Only the faintest of recollections clung to the edge of consciousness.

Desire remained, however, a burning, pulsing need that made her groan and seize one of Emma's thighs between her own, grinding her pubis against it as she sought relief. Emma's response was immediate and equally urgent. She gasped, pressed her leg up hard for an instant, then freed herself momentarily, wriggling into a sitting position and pulling her nightgown off over her head.

Now she was naked, her skin like alabaster in the misty light stealing between the half-opened window drapes.

Candice stared admiringly at such beauty. Chestnut curls tumbled over Emma's sloping shoulders and across her full, rounded breasts and pinkish-brown nipples. Her red, cushiony mouth was parted in eagerness to taste kisses, and below the swell of her belly, her wet delta was exposed, fringed by a luxuriant bush.

Candice bared her own fair-skinned body and cradled her breasts in both hands. They were smaller than Emma's, firm and high, the coral peaks rising from blush-pink areolae. She caught the scent of her own arousal, a rich brew like honeysuckle borne on a sea breeze. And perfume wafted from Emma's cleft, too, a deeper note, reminiscent of wood-smoke.

'I had a dream,' Candice murmured, her voice husky in the dimness. 'It was so strange... like a poem... Coleridge's *Kubla Khan*, perhaps.'

'You're a funny old thing... so romantic, with your nose always buried in a poetry book. Tell me about your dream,' Emma replied indulgently, leaning forward and opening her legs to wrap them round Candice's body, while her arms embraced her, breasts brushing against breasts.

'I can't recall much, but there was a man,' Candice continued, wanting to speak of it in order to give it substance, even as she allowed her hands to wander over that magnificent body offered to her so generously.

'Was he handsome?' Emma asked, then moaned softly and lifted her ribcage as Candice took one nipple between her thumb and forefinger and rolled it gently.

'I think so,' Candice said, struggling to pull together the tattered remnants of memory. 'Powerful... harshly

14

handsome... cruel. Like that statue of an avenging angel that stands in the chapel at Hightor.'

'A holy warrior with a sword?' Emma murmured, taking Candice's aching tips into her fingers and mirroring the exquisite pleasure her friend was lavishing on her.

'No... not exactly... perhaps once... but not any more. Oh Emma, I dreamed that he put his masculine organ into me.'

Emma paused in what she was doing, her full lips open in surprise. 'He did?' she exclaimed. 'But how do you know? Have you ever seen a man's part?'

Candice shook her head, 'Of course not... only in paintings and on marble images at art galleries, and then it's usually covered by a fig leaf.'

'How can you dream about it, then?' Emma demanded sensibly, and slid down beneath the covers, drawing Candice with her.

'I don't know,' she answered, going limp as she felt the familiar stroking of Emma's hands working across her waist, past the flatness of her stomach, then pausing so she could play with the curling blonde hair that coated the plump mount of Venus.

'Did you reach spasms of delight, as you do when I touch your little button?' Emma asked, close to her ear, her breath sending a frisson of excitement along Candice's nerves. 'Did it hurt you? Was it huge and hard? Remember Rosemary telling us how one of her brother's friends had unbuttoned his trousers and shown her his? She said it had reared up stiff as a poker and, after he had stroked it a few times it had suddenly spurted out creamy liquid. Is this what happened in your dream?'

'I think so, but I can't quite recall,' Candice cried, her excitement mounting as Emma's middle finger worked between the silky wings of her labia and found the sliver of flesh that was the seat of satisfaction.

She lifted her pelvis from the feather mattress, and Emma increased that enticing friction, bending to suck one of

15

Candice's nipples into her mouth, lapping at it with the point of her fleshy tongue. A well of delight fountained within Candice, and she clawed at the sheet with her fingernails in the convulsions of release.

As she died in that instant of supreme bliss, the image of a dark, saturnine face appeared behind her closed eyelids. Longing stabbed her, and her heart was like a raw wound, aching for something unattainable. Tears welled up, streaking across her temple and dripping on to the pillow.

'Don't cry, darling,' Emma soothed, catching a tear on her fingertip and touching it to her mouth.

'That was so wonderful... I thought I was dying...'

She felt Emma opening her with her thumb, pressing into the soft notch and meeting an obstruction, then heard her say with a chuckle, 'Well, whatever you dreamed, my love, your maidenhead is still intact. No man has thrust his appendage into you yet. You're ready for it though, if it's tormenting your dreams. So long to wait, too. The wedding isn't till next year.'

'I'm glad it's delayed,' Candice confessed. 'I don't think I want to be married.'

'Nonsense,' Emma retorted briskly. 'I can't wait to lose my virginity and start enjoying freedom. No more tiresome chaperons. As a respectable married woman I'll be able to go about alone, apart from my maid and coachman... and entertain anyone I fancy in my drawing room at tea-time. I was rather wondering if your brother might propose.'

'But you haven't met him yet. He's been away finishing his studies, in Paris,' Candice pointed out.

'I'm sure he'll do, from what you've told me about him,' Emma replied carelessly, adding, 'How splendid it would be if I became your sister-in-law.'

'Oh, yes. We could still be together,' Candice enthused, the last waves of orgasm rippling through her loins reminding her of how dear Emma was to her.

'He arrived late last night, after we had retired, didn't he?

16

I shall take special care with my appearance when we go down to breakfast this morning,' Emma announced. 'The Fortescue heir, and I'm sure my parents would consent. Two ancient families united. What could be more appropriate?'

'But you may not like him,' Candice demurred.

'Of course I shall. Haven't you told me he's very handsome? Now, tell me more about your dream lover. If you ever found him would you share him with me?' Emma asked, hazel eyes sparkling with mischief.

'Naturally,' Candice asserted, yet deep inside she knew that she would want to keep him entirely to herself, his every energy directed towards her and her alone.

'And we'd be able to go on making love, sisters by marriage who enjoyed each other's company,' Emma said. 'I adore stroking you, seeing your expression at the sublime moment, feeling you tremble as you peak... completely out of control.'

'It's almost frightening,' Candice breathed. 'I can't help myself. Even if Papa walked in, I'd still have to climax. You satisfy me so beautifully.' As she spoke her hands were on Emma's milk-white thighs, parting them slowly but firmly, and then she said, 'Now I'm going to return the favour.'

She knew she would have to hurry. Already she could hear the servants going about their chores, dusting, lifting ashes and re-laying fires, while breakfast was being prepared in the basement of the impressive Mayfair mansion. Soon Miss Turner would be coming in to disturb them, bringing Maisie, the chambermaid, carrying a jug of hot water for their ablutions. But the temptation to indulge in further passionate embraces was too strong to resist.

'I'm ready for my special treat,' Emma murmured as Candice's fingers combed the tangle of russet curls adorning her pudenda.

'Do you really like it?' she teased, and spread the silken petals open to expose the rose-red avenue nestled between.

'You know I do,' Emma gasped, her thighs slack and knees fallen apart to show herself even more. 'Kiss me there.

17

Please.'

Candice lowered her head, breathing in the strong aroma of her friend's pleasure garden, seeing the silvery moisture dewing the moist flesh she had revealed. She examined every nook and cranny, each soft fold, then the tip of her hot tongue licked slowly and sensually across the dewy surface.

Emma's moans became cries of distress, and her hands clasped Candice's head on either side, drawing her closer to that magical spot wherein lay the fount of joy. Candice took pity on her, yet delayed the moment of completion. She fondled each side of the swollen nub with her tongue, while stretching the labia back so that Emma's clitoris protruded like a large pink pearl.

'Ah... ah...' Emma cried in her extremity. 'For God's sake, suck it! Go on... give it to me... please...'

With her eyes closed, her own bud throbbing with desire, Candice fastened her lips round the hard gem and sucked strongly, feeling it pulse, tasting the increased flow of juices from Emma's vulva. She tongued it smoothly till she felt Emma convulse and moan inarticulately in the throes of rapturous climax.

They slumped, sighing and laughing in each other's arms, radiant with youth and all the wonder and anticipation of life.

Then, with brutal abruptness, the door swung open.

There was a startled pause, a deathly hush, before, 'Good heavens! What on earth are you doing?' cried a loud voice.

The window curtains were jerked back with a rattle of rings on brass poles and Candice looked across the room into Gwenda Turner's flinty eyes.

At once everything she had done with Emma that had seemed so harmless and natural was besmirched.

She gathered herself into a crouching position, dragging the sheet up over her breasts. 'Doing? Waking from slumber, that's all,' she retorted loudly.

'I don't think so, missy,' Gwenda returned, striding across

to stand by the bed, knuckles planted on her hips. 'You were doing more than that. Indulging in dirty practices... playing with one another. It's disgusting!'

Even as she mouthed the words, her contemptuous expression making her plain face even plainer, so Candice was aware of a hidden agenda. It came as a shock to realise that this hard-featured disciplinarian found the situation arousing.

There were two bright spots of colour on either bony cheek, and a glitter in her pebble eyes. She hovered over the bed like a scrawny bird of prey, feasting on Emma's bare, curvaceous body, and gloating on Candice's shapely shoulders that rose from the top of the sheet.

Maisie stood in the background as if turned to stone, mouth gaping. Gwenda rounded on her, flexing the thin, whippy cane she invariable carried and shouting, 'Stop staring! Get about your business, girl!'

'Yes, ma'am,' Maisie rejoined, ducking and bobbing before leaping to her task. With trembling hands she poured water into the flower-patterned china basin standing on the mahogany washstand.

She was a pretty girl who no doubt caused havoc among the menservants below stairs, but she was in awe of the formidable Gwenda Turner, as was everyone.

Even Cook, that despot who ruled the kitchen with a rod of iron, was respectful when she hove into view. Once she has been Candice's governess, but this had changed when, at fourteen, she was sent away to boarding school. Gwenda had remained as part of the household, however, sometime companion to Lady Sarah, always available to escort Candice during the vacations.

A middle-aged, embittered spinster, she had a powerful personality and it seemed that her ladyship leaned on her a good deal. Candice had never liked her, but she was not a person to be gainsaid, almost a spy in the camp, ever running to Lady Sarah with exaggerated tales of misdemeanours.

19

Added to this was her frequent use of the cane.

She firmly believed in the old adage, 'Spare the rod and spoil the child.'

Well, I've certainly not been spoiled, Candice thought ruefully, wondering what form her punishment would take.

'Get up, get dressed, breakfast with his lordship and Lady Sarah, and then come to see me in the schoolroom,' Gwenda commanded, and ran the cane through her raw-boned fingers, eyes narrowed thoughtfully. 'I shall not upset your Mama by reporting this rude behaviour to her, and will myself decide how best to deal with you. Such ungodly acts must stop forthwith. As for you, Lady Emma! Well, I'm shocked and surprised, but it's not for me to correct you. As a guest in this house, I assume you have been influenced by Lady Candice.'

Yet even amidst this tirade, her lean breasts were rising and falling quickly beneath her blue striped tight-sleeved blouse. She moved her legs in an agitated manner under the long, bell-shaped black barathea skirt, clinched at the waist by a wide leather belt with a silver buckle.

These were the only signs of inner turmoil. Apart from that, her dun-coloured hair was piled high round hidden horsehair pads and kept in place with sharp pins and tortoiseshell combs, and her whole appearance one of neatness and rigorous control.

Candice shivered, her palms and bottom stinging with the memory of former canings, and she thought of Clive with a sense of relief. Once she was married, Gwenda Turner would no longer hold sway over her. But would he? Her spirits sank as she wondered if she would be replacing one dominating person with another.

The tall dark man stood on the battlements, the strong breeze whipping at his enveloping black cloak.

The castle clung tenaciously to the top of a precipice that plunged in a sheer drop for hundreds of feet. Below, jagged rocks projected like giant's teeth, and a cataract thundered into the ravine, spray rising in a fine mist. A drawbridge spanned the dizzying drop, connecting the frowning edifice with the mainland.

He leaned against a stone bastion, positioning himself so that he might survey his domain. The roof was massive, flat and leaded, with buttresses and balustrades and nests of tall, twirled chimney pots. Mythical beasts, part griffin, part dragon, guarded each corner. He smiled sardonically and saluted them. They stared back at him, stone shields gripped between stone talons.

A banner streamed in the wind from the top of a central tower. The gold of its crest flashed in the first rays of light creeping over the horizon, and the crimson markings shone like fresh blood.

As the sky paled he could see an ocean of green covering the slopes away to the right. The hollows were still dark, while the peaks glistened, their snowy caps reflecting the dawn. It was spectacular, this Carpathian Mountain fastness, with vales and waterfalls and rocks tossed in wild confusion by some prehistoric eruption. The air was like wine, and sounds travelled clearly; the lowing of cattle, the distant tinkling of goats' bells.

Her presence was everywhere. He could feel it bubbling inside him like the volcano that had shaped his land. So close now. He could almost reach out his hand and touch her. He had done so in spirit in the night just past, but now the hunger was in him and the time had come for a closer, more intimate, physical as well as spiritual unity.

The power was strong. He had rested well, his vigour renewed, and was preparing to go forth into the world again. Once more he would seek she who had been born to be his, and he vowed that this time he would not lose her. Nothing should part them, neither God nor man nor Armageddon.

The wind was fierce, blowing his long black hair away from his face, throwing the high cheekbones into strong relief. His eyes gleamed pure green against his pale skin, his keen expression and aquiline nose like that of a raptor; beautiful – mesmeric – dangerous.

And he *was* dangerous. Aware of it and revelling in it. Once, maybe, he might have had regrets, once – at the beginning – but that was long ago.

His own omnipotence thrilled him. Wanting burned in him like an insatiable thirst; a human hunger, the primal force of lust that over-rode that other appetite by which he survived. He wanted to claw and fuck and possess – *sexually, basically – like a living animal*. And this precious hour before dawn was his moment to do so.

He closed his eyes and his right hand moved to the front of his black trousers. There he paused, savouring the sensation as his phallus stirred, rising against the inner surface of the material, the glans bulging from the foreskin. A sensualist, greedy to snatch at every experience, he relished the contrast of flesh and fabric.

Pleasure coursed through him, and he braced himself, legs astraddle as he opened his flies and withdrew his fully erect member. His eyes gleamed as he glanced down at it, and he pictured the girl in his mind, almost feeling her mouth closing over his swollen cock-head.

A single clear droplet appeared at the slit, and he massaged it over his organ, his touch slow and contemplative, rubbing the helm and down the rigid, vein-knotted stem, then up again, circling the ultra sensitive frenum.

The girl! He sent his mind out to her but met nothing.

His body yearned for release. He felt the burn of passion, his testicles surging, his cock slippery between his fingers. Now, surely, she must be aware, lying in her virgin bed? Surely she must feel his urgency and move heaven and earth to come to him?

He lifted his head and snuffed the air. The miles between them were nothing. He could smell her, that warm, perfumed essence of love-juice, and the bitter-sweet odour of the blood

22

that pulsed in her veins and oozed from her uterus during her monthly cycle. He wanted to drink of it.

He longed for their union of flesh, his hand becoming the velvet soft glove of her vagina, his fingers speeding him towards his crisis, even as he imagined her swooning in his embrace. He felt himself melting, dying, drowning in her vaginal depths, experiencing supreme spasms of the flesh that resembled pain as he reached his apogee.

His libation shot from him, arcing against the sky in a luminous spray. He collapsed against the wall, trembling from head to foot, his ice-cold semen searing his hand.

A rooster crowed in a barnyard far below in the valley. He started and flung up an arm, shielding his face from the ever strengthening rays of the sun.

Swift as thought he removed himself.

Now he was inside the fortress, descending by a treacherously winding staircase and reaching a passage flanked by arches. It yawned ahead, filled with inky darkness. There were mouldy stains on the slippery flagstones, and the damp air was heavy with rotting undertones.

The drip, drip of water was familiar to him, as were the crops of pale, sickly looking fungi that festered in corners. The walls glistened with an unwholesome slime, and torn pennants drooped overhead, still attached to the lances that had carried them into battle centuries ago. They rustled slightly, whispering of past glories.

He came to a door, studded with nails and banded with iron. He focused his power, passing through it effortlessly and then slipped along deserted galleries and across echoing, sombrely magnificent reception rooms, each richly ornamented with gilt and carvings and treasures worth an emperor's ransom. Not a finger of daylight filtered through the heavy wooden shutters and enveloping drapes that covered every window.

Finally he reached his destination, a secret chamber in the very heart of his kingdom. Huge white ecclesiastical candles wept waxen tears from wrought-iron holders, the smoke from their wicks rising straight to the vaulted ceiling, as if pulled by invisible strings. The pungent smell of incense wafted from beaten gold chafing dishes, and every rare and lovely object in his possession, acquired down the ages by fair means or foul, had been gathered there.

Dusty, though still luxurious purple curtains shrouded the arched embrasures and poured like velvet rain over the centrepiece of this fantastic chamber – the great, canopied seigniorial bed.

His eyes went to it, and he staggered with the force of emotion rushing from that wounded, abandoned place which once his heart had beaten.

He wanted her there with him, sharing his couch. He was desperate for this beautiful, innocent girl who would love him and not cringe from him. He longed to warm his freezing hands in the heat of that vital fluid pulsing through her veins, bathe in it, feed off it, make her companion for ever.

He was tired of being condemned to an eternity of wild, howling loneliness. Oh, yes, he was surrounded by creatures of his own ilk – creatures as lost as himself, but this was not enough. Caught in a vortex from which there was no escape, he would always suffer longing and frustration unless he could persuade her to join him. With a sigh, he mounted the shallow steps leading up to the bed.

He entered the womb-like interior and lay back against the black satin pillows, his long, elegant limbs stretched out. His eyelids closed, weighted with a catatonic sleep that resembled death.

Just for an instant he saw her again, then felt himself falling, helpless, tossed like a leaf, sucked into the utter blackness of oblivion.

The breakfast room was filled with sunshine. It ignited sparks off the silver entrée dishes containing liver and bacon, boiled eggs, kedgeree and porridge that crowded the massive sideboard.

Silver racks bearing slices of toast were set on the pristine damask covering the long, lyre-legged table. Silver cutlery flanked each Royal Doulton place setting, and a silver tea-pot nudged a silver coffee-pot next to delicate, gilt-edged cups and saucers.

Binns, the hatchet-faced butler, stood to attention, his eagle eye scrutinising the footmen. He had already placed a copy of *The Times* by Lord Oliver's plate, one he had taken to the butler's panty after the paperboy had delivered it to the backdoor. There he had opened it up and stitched it down the centre before removing the lightest hint of crease with a hot smoothing iron.

It was a gracious room, a fine venue wherein to begin the day. The walls were papered in gold and white stripes, the portieres fashioned of honey-hued brocade. The ceiling rose high, ornamented with plaster friezes and cornices and primrose yellow motifs. The furniture was Regency, dating from the time when the mansion was built by one of the Fortescue ancestors. The family always used it during the Season, from February to late July, when they retired to the country, there to prepare for the September pheasant shoot, followed by a quick trip to town in order to purchase gifts for Christmas which was always celebrated in the traditional way at Hightor Grange.

Thus the pattern of Candice's life had been ordained and, if all went according to plan, a similar existence would be hers when she married Clive, the only exception being that she would spend time at Troon Hall in County Wicklow and his town house in Dublin.

A footman pulled out a chair and, after kissing her mother's cheek in passing, Candice sat down at the table. Oh dear, she thought, I do hope Gwenda has kept her word and not tattled about me.

Emma was seated beside her and they did not dare look at one another, still possessed of the slightly hysterical mirth that had taken over after Gwenda had departed, leaving them to dress. Emma, a wicked mimic, had aped the chaperon's voice and military air.

Their personal maids had looked askance at the young ladies, but shrugged and got on with their work. It was not for them to question their superiors.

Lord Oliver read the paper while he breakfasted and Lady Sarah reeled off a list of people whom she had arranged to visit that afternoon. 'You'll come, Candice,' she intoned, dabbing her lips with a napkin. 'There's your great-aunt, for one. She's in town and wants to see you. Fabian as well. She'll demand to hear about the wedding plans and will expect an invitation.'

'Oh, Mama, do I have to come?' protested Fabian, spearing a morsel of bacon on the tine of his fork and transferring it to his mouth. 'She's tiresome. Quite potty... keeps repeating herself.'

'Don't be so disrespectful, Fabian,' his mother scolded, but fondly, he being the apple of her eye. 'You'll be old one day, you know.'

'Never, Mater,' he responded, with his marvellously boyish and charming smile. 'Neither will you. We're all going to live for ever... young and lovely and healthy. Ain't that so, girls?' and he winked at Candice and Emma.

There was something very dashing about him, and Candice could see Emma melting. She reappraised him, this brother whose physical attractions she had taken for granted. Yes, she supposed he could turn a maiden's head quite easily. She suspected that he had already sown his fair share of wild oats, and considered this unjust, when her morals were guarded so fiercely.

She had taken this up with him recently when he had come down from Oxford University and they were on holiday at Hightor, complaining, 'Why is it that you can go where you like and do whatever you fancy, but I can't?'

'You're a girl,' he had answered loftily, whacking a ball

26

with the croquet mallet and sending it bowling through the hoops set in the grass.

'So?' she had challenged, lining up her own long-handled hammer and putting carefully, unwilling to have him beat her – again.

'So, my dearest sister, you need to be taken care of. That's a chap's job, don't-cher-know... looking after helpless females.'

'Is it, indeed,' she snapped back, annoyed because she had missed her shot. 'And that's what you do with our mother's maids, I suppose, look after them?'

A flush had spread over his face, from firm jawline to where a lock of errant fair hair flopped over his brow. 'I don't know what you're getting at,' he had growled, frowning at her as he leaned easily on his mallet, a lithe figure in white flannel trousers and striped blazer, a straw boater pushed to the back of his head.

She had cocked an eyebrow at him and remarked, 'Oh, don't you? I saw you the other night. You had one of the parlourmaids trapped against the wall, and your hands were up under her skirt. She was squirming and wriggling, trying to get away...'

'She didn't put up much of a fight,' he had replied, sulkily. 'A hot little piece. Every male member of staff has had her.'

'Then you should have set a good example,' Candice had answered starchily, though she had been aware that the cotton gusset of her knickers was damp with the dew engendered by memories of him seducing the maid.

She should have made her presence felt, but had stood in the shadows, watching him hitching the girl's skirt even higher so that her black stockings and pale, ample thighs had been exposed. Candice had caught a quick glimpse of the wiry hair between them, followed by the rapid seesaw movement of Fabian's hips and the maid crying out sharply. Whether in pleasure or discomfort, it had been impossible to tell.

Even now, seated at the breakfast table, Candice felt a return of that heavy, hot feeling in her loins. What was the matter with her today? It was true that she was naturally curious about copulation, but last night's dream seemed to have opened up Pandora's Box. She was hungry for carnal knowledge, greedy to taste every forbidden fruit.

Her thoughts ran wild as she looked at her brother, seeing his curling, overlong hair, his eyes that were blue, like hers, his broad-shouldered body kept in trim by rowing, sword-play and attending the gymnasium.

Not since nursery days had she seen him naked, and wondered about the bulge she could see filling his trousers in the genital area. He was sprawled in the chair, leaning back, his legs spread, that fascinating protuberance on view.

He glanced up, caught her eye and gave her a questioning look. Candice blushed and gazed at her plate, toying with a portion of kedgeree. Then his eyes returned to Emma with the keen interest he had shown when they were introduced. Now he stared openly, and she simpered at him across the table.

Lady Sarah raised her slender eyebrows under her carefully arranged fringe. Fabian was the heir, but Emma's background was impeccable, her family tree stretching back to a Norman knight who had come over with William the Conqueror. Her father had a great fortune, too, and would provide her with a substantial dowry.

Candice saw that approving look, and her spirits lifted. If Mama gave her blessing to the match, then so would Lord Oliver. Soon Emma would become a Fortescue and they would be able to continue their intimacy.

She pressed her knee against Emma's under the table-cloth, and felt a returning nudge, while Fabian said earnestly, 'What a pity I missed your coming out ball, Lady Emma. But I'm here now and would deem it an honour if you'd permit me to ask your father if I may call on you.'

'I can't do that at the moment. He's in France,' she replied, blushing furiously, an angel in a white muslin bodice and sweeping skirt trimmed with blue baby-ribbon and broderie anglaise.

The neckline was modest, but her breasts swelled invitingly and her tightly corseted, handspan waist seemed to invite a man's fingers to encompass it.

'Then the instant he returns... please,' Fabian begged.

'Really, Fabian... how impetuous,' his mother chided gently.

'Oh, I'm not offended, Lady Sarah,' Emma assured her. 'With your permission, I'll speak to Papa as soon as I can.'

'Certainly, my dear,' her ladyship replied graciously.

Candice knew that in common with all young ladies of their class, love did not come into the marriage equation, but it would be an added bonus, and it seemed that Emma was smitten with Fabian and he with her and they were looked upon with favour all round.

She sighed inwardly, wishing she felt a stirring of emotion for Clive, but lacked that tightness in the depths of her being when she thought of him. When they danced she had no desire to press against him in the swift tempo of the waltz, and the touch of his gloved hand beneath her shoulder blades did not make her mouth dry and her secret place wet.

Unlike the tumult of emotions that racked her when she thought of her dream lover.

Would she dream of him again? she wondered, and pressed her thighs together surreptitiously so the moist labial lips chafed her clitoris. Pleasure stabbed through her, and she could feel that familiar dampness wetting the pubic hair around her opening.

'You shall come visiting with us this afternoon, Emma,' Lady Sarah pronounced, 'and Fabian will escort us. When are you expecting your parents to arrive in London?'

'In a week, your ladyship,' Emma replied, her heightened colour making her eyes sparkle with golden lights.

'Then we'll invite them to dinner. Won't we, my lord?'

Lady Sarah decided, and stared meaningfully at her husband.

'What's that?' he spluttered, dragging his eyes from the newspaper. 'Oh, yes... certainly, my dear. Whatever you say.'

'I suggest, Emma, that you take the air in the garden with Fabian this morning,' Lady Sarah continued, signalling to Binns who stepped forward and refilled her coffee cup. 'With your duenna, Mrs Smythe, in attendance.'

'Thank you. That will be most pleasant,' Emma responded.

Then Lady Sarah turned her eyes to her daughter and her expression changed, becoming stern. 'I hear from Miss Turner that you've been misbehaving again, Candice. You are to go to her as soon as you've finished breakfast. Do you hear me?'

'Yes, Mama,' Candice answered very low, while the fire of rebellion simmered in her breast and she longed to be free of this restrictive regime, parents, Gwenda, and later, a dictatorial husband.

Did a place exist like that of her dream-world, comprised of rainbow colours, celestial music, magic and a lover who would sweep her away? And would she ever be lucky enough to find it?

Chapter Two

'Ah, there you are, you dirty little girl!' Gwenda shouted as Candice sidled into the schoolroom. 'Has your paramour abandoned you, then? Is she walking with Lord Fabian? Acting the lady? So she should, the slut! And you are a slut, too... a filthy, degraded, unnatural slut who should be ashamed of herself. Are you ashamed?'

Candice stood before her, spine straight, head up, hating the woman and her coarse insinuations. 'No, Miss Turner, I'm not. I don't consider that I've done anything wrong,' she answered firmly.

'Oh, you don't, eh?' Gwenda paced round her slowly and insultingly, then stopped in front of her and jabbed the end of her cane under Candice's chin, forcing her head higher. 'You think it's a commendable thing to fumble with another woman's private parts and caress her breasts, do you?'

'I see nothing wrong in it, if it's done with respect and love,' Candice replied, staring into those hard eyes.

'It's against nature and God's commandments,' Gwenda thundered. 'Woman was made to pleasure man, not her sisters.'

'I don't recall the bible saying anywhere, "Thou shalt not kiss thy dearest friend or find her body beautiful,"' Candice retorted recklessly. She was about to be punished, and severely at that, so had nothing to lose.

The cane descended, swift as light, catching Candice across the tops of her thighs. It stung, even through the several layers of cloth that covered them.

'You mouth blasphemy!' Gwenda raged, and seized Candice by the arm, thrusting her towards the table where once books had lain open and instruction given.

31

Candice remembered her former governess with regret; a kindly woman who had left to marry, replaced by this martinet. Though Gwenda's reign over Candice had been of no more than a year's duration, during that time she had taught her the power of the rod, and the humiliation of the birch.

School had been a blessed escape from this tyranny. There the girls had never been caned, and Candice had managed to avoid chastisement during the holidays by being careful to give Gwenda no excuse. But now, on Emma's second visit, they had been caught in *flagrante delicto*, and Gwenda had leapt at the opportunity to exert her authority.

Candice felt Gwenda's hard hand in the small of her back, pushing her forward till she lay face-down across the table, feet flat on the linoleum, her posterior raised.

'How dare you! You can't do this to me!' she protested, head to one side, trying to see what the chaperon was doing.

She felt Gwenda behind her, heard her quickened breathing and the words that came, jerkily, from her lips, 'Oh, yes I can. Your mother has charged me not to bother her with trivialities. I'll deal with you as I think fit. It's some long time since you received a beating.'

Before Candice had a chance to move or protest, her skirt and petticoat were whipped up about her waist. Then Gwenda seized the tie of her cambric knickers, loosened it and dragged the garment down. The air struck Candice's bare buttocks, and she pressed her thighs together in an attempt to conceal the deep amber cleft and pouting purse of her sex which she knew would be exposed between them.

She was highly embarrassed. Though Gwenda had thrashed her before, she had never been bare-bottomed. Her position was shaming and she was unable to do anything about it, vulnerable in the extreme.

The drawers slipped lower, falling below her white stockinged knees, tangling her legs so she could not kick out. Before she had time to protest she heard a swishing sound and scalding pain shot through her as the rod landed on the rosy hillocks of her bottom.

She yelped, jerked and tried to escape, but Gwenda's hand clamped across the back of her neck. Candice wriggled and fought till those ruthless fingers dug into her scalp, grabbed a handful of hair and tugged it mercilessly.

'Lie still,' Gwenda hissed into her ear, her skinny breasts pressed against Candice's back. 'You *shall* be punished. You *shall* feel the kiss of the rod. I want to see that delicious arse of yours marked with stripes. If you needed to be frigged by a woman, then why wasn't it me?'

Candice, floundering in a welter of pain, shame and anguish, could hardly believe her ears. Had she imagined such an extraordinary statement? Could the woman be such a liar and hypocrite?

She collapsed against the unyielding pine of the table top and was caught off guard. The cane rose and fell, again and again. Pain cascaded through her naked flesh, leaving numbness in its wake. Tears sprang into her eyes, as crimson roses sprang into being on her rounded hinds where Gwenda laid on the stripes with cruel accuracy. They never landed on the same spot twice.

'Oh, stop... please stop,' Candice moaned, sobbing piteously.

Her welts came to life, her whole being burned, that hot, fiery feeling spreading from her rear to her mons. Each jerk of her hips as the thin cane lashed her, forced her pubis forward against the wood, making her clitoris quiver in excited, fearful anticipation of the next blow.

Her breasts were flattened beneath her, but every movement of her tormented body caused the nipples to crimp, chafed by her muslin chemise. Each time the rod connected with her reddened rump, the frottage pleasuring her teats joined that of the pressure on her nubbin, and a dark, secret lust augmented pain.

Never before had she experienced such a devastating

sensation. But then, never before had Gwenda insisted that she receive the rod's ministrations on her bare behind. To her everlasting shame she could feel love-juice trickling between her lower lips and longed for a finger to caress her heated passion-point.

Gwenda was sweating with exertion. Candice could smell her, and the sour-sweet odour of arousal escaping from her crotch. It was a heady brew, and added to that unreal feeling of acute agony mingled with pleasure.

Now Gwenda turned her attention to the backs of Candice's thighs, marking her from the underhang of her bottom to her knees. Then she laid the cane aside and touched the smarting flesh.

Candice was aware that she being felt all over. Gwenda was smoothing the painful stripes, handling the rounded globes, then dipping into the fissure that divided them. A finger traced round the tender rim of Candice's anus, pressed on it, then ventured lower, parting the wet lips and stroking over the groove, finally finding the swollen clitoris and subjecting it to rapid friction.

'Naughty, sinful girl,' Gwenda crooned in a strange, singsong voice. 'I've found your bud. How large it is. How quickly it responds. I'll tease it to make it bigger... yes, that's right... bigger and bigger. If I rub it till you burst with pleasure, will you do something for me?'

Candice was speechless, every nerve, each spasm of pain and quiver of joy bringing her nearer to bliss. Her beleaguered clitoris swelled beneath the chaperon's fingers, pushed out like an insolently proud berry. Increasing her efforts, Gwenda pounded hard on the tiny organ. Candice yelled as she reached a crescendo that rushed into a blur as she toppled over into orgasm.

'Now me... now me! I want you to watch,' Gwenda babbled, and hauled Candice from the table, forcing her to her knees beside it.

The chaperon rucked up her skirt. Beneath it she wore a

cambric petticoat. This too was lifted, revealing thin legs in black woollen stockings and white knickers that reached the knees.

Gwenda gasped loudly and cupped her mound in one hand through the fabric, a finger tracing the deep inlet between. 'Ah, this is to be enjoyed slowly,' she sighed, increasing the pressure slightly. 'You know, don't you, Lady Candice? You've been pleasuring yourself for years, no doubt. I've tried men, you see, but have come to the conclusion that sexual congress is a poor substitute for the solitary vice.'

'But you said I was wicked to caress Emma,' Candice protested, the tears drying on her cheeks, her backside throbbing, her clitoris demanding a second climax as she watched Gwenda's actions.

'So it is... and so is *this*... wicked and forbidden,' Gwenda murmured dreamily, her finger busy. 'I shall burn in hellfire for my sins, but oh, it's worth it!'

She pushed down her drawers. Candice, pinned to the floor, could see the forest of dark hair that coated her pubis, framed between elastic and cotton suspenders attached to her corsets and clipped to the stocking tops. Now the narrow mons was visible, the cleft high and sharp.

Under the covering of hair the lips were parted, separated by the inner pair pushing through. It had been much exercised, this private place of a mature woman.

She eased a little nearer, standing above Candice so that no detail could be missed. The piscine scent of her arousal filled the air as she opened her sex with both hands, holding the red lips wide apart and displaying a thick, engorged clitoris that emerged like a miniature penis from its hood.

'Look at it,' she breathed hurriedly, her eyes unfocused, her slack mouth glistening with spittle. 'Isn't it splendid? And it's mine. I'm not dependent on anyone for pleasure. Who needs a man when you've got this? I can do it whenever I like. Look... look... I'll rub it hard and make it stand up even more proudly. Not too much, though. I don't want to come off yet.'

Deftly, she coaxed her gem to rise, gravid with need. 'I just want you to watch,' she went on. 'I like to handle it myself. No one else knows how to do it as well as I.'

'But why did you ask me why I hadn't made love with you, instead of Emma?' Candice questioned, her hand straying to her own wet and slippery delta.

'I sometimes fancy the idea of another woman toying with my clittie, but this is best. You've excited me. When I saw you in bed with Lady Emma... and all the time I was beating you, my nub was tingling and my blood running hot,' Gwenda panted, her finger sliding up and down, round and round, subjecting her clitoris to vigorous treatment.

'And this is considered wrong?' Candice asked, wonderingly.

'You know it is, else why try to hide it? And confess to me, Lady Candice, that you wanted this when the cane landed on your buttocks.'

'I'm not sure... I can't tell. It hurt. It marked my flesh...'

'And it roused your naughty button, just as I am rousing mine.'

In the throes of wild delirium, Gwenda no longer seemed aware of her audience. She tossed her head from side to side, her eyes rolled up and her finger moved faster and faster.

Then she gave a shuddering gasp. Her body jerked, her pubis thrust up against her hand, and she hung there for a long moment, a wailing cry escaping her mouth. 'I can't hold back! Ah... ah... ah... Yes. I'm there. It's upon me. Oh, God... God... God!'

Candice forgot her sore rump, even forgot her dislike of this woman, feeling privileged to witness her reach her awesome crisis.

Gwenda came down rapidly from the heights, wiped her fingers on her handkerchief and adjusted her clothing. By the time she had finished it was almost impossible to equate

36

her with the frenzied wanton who had just enjoyed a mighty orgasm.

'You'll tell no one about this, and what you have seen makes no difference to my opinion of you, Lady Candice,' she said crisply, her face set in severe lines once more. 'You will desist in your debased dabblings with Lady Emma. If I find out you've disobeyed me, then I'll whip you again. Never doubt that for a moment. You'll thank me for it when the time comes for you to submit to your husband.'

'I'll never submit to a man!' Candice declared stubbornly, her emotions in chaos. Uppermost was confusion: this woman – the cane – her own reactions, all were bewildering.

'Oh, you will, missy, if you know what's good for you,' Gwenda returned. 'Now put yourself to rights, wash away the tear-stains and prepare to accompany your Mama when she goes out after luncheon.'

Fabian stepped out into the road and hailed a hansom cab. It rocked to a halt at the kerb, its twin oil-lamps adding to the hazy glow of the gas globes that penetrated the gloom.

It was a lightweight vehicle, slung between two large wheels, with a blinkered, patient nag standing in the straps and blowing down its nostrils.

The cabby, perched on a lofty seat at the back, mackintosh cape covering his burly shoulders, slid his long whip into a metal slot near his right hand and asked, 'Where to, gov'nor?'

Fabian gave an address, sprang on to the footrest and, followed by Clive, opened the door and seated himself. He rapped on the roof with the silver mount of his cane, and the hansom moved off.

Fabian passed a cigar to Clive, and put one between his own lips. A match flared briefly, illuminating his companion's face as he applied the flame to the tip of each. The scent of Havana's finest tobacco infiltrated the interior, sweetening the overpowering fusty smells – cheap perfume, male sweat, the feral whiff of coition – the underlying sourness of vomit.

'We've done our duty, Clive, old man,' he commented as he stared out of the window in front. He could see the sheen of sweat on the horse's flanks as it moved in steady rhythm. 'We sat through *Aida*, took our mamas and fiancées out to supper at the Café Royal after the opera and delivered them safely home. The rest of the night is ours.'

'I feel a trifle uncomfortable,' Clive confessed, the end of his cigar like a small red eye close to his mouth. 'I respect your sister, Fabian, and am looking forward to marrying her. She'd be disgusted if she knew we were going to a whorehouse.'

'Goddamnit, she won't know,' Fabian growled, his eyes hooded under the curved brim of his top hat. 'I, too, admire Emma. In fact, one might almost say I love her, but we can't hump 'em till after the ceremony, that damn' double wedding the parents are insisting on. It wouldn't be the done thing, anyway. Girls of our class become our wives, not our whores. There are plenty of common women to fulfil this role.'

'I suppose you're right,' Clive conceded uneasily.

'Of course I am,' Fabian said decisively. 'Stop fretting. Don't tell me you're developing a conscience? What a bore.'

He had always been the ringleader, he and Clive gaining the reputation of being two of the most daring, reckless and scandalous undergraduates in Oxford's history. Even so, they had managed to pass their exams, though how they had achieved this was something of a miracle. Their social life had taken precedence over studies, as they racketed round the old city, drinking hard, gambling feverishly, and fornicating as if sex had been invented especially for their pleasure.

Though engaged to Emma after a whirlwind courtship, Fabian had no intention of mending his ways, and fully expected Clive to carry on the same. The fact that he was to marry made no difference to Fabian's one-pointed search for gratification. He saw no reason why it should. A gentleman had a God-given right to exercise the powerful instrument that nature had placed between his legs, finding comfortable lodgings for it any time the fancy took him.

The wide, well-appointed streets of the West End gave way to those which were narrower and less well lit, bordering the River Thames. It was almost midnight when the cab stopped outside the iron gates of a house set in its own grounds.

'Is this the place?' Clive asked, as Fabian climbed out and paid the fare. The cabby touched his bowler, clicked his tongue and the hansom rolled away into the darkness.

'It is. We're about to enter paradise,' Fabian answered with a grin, settled his black opera cloak around his shoulders and lifted the latch.

The front door was attained by a flight of steps and opened by a liveried major-domo. They entered a softly lit foyer. Music drifted from one of the reception rooms: a waltz played on the piano.

The atmosphere was like a hothouse, and heady perfume rose from the orange stamens and waxen trumpets of white lilies. These stood in blue Wedgwood vases on the mosaic tiled floor, next to the glossy green leaves and purple flowers of aspidistra plants.

A girl stepped forward to take their toppers, white silk scarves, gloves and cloaks. She was blonde and fresh complexioned, and smiled at them shyly, even though her breasts bulged over the edge of a scarlet satin basque, squeezed high by whale-boning, the nipples peeping through the black lace trim like ripe raspberries.

Her short shirt was made of layers of stiff muslin that stood out from the waist. Every time she moved it lifted, dipped and swayed, giving teasing glimpses of the scanty hairs on the full, split fig of her naked pubis, or the curves of her ample buttocks, marked with the latticed stripes of a recent whipping.

Fabian pushed a hand between her legs and discovered to

his delight that she was wet there. He inserted a finger into her tight channel, up to the first knuckle. She gave a shrill scream and tried to push him away. He smiled thinly and continued to torment her, finding the puckered entrance to her rectum and forcing his digit into this forbidden realm. She squealed even louder, her cries attracting the attention of a tall, svelte woman who had appeared at the head of the deeply carpeted staircase.

'Ah, Lord Fabian,' she said, descending gracefully, her lips curving in a smile that did not quite reach her observant grey eyes. 'You like her? Our little Susan who has only just come up from Devonshire? She's a virgin, sir, I promise you, and will cost you deep in the purse. What do you say? For I must warn you that if you don't want the goods, then don't maul them.'

'Madame Carenza...' he said, releasing Susan abruptly and making an ironic bow. 'Virgins are not for me. I prefer more experienced lovers. Alas, I shall have to cope with a shrinking violet on my wedding-night, and am not relishing rupturing her maidenhead.'

Madame Carenza was a fine woman in her early forties, with dyed black hair and a statuesque figure, and she swept towards him with a rustle of lilac taffeta, as fashionably attired as a duchess at a state ball.

She extended her gloved hands, saying with a melodious laugh, 'How ungrateful! Why, most gentlemen who frequent my establishment would give their right arm for such an opportunity.'

Fabian was already looking beyond her at the wealth of woman-flesh on offer. She kept a high-class bordello patronised by the nobility, her girls renowned for their beauty, intelligence, discretion – and health. The latter was of paramount importance. No gentleman relished a dose of the clap.

'May I introduce my friend, Lord Clive?' Fabian said, his manners as impeccable as his faultlessly tailored evening suit.

'My lord,' she replied, curtseying as she looked at Clive with her lustrous, heavily-painted eyes. 'Welcome to my Temple of Joy.'

He seemed overwhelmed, and Fabian, who had become accustomed to the sumptuous bordellos of Paris, was amused by this and determined that he should enjoy himself. He had become serious of late, following Candice around with doglike devotion. It boded ill for their marriage, in Fabian's opinion. She was already far too spirited and argumentative.

'Come on,' he urged, clapping him round the shoulders. 'The night is yet young and we've a lot of rogering to do.'

'You're not too late for the entertainment,' Madame Carenza said brightly, holding his arm in her beringed fingers and leading them into the salon. It was furnished with much gilt, crimson plush upholstery and floral patterned rugs.

'And what may that be?' Fabian asked, a thrill knotting his gut and arousing the serpent that slumbered in his crotch.

'Ah, ha!' she said mysteriously, and tapped his cheek with her furled fan. 'Wait and see.'

Light scintillated on the hundred glass drops dangling from gas-powered chandeliers, and there were wall-lamps, too, each sending out dazzling diamond points. Murals decorated the walls, depicting lusty scenes from Greek legends.

Here, the Sabine women struggled in the arms of muscular warriors, their naked breasts and shapely limbs shamelessly exposed as they were subjected to the thrust of mighty phalli; there, Venus lay with a handsome shepherd boy, her lecherous hands holding his erect manhood and guiding it to her lips.

Over the green-veined marble fireplace hung an oil-painting of the mighty god, Jupiter, revelling at ease amidst the lush breasts, eager loins and generous buttocks of a bevy of amorous nymphs. In the background, amidst temples and cypress trees, lurked leering satyrs cupping the weighty balls that dangled between their goat legs, or flaunting the

41

engorged penises that reared from the hairy thickets of their underbellies.

Not only were there erotic paintings but statues to excite the senses. Skilfully executed, they represented men with women, women with women, men with men, all straining in ecstasy. Everywhere one looked there was some reminder that this was indeed a shrine dedicated to fornication.

The salon was already filling up, gentlemen arriving from their clubs to feed their basest appetites in the underworld of vice that flourished beneath the surface of respectable Victorian London. There were officers in military uniforms, politicians fresh from a late-night sitting at the House of Commons, dog-collared clergy, men of letters, and a university don or two.

They were all the same to the high-priestess, Madame Carenza, and her vestal virgins – simply men, with egos that needed boosting and lusts that required appeasing, be they never so perverse. She did not ask their surnames, but knew most of them nonetheless. Many a state secret had been divulged during pillow talk, but never left the walls of her house. In return, grateful gentleman of power and influence made sure that she was not harassed by the Chief of Police. In fact, he was one of her most regular clients.

Her ladies strolled about or sat with customers on the brocaded couches, fondling their jutting nipples, or disposing their legs in such a manner that their clefts were revealed. Champagne was served by maids wearing lacy knickers, brief corsets, black stockings and shoes with high heels.

There were a number of handsome striplings acting as waiters, in incredibly short tunics that exposed their tightly compact balls and vigorous pricks in a permanent state of erection. As they passed among the men, so they meekly allowed themselves to be handled by those of a certain persuasion.

Fabian was spoilt for choice, enchanted by the sirens with sultry eyes and pouting lips, their bodies open for inspection.

His fully aroused penis quivered as he noticed that several of them bore the marks of the whip, particularly those in a servile role.

His heart beat like a drum at their provocative gestures, and he was particularly attracted to a striking brunette with a haughty stare. She wore a magnificent hat cocked at a saucy angle and nothing else, except tight black satin elbow-length gloves, stilt-heeled ankle boots and silk stockings upheld by diamanté trimmed garters.

He nodded to Madame Carenza who held out her hand. He dropped several gold coins into the white gloved palm. 'Here's a treat for you, Miranda,' the procuress said to the girl of his choice. 'Be nice to this gentleman.'

Miranda nodded and sashayed towards him, coming to rest between his opened thighs, her depilated and perfumed mons on a level with his mouth. She lifted one leg and draped it over him, affording him an uninterrupted view of her dark pink slit. Then she nudged his knees together and sank down on his lap, her parted cleft pressing against his throbbing groin. She gave a superior little smile, unbuttoned his trousers and took out his tumescent member, sliding her fingers up and down his shaft, then licking the plum. Jism trickled from the single eye.

'D'you fancy me, love?' asked a copper-headed whore with enormous breasts, her tongue working gently round the rim of Clive's ear.

'Go on. Have her. She's good at it. I know. I fucked her last time I was here,' Fabian urged, holding on to his control with difficulty, reluctant to pour forth his emission into Miranda's hand, willing it to last. Though he might achieve several orgasms, he would have to pay for each one and, anyway, the first was always the best. Then he added caustically, 'What's wrong? Afraid Candice will find out?'

'No, I'm not,' Clive snapped belligerently. 'God, you talk as if I'm already the henpecked husband. I'll have her, and that one, too,' and he pointed recklessly at a girl seated on a tapestry cushion near his feet, a doe-eyed tart with little pointed breasts. She was smoking a cigarette in a long, jade holder, and was nude apart from a jewelled cache-sexe that clasped her furry mound.

'That's more like it,' Fabian shouted. 'Two at once, eh? What a stallion!'

The music had changed, an Indian drummer and a flautist supplying Eastern rhythms. A plump, dark-skinned houri stood on a platform at the end of the room, gyrating her hips, her belly undulating, the tinkle of the little bells round her ankles ringing out every time she moved her feet. At first she was shrouded in diaphanous veils, but she gradually dropped the scarves one by one, her splendid body glimpsed tantalisingly through the spangled gauze, till she tossed the last away and posed naked.

Her nipples were gilded and gripped by metal clamps from which hung more bells. Every hair had been plucked from her body, and her palms and the soles of her feet were traced with coloured dye. The men roared in approval and stamped on the parquet.

Money showered on to the stage, and Madame's slave-boys hurriedly gathered it up, taking it to her on silver salvers.

She clapped her hands and the dancer jumped down. Two of Madame's helpers assisted a fair-haired girl to mount the platform in her place. They were big, strapping lads in leather jock-straps, and though she dragged back reluctantly she could not prevent them from positioning her centre stage, helpless in the face of their sleek muscular strength.

The audience voiced their appreciation, admiring the tableau as they sprawled in deep chairs or on couches, attended by the whores. The atmosphere was tense, the men already inflamed, the bulges in their trousers betraying the need swelling their cocks.

With a drum roll on the piano, the slaves fastened manacles to the girl's wrists, linked by chains. A rope dangled from the ceiling by a hook and she made frightened, choking noises as they fastened her to it, suspended with tethered arms stretched taught above her flaxen head.

The little silk shift which was her only garment rode up over her straining body, the flimsy material clinging to her raised breasts and puckered nipples as if it was wet. Her white, slender legs stayed still for a moment, then her bare feet scrabbled for a purchase on the floor, but only the tips of her toes made contact.

The spectators whistled and hooted as the hem of her tunic settled just above the tufted mound. Frantically realising this, she clamped her thighs together, trying to hide the sensitive niche between her love lips.

The taller of the young men reached out and spun her so that she could be viewed from every side, then he grabbed the top of the shift and pulled sharply downwards, ripping it from her. He then seized the rope, holding her still so she could not move. She screamed and struggled to no avail.

The other youth, stocky and dark, paced round her, then picked up a short wooden paddle with a rounded handle and a smooth, four-inch blade. He caught her across the bottom with it. The white leather surface met tender flesh with a sharp, smacking sound that reverberated throughout the room.

The girl howled; the audience cheered; Fabian nearly came, but Miranda squeezed the base of his penis and prevented it. His tribute remained unspilled, a hot pool of lava within his testicles.

The slaves revolved the girl again, showing her tightly clenched bottom cheeks and the rosy flush suffusing them. This excited the onlookers to a frenzy. One man spurted all over the front of his trousers. And he was not long alone, as both slaves set about her with the paddles, reddening her rump and forcing further cries from her, tears rolling unchecked down her face.

They threw the paddles aside. The tall lad wrapped his arms around her hips and took her weight from behind. He tore off his G-string and his cock was at full stand, long and circumcised, the bare knob red and shiny, the shaft so stiff that it pointed upwards to his navel. He flaunted it, turning to the crowd and making it hop without even touching it. Next he rubbed it against the girl's bottom, and worked it into the groove between.

His hand came round, skimming over her breasts and darting down to divide her labia, stretching her wide, finding her nubbin and stroking it relentlessly. He held her in such a way that her hindquarters jutted against his rigid phallus, making access easy. A heave of his powerful thighs and she was impaled, screeching as his weapon penetrated her to the cervix, her own weight forcing her down to receive it.

Ribald advice was hurled at him from all sides. He made no response, frowning in concentration, grinding and pumping, his knees slightly bent, his pelvis working like a piston. The audience were in an uproar as the other slave got behind him, took out a large and meaty appendage from his genital support and, seizing his companion round the neck, plunged this well lubricated tool up to the hilt in his arsehole.

Fabian, watching the three of them playing the humped backed beast, could feel a surge of tremendous heat rushing down his spine and gathering in his groin. He could see Clive sprawled on a divan between the Arab girl and blonde harpy. They had his shirt and flies undone and were tweaking his nipples and massaging his fiery-red prick.

A haze passed across Fabian's sight, and he groaned as he felt Miranda's wet mouth encompassing him, stretched lips sliding round his helm, almost taking the whole of him, his knob butting the back of her throat. The lips slid up and down, sucking strongly – releasing him on the upward stroke, swallowing him on the downward.

With astonishing abruptness he felt the unstoppable, explosive rush of orgasm. Too late, Miranda tugged herself free. He shot his semen all over her face, her breasts and those elegantly gloved hands, marking the black satin with white stains.

Later, she took him to her room, a neat, functional place with a single bed, a washbasin and clean towels. There she straddled him, rubbing her pussy against him and talking dirty, almost convincing him that the encounter was an enjoyable rather than a monetary transaction.

By that time the edge had gone from his appetite and he was entering that cheerless phase of satiety. He was sickened by her and as soon as she had drained him of the last drop of fluid, he left her bed.

'I'm tired of London,' he growled as he and Clive sat in a cab, leaving the brothel in the small hours and heading for the Fortescue town house. 'Nothing exciting ever happens here. Same old round. Same old faces. I want to go abroad again.'

Clive, dozing in the corner, opened one eye and regarded him through the dimness. 'Hell, you've not been back long,' he reminded.

'That's true, but they know how to live on the Continent,' Fabian gloomed, giving in to the melancholy engendered by too much alcohol and loveless sex. 'I need to get away from here before I go stark, staring mad. I'll speak to Mama about it.'

'Get out your Baedekers',' Fabian shouted, bounding in at the French doors of the library.

'Why on earth should I do that?' Candice answered lazily, looking up from a calfbound volume of the *Rubaiyat of Omar Khyyam*, a book of Persian poems she had discovered on a second hand stall in the Caledonian Market.

Fabian flopped down in one of the wing chairs near the fireplace, pushed back his unruly quiff and answered, 'You'll need the guide book to Northern Italy. Venice, to be precise. We're going there at the end of the month.'

Candice sat up and laid the poems aside. She drew her

legs under her on the deeply cushioned couch, and stared at him with bright, enquiring eyes, saying, 'To Italy?'

'Absolutely,' he stated, then looked towards the bell-pull and asked, 'I say, d'you suppose old Binns would bring me in a whisky if I rang for him?'

'I doubt it, at this time of day,' she said, grinning at him. He was always making outrageous suggestions.

'And a fellow can't smoke in here,' he grumbled, taking out his gold cigarette case, turning it over in his hands regretfully, then replacing it in his pocket.

'Tell me about Italy,' she said, leaning forward eagerly, her honey-blonde hair piled high on the crown of her head, with little tendrils falling each side of her face and wispy fronds caressing the slender nape of her neck. 'Where did you get this idea?'

'I've been talking to Mama and she agrees,' he said, lounging low on his spine and stretching his long legs before him. 'It's all arranged. I suggested that we should go abroad on an educational, sightseeing trip. All four of us... you and Clive, Emma and myself, with Miss Turner and Mrs Smythe along to guard your reputations and make sure we don't corrupt you. I think Mama's quite pleased to get rid of us. She wants to spend time at the villa in Brighton, playing cards with her cronies, and strolling on the promenade and taking tea in the Winter Gardens.'

'And why wasn't I consulted?' Candice demanded, her voice rising an indignant octave as the initial excitement was replaced by anger. 'Am I allowed to have no opinion on where I go or with whom?'

He frowned, forming his hands into a spy-glass and staring at her through it. 'I say, what's wrong? I thought you'd be over the moon. It'll be no end of a lark... Venice is wonderful, so I've heard. I can't wait. Think of the fun you'll have there with Clive... dances, parties, masked balls and the casinos.'

She bit her lip, eyes stormy, and said, 'That's just it, Fabian.

I think I'd rather go without him.'

He shot her a worried glance, his handsome face unusually serious. 'That's not on, and you know it,' he said sternly. 'It's a bit late to start thinking like that. He's one of the best.'

'I know. I'm being unfair,' she conceded, ashamed of herself and worried by her lack of enthusiasm. Venice appealed to her, but not with Clive.

'We're all feeling a little stale,' Fabian insisted. 'A holiday away from England will be capital. You'll get to know Clive better, find out more about him. I must say, I can't wait to whisk Emma away from her bossy Mamma and doting father. All these complicated wedding plans can get a chap down.'

Candice leaned her head against the back of the couch and closed her eyes. Visions of gondolas and magnificent buildings drifted across her inner eye. She had seen pictures of Venice in books. She imagined she was walking across St Mark's Square and staring up at the Basilica. It was night, and she was wearing a heavenly blue ballgown, and diamonds round her throat. There was someone with her, and it was not Clive.

She glimpsed the stranger as they stepped into a gondola and were transported to a palazzo. An extremely tall, handsome man, elegantly dressed, his black hair curling to his shoulders, his thin, almost aesthetic face turned towards her, his eyes burning green, with little flames, jets of amber, in their depths.

Venice! Yes, yes! cried her soul.

'Venice,' said her brother, smiling, but rather wary after her outburst. 'Why, maybe I should have waited and we could have had a double honeymoon there. Never mind, we can go again next year.'

She stared at him, like a sleepwalker who has been awakened. The room came back into focus, and she felt a sense of loss that made her want to weep. Then hope flared up, making her body burn and tingle. Maybe she would meet him there, the man destined to shape her future.

And in the depths of his ancestral bed, high in the mountains, something disturbed Prince Dimitri's deathlike sleep. A tremor, an instinct, yet less substantial than either, and the ghost of a smile touched his full, red, sensual lips.

Chapter Three

The steamer was an old one, belonging to an Italian line. It was crowded, noisy and grimy, but Clive had become accustomed to the inconveniences of travel which were impossible to avoid, even on first class tickets. He and his party had left Dover for Calais by ferry, and then taken the train across Europe.

To him, every moment had been exhilarating, for he was with Candice for hours on end, day after day. He asked for nothing more, though suffered continual frustration, his penis threatening to come erect whenever she was near. Nevertheless, he and Fabian had seized the chance to relieve their sexual urges whenever they could.

During breaks in the journey they had slipped away late at night when the rest were asleep. It had been easy to find prostitutes: language had proved no barrier. All they had to do was grease the palms of the hall porters in the various hotels in which they stayed, for addresses to be given and assignations arranged.

But Clive took little joy in this basic gratification of the flesh, itching for union with Candice. It was her face he saw as he humped a foreign whore, her virgin niche he pretended to enter instead of a well-worn pathway.

Now he stood with the object of his desire on the deck of the steamer which would take them to Venice.

'We're almost there,' he remarked, leaning his elbow against hers on the rail, achingly aware of the perfection of her face under the becoming little hat that topped her shining hair, and of her shoulder brushing his.

Though it was covered by her cape, that touch burned into his skin through his overcoat, and the wayward beast that rested along his left thigh started to stir and swell, threatening to spoil the cut of his tailored trousers. Sweat beaded his brow. The weather had grown steadily warmer as they went further south. As soon as they reached their hotel he would order his valet to unpack white linen suits and poplin shirts with soft collars.

Candice turned her head and smiled at him as the deck juddered beneath their feet. The people standing on the quay waved farewell to those on board as the boat's dark hulk slowly left the jetty, propeller churning up the dingy water as it manoeuvred towards the open sea.

'I'll be glad to stay in one place for a while,' Candice observed. 'We've packed in so much during the last ten days that I'm quite exhausted. I want to visit the Lido. A long, lazy sojourn amidst sand and sea will be delightful.'

'But there are fine buildings we must see,' he insisted. 'The Rialto, the museum and churches.'

She lifted her hand and placed it teasingly over his bearded lips, saying, 'I know. You don't have to reel them off. But for heaven's sake, Clive... just for now I've had a surfeit of frescoes and picture galleries and awesome architecture. It's time to have some fun. We can go bathing together.'

The prospect was so thrilling that Clive gave up trying to control his organ. Now it rose straight against his belly, conquering both underpants and trousers, its wet tip brushing his waistband. He leaned further over the rail in order to hide this strident evidence of lust.

To see Candice in bathing dress! Her body would be modestly covered in a navy-blue serge tunic that covered her hips, and matching bloomers to her knees, stockings, pumps, even a frilled cap, but never mind – when the fabric became wet it would cling to her. He might glimpse the outline of her nipples, crimped by the chilly water, and the division of her buttocks, should the tunic shift out of place and – bliss! – the line of her cleft.

He was trembling like a boy who has just had his first

wet-dream, and could not help catching her hand in his and covering it with passionate kisses, tasting her skin, smelling her perfume.

'Your beard tickles,' she said, and her azure eyes danced under the long, curling lashes. 'You'd better not let Miss Turner see you doing that.'

She did not withdraw her hand, however, and he had the wild notion of transferring it to his trouser closure, making her aware of his hot, swollen rod. What would her reaction be? One of horror? Surprise? Interest?

He groaned and concern flashed across her mobile features, as she asked, 'What's wrong? Are you seasick?'

'No, no...' he said, shaking his head and gripping her hand so tightly that the flesh whitened under the pressure. 'Oh, Candice, if only we were on our honeymoon! I want you so much. I'm sorry to startle you, and am sure you don't know what I mean but, my dearest girl, a man has needs that you can't possibly comprehend.'

'What would you like me to do, Clive?' she asked quietly, and the colour rose in her cheeks.

This was too much even for his iron self-control. He was on the very brink, his crisis a heartbeat away. 'Don't be frightened,' he muttered and pulled her hand under his overcoat, pressing it to the high ridge of his phallus.

She did not resist, merely remarked, 'What are you doing, Clive? And what is that lump in your groin?'

'I'm not doing anything,' he panted, rocking his hips slightly so that her palm slid over his frantic member. 'I just want to feel your hand there... for a moment... no more. You don't mind?'

'No,' she said, her face serious and intent. 'But someone may see us. This is a public place.'

'They won't notice. They are watching the harbour disappearing in the distance. Please, darling...'

He could not restrain a moan as her fingers felt round the cloth concealing his thickened stem, then started sliding up and down, the motion drawing his foreskin taut and increasing the friction on the engorged glans.

She was staring out to sea, a faraway look in her eyes, and he could not contain himself, a mighty spasm of bliss shooting through him as his cock discharged its load into his silken underpants.

Candice must have felt the dampness that penetrated his trousers, but she continued to stroke the now subsiding bulge, her attention on the horizon and the blue vault of the sky that spread over the empty sea.

'Darling,' he murmured close to her lobe, setting the pearl ear-drop swinging. 'Oh, my lovely girl... thank you... thank you...'

'What did I do?' Candice asked guilelessly, and he met the full blaze of those marvellous sapphire eyes. She withdrew her hand and ran it down the side of her cape fastidiously.

'You gave me a glimpse of heaven,' he said, adoring her. 'And one day, soon, I shall take you there, too... my innocent child-bride.'

The glance she now gave him was charged with mischief, and a secret knowledge that he would rather not have seen, wanting to believe her to be unsullied. 'Did you come off in your trousers, Clive?' she asked him boldly. 'Was that what happened?'

He could feel the heat rising into his face under his neatly clipped brown beard, astonished and shocked by her answer. Could she possibly be experienced? Surely not. Her honour had been cherished most carefully, as far as he was aware.

'Well, yes,' he admitted, fidgeting uneasily, her artless question putting fresh life into his flaccid cock. 'I did "come off", as you put it. I'm surprised you know that crude term, or what happens to a man.'

'Oh, don't bother about it,' she returned carelessly, tucking a rebellious curl under her hat brim. 'I'm a virgin, I assure you, but am not entirely ignorant of the needs of the flesh.

Women have urges, too, you see. If you were to put a hand in my drawers right now, you'd find I'm very wet.'

He stood there, rooted to the spot, but before he could recover speech a gong sounded for luncheon and they went to join Fabian and Emma in the dining saloon.

Later they occupied deck-chairs and talked, read or dozed till at last the flat coast appeared, and fishing boats bobbed on the water, their colourful sails and swarthy, red-capped crews making Candice think of pirates.

She was alert at once, running to the rail, and catching sight of glittering minarets in the midst of the water, and then Venice itself, rising slowly from the sea, the marble city taking form, the slim towers and great domes outlined against the clear, cloudless beauty of the evening sky.

Her heart contracted, and she clung to the cool iron, another landscape superimposed over the present one – that strange, celestial place she had seen in her dream. Had this been Venice? Had she been granted a glimpse of the future?

Clasping her knotted hands to her breasts in excitement, she cried over her shoulder, 'Emma... look! It's like Tennyson's poem when he describes Camelot: "Fairy Queens hath built the city, they came from out a sacred mountain-cleft towards the sunrise, each with harp in hand; and built to the music of their harps."'

'It's breathtaking,' Emma agreed, coming to stand beside her, an arm looped around her shoulders. 'How mysterious and wonderful. Makes one think of feverish liaisons, duels and plots and illicit love in secret hideaways.'

'And what do you know of forbidden love?' Fabian asked patronisingly, as he came up behind her. 'You'll find, you sweet romantic little things, that Venice stinks in the hot weather, and is rather unpleasant during the sirocco, a scorching wind that blows from Africa.'

'A girl can dream, can't she? And use her imagination,' Emma replied, with a toss of her head.

But Candice hugged her dream to herself as the steamer chugged at half speed through the narrow harbour and anchored in the lagoon.

She had thought of it often, longed for it every night, but it had never returned. Yet a weird kind of certainty had bubbled inside her since she left England, every turn of the train wheels or revolution of the ferry's screw, bringing her closer and closer, but to what she had no clear idea.

In defiance of Miss Turner's edict, she and Emma still pleasured one another whenever they could, though the chaperon had made it difficult. Whenever Candice glanced at that stern, plain face she recalled the way she had beaten her and then brought her to climax, but she did not tell Emma the whole story, only that she had been caned.

The memory was one she brooded over in the privacy of her room, her buttocks stinging even though the bruises had long since vanished, the dichotomy of burning pain and extreme pleasure one which bemused and fascinated her.

She used these thoughts as aids to masturbation, pinching her nipples into peaks, then cupping her mons, her finger finding her slippery delta and rousing her clitoris. As she did so, she visualised a man spanking her – not any man – only he who had appeared to her in that never-to-be-forgotten dream.

Emma's chaperon, Mrs Flora Smythe was easy to deal with, the complete opposite to Gwenda. A plump, comely widow with an eye for the men, she had been in a ferment of excitement ever since they stepped aboard ship at Dover. There were men aplenty in foreign climes, so she said, gay and dashing, a cut above their dour, conventional English counterparts.

Candice could not wait to tell Emma about Clive's behaviour and how she had stroked his serpent and made it spit. Fabian, apparently, was being the perfect gentleman, much to Emma's chagrin, but there was plenty of time to change all that – and a plethora of other suitors, no doubt.

They were booked in at Danieli's Royal Hotel, but Lady Sarah had written to an acquaintance of hers, Baroness Orville, who resided in Venice and she had promised to insure that no ball or function was held without them being invited.

Their trunks were full of new clothes. They had indulged in an orgy of shopping before leaving London, purchasing everything that a wealthy young lady would need on a Continental holiday. They had already worn some of the evening gowns when dining in luxurious hotels on the way, but even grander ones had been reserved for Venice, to say nothing of morning dresses and afternoon dresses, swimming attire, delicate underwear, nightgowns and negligées.

Shoes, hats, stockings and scarves were theirs in abundance, and their fathers had given them *carte blanche* to shop at jewellers in Bond Street for gems to set off their beauty.

'We're going to have a marvellous time,' Emma said, and squeezed Candice's waist.

There was a delay while the medical inspector came aboard, but soon the landing-stairs were let down, and after the customs officials had done their work, passengers started to disembark. Gondolas came alongside like superb swans. Long, graceful, agile and flat-bottomed, with a curl at the stern and a decorative comb at the bow, some of them had hoods or canopies in the centre to protect passengers.

The gondoliers thronged the steps, their craft moored to thick striped poles that rose from the water. They were touting for business, arguing in dialect, tough, dark men with brawny shoulders and flexible waists. They smiled broadly with a flash of white teeth at Emma and Candice standing on the landing stage with the baggage, their ladies maids, the valets and the chaperons, while Clive and Fabian searched for a representative of the Hotel Danieli.

Mission accomplished, 'It's all arranged,' Fabian said, returning to where they waited. 'The hotel has its own fleet of gondolas. We'll take the leading one, Miss Turner and

Mrs Smythe in another with the hand luggage, and the servants and trunks bringing up the rear.'

With a momentary tremor and hesitation, Candice held out her hand to the young, smiling gondolier. He was attired in white, with a blue scarf round his supple waist, trimmed with silver lace, and a plaque bearing the hotel's escutcheon on his chest. His black ringlets were part covered by a wide-brimmed straw hat.

His grip was firm, his hand warm and dry as he helped her into her seat with solemn politeness, yet she sensed that, if the truth was known, he would really have liked to lay her back against the plush cushions and undress her, then plunge his tool into her warm haven.

The thought made her vagina contract and as she glanced at him from the tail of her eye, she could see a promising fullness at the front of his trousers. A smile flitted over his bronzed countenance.

'My name is Giacomo, *signorina*,' he said, his voice heavily accented. 'Ask for me if you need a gondola. At any time, day or night.'

He spoke low, a purring inflection in his tone as he lingered on the last word. Blushing furiously, she made no reply, and he released her hand after detaining it longer than was necessary.

Emma and Fabian settled themselves opposite Candice in the comfortable padded chairs under the canopy, and the boat glided rapidly between rows of great houses and palaces which rose out of the water on either side. The sunset struck them dramatically, bathing the Palladian facades in crimson, and reflecting on the water so that the gondola seemed to be skimming through a river of fire.

'Look!' Fabian said, pointing to a massive standard in red and gold hanging from one of the balconies. 'See the Lion of Venice, that strange, winged beast?'

They dutifully looked. Fabian had been mugging up on the guide books.

The watery road to their hotel lay some distance down the Grand Canal, and then turned aside into one of the numerous narrow lanes that branched off in every direction.

Candice's admiration of Giacomo's graceful movements in propelling the gondola rose by leaps and bounds as he skilfully negotiated the rectangular corners, uttering warning shouts as they shot round, in case another boat approached from the opposite direction. A lamp hung on its prow, and every other craft was now illuminated, too. Some were ornamented with flowers, carrying revellers who were singing and playing guitars.

Candice was enchanted, falling rapidly under the spell of the ancient city, while Fabian droned on about its thousand years of glorious, active life.

'Hush, dearest, don't be such an old bore,' Emma chided gently, her hand in his as they sat close together. 'It's all too terribly romantic. I feel as if we're back in the past and can't wait to go to a ball wearing a mask.'

Clive had succeeded in ensconcing himself next to Candice, but she wanted no distractions, every iota of her being concentrated on her surroundings.

'The Hotel Danieli was once one of the Doge's palaces,' Fabian went on, refusing to be silenced, sliding an arm along the back of Emma's chair, then turning to shout at Giacomo, 'Are we nearly there?'

'*Si, signor,*' he answered, pointing ahead.

They were suddenly brought back to the nineteenth century, seeing the dazzling lights of the hotel, where numerous visitors strolled on the walk outside it, and a private flight of steps led from the canal.

Candice rose and prepared to alight. She was just about to place her hand in Giacomo's when she paused, riveted by the sight of an ornate gondola that swept passed them and glided towards a side turning.

It was pitch black, and reminded her of a coffin. Its cabin was of carved wood with curtains at the sides and a shuttered door. A hooded and cloaked figure stood at the stern, working the pole.

An icy finger trailed down her spine. That silent, swiftly moving craft suggested dank alleyways and lawless encounters in the night – even visions of death itself, the bier and solemn rites and a last soundless voyage.

'Is that one for hire? Is it owned by a hotel?' she asked Giacomo, nodding towards the funereal craft as it nosed into a water lane and disappeared.

He grimaced and crossed himself, saying, 'Is a private boat, *signorina*. It belongs to Prince Dimitri. Some say he is the devil. Who knows?'

'So, what gossip have you brought me?' asked Comte Henri Merlion of the man who had just been shown into his private apartment.

A sneer crossed his olive-skinned, classically handsome face, and as he spoke he idly drew the thongs of a supple Spanish leather whip through his slender hands, regarding his visitor through narrowed, slate-coloured eyes.

He leaned nonchalantly against a pillar in a chamber the size of a ballroom, in no way concerned because he had been interrupted in a stimulating encounter with his mistress who was tethered to a cross-piece placed near the marble fireplace. He flicked a glance at her, this glorious Titian haired creature, the toast of Venice, a spoilt darling wooed by kings, but his alone – his slave to treat as he willed.

The person he addressed was a slight, wispy, boyish-looking man dressed in the last extreme of fashion, his willowy figure displayed to perfection by a tight waisted velvet tailcoat and exceedingly form-hugging, dove grey trousers.

'Gossip, comte?' he exclaimed, pantomiming with his manicured hands. 'You know I never prattle. The soul of discretion, me.'

Henri's sneer deepened, and he moved his lithe body from

its resting place, as steely and supple as one of the rapiers he used with deadly affect at the fencing school.

'Gaston, you're a bad liar,' he snapped, and approached him, tapping the whip against the side of his black riding boot as he did so.

'Only joking,' Gaston Laveau murmured nervously, swallowing hard as he eyed it.

'Well?' Henri stood still as a panther stalking its prey, and his lips curled in a thin smile as he observed Gaston's distress, and the dew of fearful anticipation breaking out on the delicately painted face.

'Well,' the unfortunate young man answered, running a finger round the inside of his collar and easing his colourful cravat. 'The talk is of a party of young English people who have just arrived. I had it from Baroness Orville whom I attended before coming here. She knows the mother of two of them... Lady Sarah Fortescue, whose daughter, Lady Candice, and son, Lord Fabian are among the visitors.'

'Young, you say? And good looking?' Henri mused, watching the ripple of lights on water dappling the ceiling. Wherever he went in his splendid palazzo, it was to be reminded of the canals outside, the arteries of Venice.

Gaston recovered his aplomb, preening himself as he gazed at his reflection in one of the dozen mirrors gracing the walls. He pushed back a lock of blond streaked hair and touched a finger to his arched eyebrows, playing for time as he struggled to remember precisely what the baroness had told him.

'I'm not sure about their looks. It was rather a trying meeting,' he said in mitigation. 'She's a domineering woman, a demon of libidinousness. Although I'm only her coiffeur, and she knows perfectly well that I'm interested in members of my own sex, she always tries to seduce me. She expects me to be her *cavaliere serviente*, worshipping her as my *amico*. It's too, too ghastly. If I don't, she beats me.'

Henri snorted down his nose impatiently and cracked the

whip. 'And you love it! Get to the point. The English visitors!' he reminded harshly.

'Oh, yes... besides the two I've already mentioned, there is a Lord Clive and a Lady Emma, so I was given to understand.'

'Humm,' Henri murmured thoughtfully. 'They might be worth viewing. What d'you think, Bianca?' And he swung round to the manacled woman.

'Whatever you say,' she breathed, daring to glance up at him through the tumbled mass of flaming auburn locks that had fallen forward over her face.

He was worth looking at with his dark hair winged with silver at the temples. His broad-shouldered body was clad in a white, full-sleeved shirt and his long, strong legs were covered by black leather breeches that fitted without a wrinkle, emphasising the generous bulk of his phallus at the apex of his muscular thighs.

He strode over to her, his cock thickening as he observed her helplessness. She was chained to the cross, arms outstretched, her wrists circled by metal cuffs and clamped to the wood. This position raised her full breasts high. Stopping in front of her in an arrogant, spread-legged stance, he flicked her nipples with his fingers, the hardness in his groin increasing as he watched them peak, eager for more.

'Aren't you forgetting something?' he asked, shaking his head, and tweaking her teats till she yelped.

'Master,' she cried. 'I didn't call you master.'

'And are you sorry?'

'Oh yes, master. Very sorry.'

'And how many lashes shall I give you for that omission?'

'Three, master.'

'Is that enough? What do you think, Gaston?' Henri asked, spinning round on his heel and fixing the cringing catamite with his hard eyes.

'No, master. Give her six,' he stammered, hypnotised by the whip and the powerful man who flourished it. He bent double, his hands clasped to his crotch wherein lay his plump penis.

'She hasn't answered my question,' Henri said, prolonging the moment, the tail of the whip snaking across her thighs, barely touching her. 'I repeat, Bianca... shall we seduce these young English folk?'

'Yes, master,' she whimpered, and then added, 'Can you let me down, please? I need to empty my bladder.'

'Certainly not!' he snapped, and implemented his words with a swift, stinging lash. 'You'll hold your water. If the slightest drop stains my precious Chinese silk carpet you'll be thrashed even more soundly. Do you hear?'

'Yes, master,' she whined and wriggled her hips.

She could barely move, her legs splayed, ankles fastened to the foot-rest. Her body was naked, apart from a tight leather belt around her waist. Two straps ran down from it, framing her taut belly and luxuriant copper-hued bush, and then running up the exposed avenue of her arse to be clipped to shining metal rings at the back of the restrictive band.

Her breasts were forced up by further leather bindings, and now Henri tormented them even more by fastening clips to the nipples, the sharp little teeth biting into the tender flesh. He measured her endurance, an experienced controller, knowing that she was enjoying every moment of her torment. He felt between her legs, his fingers encountering the hair fringing her labia and the wet, swollen flesh.

He rubbed his middle digit over her nubbin. It was hard as a pea, poking from its place at the top of her delta. Henri loved to feel a woman's arousal, rejoicing in bringing her to a state of frenzied lust. Be she commoner or princess, few could resist being finger-fucked by a man who knew what he was doing.

Henri had travelled far and wide to acquire his skills, studying the art of love in such diverse schools as the brothels of Paris and the temples of India – and not only those of love. He had also been trained in the delights of perversion

– of how to bring the body to blissful heights through pain, and how to conquer even the most stubborn, forcing them to admit to their desire to be dominated.

Bianca was such a one. Proud, wilful, high-handed, a law unto herself – until she met Henri.

Now she was his victim, hanging on the cross-piece, awaiting his pleasure. It was almost too much, and his cock rose inside his breeches, throbbing with need. Whatever he fancied was his for the taking. Her nether hole, perhaps? Or he could come between her breasts, pressing them together and using them like her vagina. Then there was that velvety channel itself, so warm and wet and encompassing. He was spoilt for choice.

Then he glanced at Gaston, who was gazing at him with adoring eyes while he rubbed his penis through his trousers. Here was a further alternative – Gaston's tight orifice.

Henri twirled the cross round, so that Bianca's back and buttocks faced him, then he raised the whip, his excitement soaring as he heard it whistle though the air and the satisfying sound of it landing on bare flesh.

Bianca screamed and jerked in her bonds. He struck her again, bringing further agonised cries from her lips and seeing dark red patches appearing on the rounded globes of her white bottom. She moaned and sobbed, but having been on the receiving end of the whip, he knew that she would soon be entering that plateau where anguish and pleasure overlapped.

Gaston was counting, his voice a monotone accompanying the song of the whip. 'One... two... three... four...'

Henri moved round till he stood before her, plunging his hand into those glossy curls and lifting her face to his. Tears streamed from her eyes, and he brought his mouth to hers, possessing it, plundering it, feeling her tongue answering his passion.

Then he withdrew, took up his position and lashed her across the thighs. She moaned piteously and her water gushed out. Henri dropped to his knees between her parted legs, holding his face up to receive it, that warm, fragrant rain washing over him.

When it was no more than a dribble, he stood up, shook back his wet hair and administered the final blow. While she was still agonised by it he seized her swollen clitoris between his forefinger and thumb and rolled it vigorously. She came at once, convulsing and trembling, her pubis thrust against his hand.

'Oh, master... master...' she wailed. 'I'm sorry about the carpet... I couldn't wait any longer.'

'Never fear, my love,' he murmured, his smile as cold as the Arctic Ocean. 'You shall pay for your lack of control. It will be twelve lashes next time.'

He smiled into her love-drugged eyes and kissed her lips once, then turned away.

Gaston was waiting on hands and knees, his trousers pulled down, his pale, skinny posterior raised. Henri unbuttoned his breeches and straddled him, reached round to coat his fingers with the pre-come juice dribbling from Gaston's cock, and then worked it into his puckered anus. Gaston groaned, and rubbed his own stiff organ in search of orgasm.

Henri spread him wide, his fingers penetrating the tight anal opening, stretching it to receive something much bigger. His chest was heaving and his heart beat a rapid tattoo, his penis rearing up, seeming to search blindly for a nook in which to bury itself.

Gaston grunted, his hand flying over his own appendage, and Henri withdrew his fingers, then lifted his mighty, engorged rod and thrust it into the prepared aperture. Slowly, inch by inch, he watched his cock disappearing, while Gaston cried out and bucked against him. There was a moment's resistance, and then Henri felt the passage yielding as he penetrated it fully.

He ground his hips roughly, and began to pump. His thrusts were savage, the master out of control, his lust placing himself at the mercy of the slave. His lower belly slapped loudly against Gaston's buttocks with each forward slam.

The madness was in him, that compelling impulse rushing him towards completion, and he gave himself up to it, feeling the force searing his spine, filling his loins, making his balls tighten and his cock spasm, shooting forth a stream of semen.

He ripped himself out of Gaston's arse, watching the final spurt spattering the pallid flesh. Gaston had come, too, white strings of fluid hanging from his penis.

Henri recovered quickly, bending and wiping his deflating member on the tail of Gaston's shirt.

Bianca smiled at him, her face relaxed and peaceful. Once more in charge of himself, Henri began to make plans.

'Well, my sweet,' he said to her. 'I think we'll ask them to the ball we're holding tomorrow evening. The baroness is coming and you'll suggest that she brings her protégés as guests of honour. See to it.'

'And Prince Dimitri, and his three lovely sisters?' she asked as he unfastened the cuffs and helped her from the cross. 'We met them at a soirée not long ago. Do you remember?'

His strongly marked brows drew down in a frown. 'Yes, I remember very well. They left early. Ask him if you wish, though he's a deuced unsociable fellow by all accounts. His sisters are indeed incredibly beautiful.'

'And he is one of the most handsome men I've ever seen,' she said, dimpling up at him. 'Except you, of course... master.'

'They come from somewhere in Eastern Europe,' Gaston put in, adjusting his clothing and patting his hair into place. 'Hungary, Rumania or some such. I hear that they own the Palazzo Tassinari, a magnificent mansion, though rather fallen into disrepair. It's rumoured that members of their family have visited there occasionally for the last hundred years at least, but are somewhat reclusive. The palazzo lies empty for much of the time.'

'Trust you to come up with fascinating details,' Bianca purred, slipping a semi-transparent robe over her nakedness, her bottom showing through it, rose-red and glowing. 'I shall send the prince an invitation. You will attend, too, Gaston, and act the spy, a role I know you'll enjoy.'

'Thank you, madame,' he said, bowing low, their creature happy to obey every command.

Candice slept, or was it sleep? She was in the open under the glare of a gibbous moon. The ground was spongy beneath her bare feet. Someone had her by the hand and they were running – gliding on ice – faster and faster.

A grey mist swirled. Voices were singing. Fingers touched her, small fingers pattering over her body, teasing her nipples, a tongue tip tasting her wet fissure like a small hungry animal.

She was being prepared for someone, roused, inflamed, made receptive.

He was coming. She could feel the shockwaves of his approach.

The sky glimmered like spangled gauze, and from the sulphurous spaces of the universe he flew towards her. A radiant being, dazzling her eyes, his wings flaming, his hair coiling upwards to become one with the impenetrable darkness permeating him.

The firmament lit up with the blaze of his arrival. He had travelled from infinity to reach her and she waited, breathlessly.

Then she was swept up in iron-muscled arms, held against the hard wall of his chest, part of the scarlet and black, feeling his mouth feeding on hers. Heavenly mouth, magical tongue stabbing, the sweet thick flavour of nectar flowing over her taste buds.

His hand thrust between her legs, parting her labia, fingers plunging inside her, rapidly moving, betraying impatience. The hot wetness of her sap bathed her thighs as he withdrew his fingers from her tingling vulva. Then his phallus drove into her savagely, wringing a cry from her lips. Still wailing, she was lifted high on this cold, impaling stake.

Against a purple aurora laced with shooting, crimson stars, she felt it rending her, penetrating her to her heart – freezing – inhumanly cold – making her ache and burn, heating her into frenzied desire.

She clung to his mighty shoulders, legs wrapped round his waist, arching her hips away from the tremendous pressure of his organ, ecstasy pounding through her as his shaft chafed against her clitoris. She was fervently filled, stretched and invaded, the entity opening her as if he wanted to rip her asunder. She welcomed it as a saint welcomes martyrdom, the pain transmogrified into ecstatic bliss, of no account against the will and passion of her superhuman lover.

It did not hurt any more. The godlike phallus warmed her into pleasure so intense that she thought it might kill her.

'Ah... ah...' she screamed, on the splintering edge of orgasm. 'Ah... ah...' as she exploded against his stalk, the icy gush of his essence like a tidal wave drowning her.

She clawed at his back. Her fingers were wet with blood. Her maddened cries were muffled by the ebony mass of his hair. His movements slowed, the spear of power still buried to the hilt in her pulsating sheath. She heard his husky voice whispering her name.

'Candice... beloved...'

The voice changed. She was shooting away, holding out her arms to him, crying. A moment of blackness, disorientation, and then:

'Hush, dear... it's all right. You were having a bad dream,' said Emma, leaning over the bed, ghostlike in her white nightgown. 'I heard you cry out and came to you. Hush, hush... you are safe now.'

Chapter Four

Emma was worried about Candice. There was no one in whom she could confide her anxiety, but was determined to keep a close watch on her.

Once again she found herself adopting the role of nursemaid to her friend. Though she put on a brave front, there was something so vulnerable about Candice, betrayed by her eyes and the tender line of her mouth. Her interests, too, showed a bright mind which could easily become disturbed. A romantic, a dreamer, sometimes she did not seem to be quite of this world. But only sometimes, as in the hours following her nightmares. This is what Emma had labelled them, those eerie visions that had twice haunted her sleep. She was convinced Candice had been having another one – her piteous cries – her distress.

But when Candice had awakened the next morning she had embraced Emma, saying, 'I'm so glad you're here. Were you lonely, my love? How is it you've braved the dreaded Gwenda to be with me?'

Emma had pressed her close, running her hands over the tangled fair curls and looking anxiously into Candice's eyes which were still misted with sleep. 'Don't you remember?' she had asked, responding to that lovely scent which breathed out from between Candice's breasts.

Candice had shaken her head, snuggling in Emma's arms, 'No, what was it?'

Emma had been reluctant to say anything that might jog Candice's memory, choosing her words with care. 'I heard you calling out, and thought you might be frightened, finding yourself in an unfamiliar room. That's all.'

'Is it?' Candice murmured, and to Emma's alarm appeared

to be groping around in her mind for that dreaded dreamscape.

'Yes, entirely all. I thought it best if I stayed with you,' Emma had replied and, to divert her friend, and also satisfy her own cravings, she had caressed Candice's firm breasts.

The nipples had hardened through the thin lawn of her nightdress, and she had undone the ribbon fastening and bared them to her lips. At the same time her hand had idled down to where the skirt had been rucked up as Candice thrashed in slumber. The fronds of hair on her pubis were wet, and as Emma explored further she had discovered that her labia and inner thighs were slippery with the honeydew of arousal.

Even while she had brought her to climax and then taken her own pleasure, so she had been aware of a niggling unease, as she wondered what had caused Candice to be so ripe and ready, or rather – who?

The Hotel Danieli was well appointed, with lofty rooms decorated with baroque exuberance. Only the rich could afford to stay there, and the suite prepared for the Fortescues lay on the second floor, the walls ablaze with murals in the style of Tintoretto. The furniture was heavily carved, the chairs deep and comfortable, the beds broad four-posters with mosquito nets hanging from their testers, the bathrooms luxurious.

'I like it,' Fabian said, glancing round as they breakfasted in the imposing dining room where fluted columns reached the domed ceiling, potted palms supplied greenery and a small orchestra playing light Neapolitan tunes occupied a half-moon stage.

'We couldn't have made a better choice,' he went on. 'Mater's a perfect wizard at organising foreign holidays. Our first duty is a visit to her friend, Baroness Orville. I've already sent her a calling card, so she'll be expecting us. I gather she keeps open house in the mornings, tends to hold court, quite a notable person, so Mater says.'

Emma watched the proceedings and listened to all that was being said. She often found herself in the position of observer, far more astute than her rather frivolous exterior suggested. Now she cast an eye over the room, filled with round tables sparkling with glass and silver where guests of all nationalities talked vivaciously in little, exclusive groups.

Ladies in enormous hats and *chic* gowns; children with their nursemaids, the little girls in frilly frocks, the boys in sailor-suits; gentlemen wearing white or pale grey, twirling their waxed moustaches and smiling magnanimously at their females. The *maitre d'*, a dignified figure in black, poised on the balls of his feet, solicitous of his guests' requirements as he ordered the waiters about.

The sound of lyrical Italian voices predominated, and Emma's ear vibrated to it the language of poetry, of song – and love. She felt languid with desire, even the rasp of silk as one of her legs crossed the other made her skin tingle. Her tight corset seemed to encourage that feeling of heat in her loins, and her nipples were ultra-sensitive as her every movement caused them to rub against the lace of her chemise.

Fabian smiled at her across the table. She wanted to leap up, spread her legs over his lap and rub her crotch against his manhood. He was so handsome, curly-headed as a young god. Adonis sprang to mind – all those statues they had seen in Paris – the fig leaves spoiling the view but leaving the imagination to run riot.

Her husband-to-be and as circumspect as a monk, though she guessed he was hot as fire, probably pouring out his energy into harlots. This piqued her, but she was far too practical to fall in love, eager to be in the position where daily intercourse was the norm – the blessed state of matrimony. She resolved to put a stop to his whoremongering once they were wed, making sure she exhausted him with her own fierce demands on his penis.

Clive came under her scrutiny, while she sat there

demurely, nibbling a croissant and sipping her coffee. She liked his neat beard and moustache and pomaded brown hair. His eyes were brown, too, and his body well proportioned.

She savoured the secret knowledge of his behaviour towards Candice on the ferry. When her friend had whispered to her of this incident, it had excited her so much that she had been obliged to find the bathroom, lock the door, lift her petticoats and rub her clitoris till she gasped and convulsed.

Everywhere she looked there seemed to be a desirable male – the gondoliers, the waiters, even the pageboys in their smart green uniforms with brass buttons and saucy round hats.

It's Venice, she decided. In spite of its churches, saints and religiosity it is decadent and steeped in sin.

She pulled herself together sharply. If it was affecting her so strongly, then what must it be doing to the impressionable Candice?

'Where shall we meet, my lord?' Gwenda asked Fabian when, following his instructions, she and Flora Smythe scrambled from the gondola near a waterside post-office, dispatched to buy picture-cards and stamps.

'Make for the Rialto,' he replied, attired for the visit to the baroness in a spotless cream suit with a high-buttoned waistcoat, a pale blue shirt and a bow tie.

'And where is that, sir?' Gwenda enquired frostily, as severely dressed as ever, making no concession to the climate.

A pork-pie was pinned firmly in place on her top-knot, with the brim in the exact centre of her forehead. Her cane had been replaced by a black parasol which she unfurled to protect her from the strong Venetian sunlight.

'I'm sure we can find it,' said Flora in a rush, dimpling at Giacomo, eager to escape her employers for a while.

In contrast to the other chaperon she was excessively

feminine, in a pink linen dress, flounced and embroidered, and a straw hat awashed with silk roses. Her parasol was pink, and her face glowed in its shade as she held it aloft.

'I dare say we shall, but not without some difficulty,' Gwenda said with a disapproving sniff.

'It spans the Grand Canal, near the market,' Fabian answered irritably. There was something about Gwenda that made his hackles rise. 'You can walk through the backstreets. They are connected by bridges. I'm sure even you can manage that, Miss Turner. We'll see you there in,' and he consulted the dial of his gold pocket-watch, 'an hour.'

'Very well, my lord,' Gwenda said crisply, and gave him and Clive a withering glare. 'I suppose that will be in order, though I'm not happy about leaving Lady Candice. I promised Lady Sarah that I would look after her.'

'She's with me, you silly woman,' Fabian snapped, the gondola swaying as he sat up sharply. 'I'm perfectly capable of fending off vile seducers. Do you really think I won't keep an eye on my sister?'

Gwenda gave him a stern stare, her thin nostrils flaring. 'I trust this is true, sir,' she reluctantly conceded.

'I'm confident our young ladies are in excellent hands,' Flora gushed, all of a flutter, and added, 'Come along, Miss Turner.'

Gwenda snorted and stalked off with Flora trotting along behind her, shirts swishing, parasol handle resting across her shoulder.

'Miss Turner is a ridiculous female. I can't think why Mater tolerates her,' Fabian commented scathingly. Then he turned to Giacomo who was resting on his pole in the stern and rapped out, 'To the Palazzo Mancini.'

The exterior of the baroness's mansion was less grand than that of the hotel. Its façade was narrower and its steps mossy, while its door stood under an archway of worn stone.

On reaching it, Giacomo leapt ashore, fastened the gondola to the post, and assisted Emma and Candice to dry land.

The door was opened by a footman in striped livery. Fabian, that self-appointed organiser and spokesman, gave their names.

The footman bowed, said, 'This way, *signori*,' and conducted them across a shady, flower-filled courtyard and up a flight of marble stairs.

The room into which they were shown had a long, high ceiling painted with life-sized flying cupids and plasterwork as complicated as icing on a wedding cake. The walls were hung with pleated gold silk tenting. There were upholstered chairs and matching curtains patterned in sprigs and ribbons. Gilt mirrors and tall windows gave a faint rippling view of the canal and gardens outside.

It was filled with a chattering crowd, the baroness's sycophants, some genuine aristocrats, others mere hangers-on who lived on their wits.

Esmeralda, Baroness Orville, reclined on a thronelike chair at the end of the reception room. It was placed on a dais reached by three steps. On one side of her stood an Arabian girl, in gossamer pantaloons gathered in at the ankle, a girdle round her slim waist, and a tiny sequinned bolero that barely covered her breasts. A collar and slave bangles completed her attire.

On the other was a young man in a turban, his skin chocolate-brown, his features of an African cast with wide nostrils and thick lips. He, too, wore baggy trousers, though he was naked to the waist, a spiked leather collar round his neck and damascened bracelets on his broad wrist.

Each stirred the air above their mistress's head with peacock feather fans on bamboo poles. Leashes were looped over the arms of her chair, their ends attached to the slaves' collars. Esmeralda tugged at them every so often, jerking their heads up.

She wore a flowing chiffon, heavily beaded orange gown with loose sleeves. Her black hair was twisted into a coil on the crown of her head and secured by a diadem. A string of amber beads dangled down between her breasts, the deep neckline displaying the swell of those large orbs. Matching pendants swung from her ears, and her cheeks were rouged, her lips carmined and her lids heavily dusted with greenish powder.

This unusual vision extended a hand to Fabian as he approached, and said in mellifluous tones, 'Welcome, young scion of the House of Fortescue. I shall endeavour to make your stay in Venice a memorable one. And which of these two beauties is your sister?'

Candice wanted the floor to open and swallow her, embarrassed and bewildered by this eccentric woman. She stared, wide-eyed, at the blond man crouched on the bottom step of the dais. Clad in coat and knickerbockers of violet velvet, with a lace collar and a wide-awake hat trimmed with ostrich plumes, he was licking the baroness's feet like a dog, sucking each bare toe into his mouth with a kind of slobbering absorption.

She stirred, kicked him and said, 'That's enough, Gaston. Get up.'

'May I present Lady Candice?' Fabian said, sober as a judge, ignoring this unusual performance and propelling Candice forward.

Esmeralda rose to her full height, a tall woman whose thin gown revealed that her huge breasts were naked of underpinning, and her hips as voluptuous as those of the Venus Aphrodites flaunting their charms from the canvasses that hung in alcoves.

Candice felt awkward and unsophisticated as Esmeralda looked her over from head to foot, remarking, 'Oh yes, a beauty indeed. You're not a bit like your mother. How is dear Sarah? I haven't seen her for years.'

'She is well, thank you, baroness,' Candice stammered, unable to stop staring at those massive breasts, the nipples protruding against the beaded fabric, hard as cobnuts.

'We knew one another when we were young,' Esmeralda

continued, signalling to a servant who brought over a tray containing wine in crystal goblets, and little iced cakes. 'Then she married Fortescue and became lady of the manor, while I accepted the elderly Baron Orville, leaving England for foreign climes. He died shortly after, but I didn't waste time in repining. I've seen your mamma occasionally, and we've never lost touch. Have some wine, my child, and cake.'

Candice accepted, glad to give her hands something to do. She could not understand how her conventional parent, that stickler for protocol, could know such an outrageous person, let alone encourage her children to spend time in her company. But perhaps the baroness had changed since last they met.

Emma and Clive were introduced and Esmeralda received them graciously, though there was a predatory glint in her eyes. Then she said, 'You must meet some friends of mine, Comte Henri Merlion and Countess Bianca Renzo. They are giving a ball tonight and have already requested your presence. You'll come, of course.'

'Thank you, baroness. We shall be delighted to accept,' Fabian said, daring any one in his group to disagree. Then he replaced his glass on the tray and added, 'Now we'll take our leave. We are about to view this magnificent city.'

'You will not be disappointed,' Esmeralda replied, regarding him with her ink-black eyes. 'There is everything here to delight the cultured, the ardent traveller or mere pleasure-seeker. Venice can be all things to all men... and women, too,' and she directed her gaze at Candice. 'Come to the ball. This will be your proper introduction to our society. Anything can happen and probably will. I'll meet you there. Ask your gondolier to take you to the Palazzo Barbesi.'

She insisted on kissing their cheeks, and Candice was unpleasantly aware of being held a little too long and a little too close to those enormous, overpowering breasts. Esmeralda's perfume, sickly and cloying, seemed to cling to her like a miasma even when they had left the building and gone sight-seeing.

'Soon, my darlings, soon. Be patient,' Dimitri said, lounging in his great chair in the banqueting hall of his Venetian palace.

He sat at the head of the refectory table that stretched for twenty feet, large enough to accommodate two dozen guests. The board was bare, save for a seven-branched candelabrum, the soft light reflected in the eyes of his three unusually lovely companions, his sisters by blood, not birth.

'We're hungry,' they chorused, weaving like smoke in the dimness, performing a spectral dance for his entertainment.

'Then feed before the ball,' he advised, staring at them broodingly, every line of him proclaiming hauteur and self-will. 'I shall. Nothing must distract me from my purpose.'

'But don't you desire *her* as your source of sustenance? Your beautiful victim?' asked Medea, the eldest of the three.

Jewels flashed in her ebony hair that massed like a storm-cloud about her marble-white shoulders. Her eyes were pools of darkness, with sparks flaming in their depths. Her body was lissom, limbs gleaming through the sheer fabric of her robe, her breasts firm, the nipples ruby red.

'No,' he snarled, and his voice echoed under the beams, the force of his rage seeming to shake the palace to its foundations. 'Not my victim... never that.'

'Can it be you're in love, brother?' teased Madelon, her eyes glistening like moonlight on snow. She was petite, younger than the others, dressed in a gown from a famous Paris fashion house, the epitome of grace. Her hair, silvery-white as fairy floss, was elaborately ringletted, and when she laughed, as she did now, the sound resembled the tinkle of breaking glass, enough to make even the bravest man's blood run cold.

'Perhaps,' he answered dourly. 'I want this woman.'

'As a man does? You want to possess her physically? Yearn

to drive your prick into her love-channel, is that it?' put in Allegra, the remaining sister.

The bone structure of her face was perfect, her skin deathly pale as a shroud. Her colouring was that of a vixen, her hair a fiery nimbus round her shapely head. It seemed to glow like the sun, melting from gold to orange to red. And her eyes, too, constantly changed colour, violet to darkest purple.

Dimitri experienced that shift which always happened at dawn or dusk, the time when he could function as a man. His penis swelled in his impeccable evening trousers, and the sisters saw it, smiling as they linked arms and tormented him.

'You could have us, instead,' whispered Medea, her tongue extended, running across her red lips suggestively. 'It has happened before when we've lain together... at this time... or at that hour of the wolf just before daylight. We have pleasured you and not only with mind-play, our bodies have become human again and we have known that bliss which is on a par with the delirious frenzy of feeding.'

'I know,' he said, his voice heavy with melancholy. 'But this is different. We have been companions, it's true, and will go on being so, but she must be my bride.'

'We've looked at her,' Allegra said, and her hair shot out flames. 'She's nothing special, brother. You've been offered more beautiful women, drank of them, then tossed them aside. Why Candice?'

He was on his feet, moving with that lightning speed which was a part of what he was. His face was contorted with anger, his eyes flashing viciously.

'You've seen her? When?' he demanded, threatening to shrivel them with his glare.

'We've had her under surveillance for ages,' Madelon responded, refusing to be intimidated. She flicked open her lace fan and stared at him over the edge coquettishly. 'We linked our minds with yours, Dimitri. Did you think to exclude us from your plans? That was naughty of you, and most ungallant.'

There was something so terrible in his face that even she stopped flirting and retreated to a corner of the hall with her sisters. He grew in stature, looming over them, filling the entire area, a monstrous black shadow.

'If either one of you bitches harms her, then I swear by all the dukes and earls of hell, that I'll hound you till the end of time,' he roared, flexing his hands, the fingers resembling talons, the nails long and curved.

'We won't harm her,' ventured Medea and, bolder than the others, drifted up to clasp him round the shoulders, pressing her breasts against his chest. 'It's her friends who interest us. We can satisfy both appetites at once with them... Fabian and Clive, and not forgetting the lovely Emma. Trust me, brother. Haven't I been with you since the time you were transformed? Didn't I accompany you on your dark journey into immortality?'

'Yes, you did, and that was when I left the girl behind, she who is now called Candice. She refused to come with me... too afraid of losing her soul.'

Dimitri was especially ravenous that night, and hunger lent a crystalline clarity to his thoughts. He slipped back into the past, reliving those events which had dramatically shaped his future:

Paris during the reign of Louis XIV, the Sun King—

Another night of excess awaited him, starting at the card-tables, then progressing to an eating house, roistering and drinking before picking up a lively whore and fucking her. How much more exciting was Paris than that gloomy castle in the Carpathians where he had spent his boyhood?

He had been dispatched to France by his father who, exasperated by his behaviour and wearied of his continual harping on about becoming a doctor (a most unsuitable occupation for a prince!) had obtained a place for him at medical school.

No doubt he had hoped Dimitri might get his rebelliousness

out of his system, satisfy his endless curiosity regarding the workings of the human mind and body, and return to take up his responsibilities as heir to their mountainous kingdom.

Dimitri's title opened the doors to the royal palaces. Quickly disillusioned by the ignorance of his tutors and appalled by the squalid hospitals, he neglected his studies, preferring to experiment alone.

Twenty-six and lusty, he joined those dandified rakes who gambled and whored, obsessed with fashion and prickly about their honour, quick to draw their swords at any real or imagined insult.

He had gained a reputation as a duellist. No man cared to cross him. Not only did they respect his prowess with the rapier, but recognised the other side of him – serious, brooding and with more than a hint of cruelty.

His reflection stared back at him from the cheval mirror, of above average height, with those pronounced features and passionate eyes that proclaimed his Slavic origins. He had not yet adopted the new fad for huge, curled perukes, wearing his own hair, a mane of tousled black ringlets that fell across his shoulders and halfway down his back.

His thoughts strayed to Lady Mariella to whom he had been betrothed when he was ten and she a babe in the cradle. When introduced to her in Paris he had fallen in love. They were to be married in the summer and, profligate though he was, he had not tried to seduce this lovely sixteen year old, respecting her purity.

'I was with you then, one of your many mistresses,' Medea said, reading his mind and catapulting him back to the present. 'What a time we had! I've never regretted it. So rich and sumptuous and wicked! King Louis had me, you know. Oh yes, right under the nose of his mistress, Madame de Montespan. She was a sorceress, using love-potions and sacrificing newborn babes to keep his interest.'

'So it was rumoured during the *Affaire des Poisons* when so many people were brought to trial. Her name was kept out of it,' Dimitri said, part of him in Venice, part in France during that barbarous witch hunt.

Madame de Montespan, dominating, perverted and avaricious. Dimitri wondered about her as he stepped from his bedchamber in seventeenth-century Paris and entered his laboratory.

Were the rumours true? Did she take part in obscene black-magic rituals? Could his name be linked with hers? Surely not. Though he had participated in her orgies, playing sex games with whips and manacles, he did not cast spells or brew poison and regarded fortune-tellers as charlatans.

Dabbling in the occult was the current vogue among fashionable sensation-seekers. Astrologers, palmists, necromancers, all attracted a large following, though such practices were totally against the church's teachings.

The laboratory was warm, a stove built into a recess. Dimitri tucked a small porcelain crucible in its fire-clay cradle and banked the glowing cinders round it. Faint, herb-scented vapours spiralled upwards to the groined roof. There was no sound save that of a delicate bubbling.

He flipped open his notes and studied them. He was seeking to perfect a formula which would render patients unconscious while operations took place. At the moment these were little short of butchery with the unfortunate person made drunk and strapped to the table. A surgeon's skill depended on his speed with the knife.

'It was Belphegor who saved you,' Medea reminded, and Dimitri was back in Venice, aware of her insistent fingers exploring his sex, passing through the fabric of his trousers and fondling his balls, then stimulating the phallus that lifted to meet her phantom caress.

'I did not realise what he was,' Dimitri said, the image of that elegant fiend suddenly appearing before him in the laboratory.

'How did you get in? I didn't hear you knock,' Dimitri said, happy to see this clever friend with whom he often sat far into the night, deep in philosophical discussions.

Belphegor was older than Dimitri, magnificently handsome, an aristocrat who was vague about his place of birth – giving it as somewhere in Eastern Europe. He was rich, knowledgeable and elusive, never on the scene till nightfall.

He leaned an elbow nonchalantly on the work-bench and rearranged a set of glass vessels filled with concoctions of amber and green, the touch of his hand almost caressing.

'I'm here to warn you,' he said in his rich, rolling voice. 'At dawn La Reynie, the chief of police, is coming to arrest you.'

A retort dropped from Dimitri's fingers and shattered on the floor. 'Why?' he exclaimed, that gut feeling of unease manifesting tenfold.

'For practising the black arts,' Belphegor replied, his brown eyes serious. 'You have been named by the witch, La Voisin... under torture, it's true, but her evidence is enough to damn you, my friend. The king fears poison above all else, and he is panicking. He'll protect Montespan, finding other scapegoats.'

'Like myself,' Dimitri muttered, his bowels clenching with fear.

'Exactly,' Belphegor replied and, though Dimitri did not see him move, he had come very close. 'I can help you escape interrogation and burning to death at the stake, for make no mistake, you will be condemned.'

'Can I make a run for it?'

'Alas, orders have gone out that the city gates are to be closed and guarded.'

'Then I'm doomed.'

Belphegor smiled into his eyes, and his touch was intimate. Dimitri's shock warmed into pleasure as one slim white hand reached round to caress his buttocks.

'All is not lost,' Belphegor murmured, his breath fragrant yet laced with the sickly-sweet, acrid smell of blood. 'I can rescue you, and I will, my beautiful young friend. I've wanted you for months, but you were so engrossed in cunts and bosoms. Give yourself to me, body and soul, and you will never die.'

'How is this possible?' Dimitri asked, feeling Belphegor run the tips of his fingers along his throat, lingering where the pulse beat strongly in the jugular vein.

His touch was fluid, exciting, more lust-inducing than female caresses. Immediate. Needing instant gratification. Akin to masturbation. Dimitri's penis responded, painfully stiff and rampantly inflamed.

'Have you never heard of the *nosferatu*?' Belphegor purred.

A shiver rippled through Dimitri, deadly fear and longing fluttering in his belly, tingling in the tip of his cock and spreading to the heaviness of his balls.

'Vampires? But of course. My country is rife with such superstitions,' he managed to stammer. 'I learned about them at my nurse's knee.'

Belphegor lifted his head and smiled at him, lips curling back over his teeth, the canines longer and sharper than was normal. 'No old wives' tales, my friend. We exist. I am undead... a vampire, and I'm offering this gift to you. Let me make you as myself and you will be invincible. You don't want to die horribly, do you?'

'No, I don't,' Dimitri averred, mesmerised by Belphegor's eyes. 'But I can't believe you're one of those devilish creatures.'

'I give you my word as a gentleman,' Belphegor insisted. 'Did you never wonder how I knew so much about history, science and literature? I have been around since the Middle Ages. Make up your mind, Dimitri. We have no time to lose. Is it to be life everlasting, or an ignominious death?'

'I've little alternative, have I?'

'And you believe me now? You want me to do it?'

'Yes... yes,' the words left Dimitri's lips like a sigh.

In that instant he felt himself possessed. He was helpless

as a babe against the other's superhuman strength, and did not want to resist. The creature's phallus slipped between his arse cheeks and invaded his forbidden hole, bringing him to a screaming crisis of pleasure. At the moment when his semen spurted and Belphegor's cold fluid pumped into the depths of his body, those vampire fangs sliced through the skin of his throat like a hot knife through butter.

His life-force was flowing away in a stream of exquisite ecstasy. He was fading, fainting, as Belphegor drained him to the threshold of death, then abruptly released him.

Dimitri dropped to the ground, watching through half-closed eyes. The vampire tossed back the frill at his wrist and bit into the flesh, then thrust it forwards, the hot blood dripping into Dimitri's mouth.

'Drink of me!' Belphegor muttered urgently.

Snatched back to Venice, he heard Allegra saying, 'And when you fed on his blood, he gave you all the vampire powers – great strength, the ability to travel through time, to be invisible, to read minds, to hypnotise... and to make others undead.'

Madelon had joined her sister, her tiny hands slipping through Dimitri's shirt and teasing his nipples, her succulent lips following their path. Strung on the rack of pleasure, Dimitri almost forgot the other driving need that must be satisfied, and quickly, lest he become frail.

'You accepted his gift,' Medea whispered, on a sigh that could have been the night breeze wafting between the shutters. 'You became a vampire and, my dear brother, passed on the blessing to me... and to Allegra. We were also implicated in the witch-trials.'

'You saved us from an agonising death,' Allegra murmured, her tongue lapping at his ear. 'But couldn't persuade your betrothed to join us.'

'I tried,' he said on a note of anguish. 'She was in no danger, an innocent virgin. I had never done more than kiss her hand. After my transformation I appeared to her one night, but she screamed for her priest and I had to leave. She later became a nun and I was never able to get close to her again. When she died, she entered realms where I was forbidden to follow, and now she has been born again as Candice.'

'This time you are determined not to lose her,' Madelon said, winding her arms around his neck. 'I will help you, for I, too, owe you a debt I can never repay. You rescued me from the mob in the days of the French Revolution. They were going chop my head off on the guillotine, all because I was an *aristo*.'

'You were lovely then, and just as lovely now,' he answered, his hands holding hers as they appeared at his waist, passing through his body. 'We remain as we were at the moment we became blood-drinkers... never aging... always young...'

'And virile,' added Medea.

'And desirable,' put in Madelon.

'And invincible,' said Allegra.

'And hungry!' Dimitri concluded with a grim laugh. 'It's time to go, ladies. Time to trawl Venice for our next meal.'

'Venice is wonderful,' they agreed in unison.

'Remember when we first came here?' asked Medea, and weaved herself into the darkness which now invaded the hall as he snuffed the candles. 'We bought this house... oh, it's so useful to have helpers... the gypsies who revere us, and admirers who will not have us harmed. Our agent, Carl, did the buying, and he is still with us, betwixt and between, neither quite human nor entirely vampire. All we have to do is become succubi, enter his bed at night and drain him of his vital juices, his blood, and his semen which nourishes us almost as well. And he adores us for it.'

'There is so much to be had here, and always has been. A fine feeding ground. The narrow streets, the dens of iniquity in the shabbier quarters. We can wander at will and take our pick in the labyrinths of stone and water, streets and houses,' carolled Allegra gleefully.

'I prefer blue blood,' Madelon commented loftily. 'There's nothing so invigorating as dining on a well-bred young beau or a genteel virgin. I never drain them completely. I leave them on the point of death, so that when they awake hours later they are filled with a lassitude for which their doctors can find no cause, the tiny marks of my teeth on their flesh dismissed as insect bites. They recover after a few days, the bites fade, and they remember nothing except an absolutely amazing dream. They are too shy to confess to anyone that it was sexual.'

'So fussy!' Medea exclaimed impatiently. 'Blood is blood, wherever it comes from. I don't say no to rats, cats and dogs, if that's all there is.'

'Stop arguing, and let's go,' Dimitri ordered.

'Yes, brother,' they cried, raised their arms and, like him, disintegrated in a shimmer of mist.

'Giacomo! You're such a charmer,' breathed Flora as he clipped her round the waist and pressed her against his hot body. 'I really must go. The others are waiting for me. No, stop it.' She made a token gesture of pushing away the hand that was inveigling its way up her skirt.

'Ah, *bella signora*,' he sighed, as they stood under the bridge in his tethered gondola, a rather unstable trysting place.

Flora could feel her resolve melting, though she knew she must return in haste to the café where Lady Emma and the others were eating ice-cream and resting after the vigours of tramping round St Mark's. She had slipped away with the excuse that she had left her bag on board, but in reality had wanted to find the attractive Giacomo who had been giving her little signals ever since she had first clapped eyes on him.

A widow of thirty, she missed the comforts of the connubial couch, such as they had been, and sought satisfaction wherever she could. This trip was providing her with a wealth of lovers, of humble origin maybe, but no matter.

Gwenda was an enigma to her with her open dislike of men. Flora always felt uneasy when undressing in front of her in the room they shared. She had the feeling that Gwenda wanted to touch her, and Flora did not reciprocate. Though indulging her desires whenever she could, these always featured the male sex. It was strong arms and a big cock that she wanted.

Her late husband, a grocer, had left her reasonably off, and there was no necessity for her to work, but she found that being a chaperon enabled her to enter realms otherwise barred to her. Childless and fancy free, she enjoyed every moment of her life. Being Lady Emma's duenna had proved a golden opportunity for dalliance, and this European adventure the best of all.

What could be better than a horny young gondolier?

His mouth found hers, his breath fragrant with garlic. His tongue parted her lips and slipped inside, and he moaned under his breath as he probed and tasted. His fingers had reached their goal, brushing aside the wide leg of Flora's silk knickers and gently stroking over her bush. She hoped he would not look, for she bleached her hair and this would give the game away, her thick pubic floss several shades darker.

God, but he knows what to do, she thought, while it was still possible to think coherently. He's parting my slit and finding my bud. Oh, yes! It's even better than when I frig myself.

She was in a trance, breathless, waiting, anticipating that explosive rush of orgasm. He still kissed her, deeply, divinely, and she wished they were in bed somewhere, mother-naked.

'No, don't stop,' she murmured as he withdrew his hand. It was wet with her juices and he passed his fingers under his nose, inhaling deeply, then saying in fascinating broken English, 'Madame, lie with me in the gondola. We shall rest on the cushions and I will draw the little curtains. No one shall see us.'

She was beyond recall now, following where he led, to the velvet seats beneath the canopy. A cramped space for loving, but no matter. He sat in one of the chairs and she knelt in front of him. He took her wrist in his fingers and very gently placed them on the bulge straining the buttons of his flies.

Flora did not hesitate, deftly unfastening him and drawing out his large, olive-hued member from its nest of black curls. It pointed upwards, seeming to salute her, long and thick, veined and velvet skinned, its helm twin-lobed and shiny, wet with jism. For a moment she did nothing more than roll it in her hand, relishing the feel of his randy young manhood. Then, slowly and carefully, she lowered her head and took the tip into her mouth.

She furled her tongue round it, licking in the salty taste – sweat and pre-come. Down she went, lower and lower, her breasts bulging out of her bodice, her skirts high above her knees, taking in the whole of him until the glans bored into her throat and she was smothered in the heat and hairiness of his crotch.

Moving up a little she sucked vigorously, hair tumbling down, rosy hat tossed aside. He was pressing up, driving into her mouth, but she did not intend him to come that way. She needed to feel that solid bough deep inside her, and teasingly withdrew, saying, 'Not yet, Giacomo.'

She rose, dropped her knickers and sat across his lap, showing her lace-welted stockings and small feet in glacé kid shoes. Her fleshy thighs and ample hips swamped the slimness of the youth beneath her, but his cock jabbed against her delta, hard as a log.

He reached up and freed one of her breasts from her bodice, pulling at the long pink teat, then lifting his head and sucking it. Flora was in heaven. She rolled her other nipple in her fingers, adding to the excitement, her clitoris protruding from its cowl, frantic for attention.

And he knew. He understood.

'Madonna,' he whispered, in that velvet-dark, husky voice. '*Bella... bella...*'

Worshipping at the shrine of her womanhood, he eased her up till she was astride his face. Flora could not believe her incredible luck. Taking her weight on her knees in order not to crush him, she was rewarded by the feel of this thick, fleshy tongue working her clitoris. It flicked, it teased, it roused – driving her mad.

She threw back her head, eyes closed, her energies concentrated on those three points of pleasure – her nipples and her nodule. Flora arched her back, thrusting herself against that tongue which was exploring the sensitive groove between her love lips.

The feeling grew and gathered, tingling upwards from her toes, past her knees, her thighs and into her throbbing depths. She cried out as his teeth fastened lightly on the very nexus of her pleasure. She peaked, carried to bliss by the sweeping torrent of orgasm.

As she rose, gasping in her release, Giacomo slid her over his body and lifted her on to his organ. Then he drove it in, filling her as she had wanted to be filled since first seeing him. Now all gentleness had gone and he plunged in violently, thrusting and pumping, jabbing and working her. Flora bounced up and down on his ardent phallus, her slippery channel stretched wide, feeling her aching inner muscles contracting in the final spasms of climax.

The gondola rocked. Passers by observing it must guess what was taking place in the curtained cabin, but she did not care. The madness was in her – that blind urge to absorb him into her very depths, and hold him there for ever.

He gave a final thrust and his penis jerked. Hot fluid gushed into her, and she collapsed on him, gasping.

After he had withdrawn she pulled down her skirts and sat beside him while her pulse slowed and the tremors in her body subsided. He tucked his weapon away and held her in his arms, then whispered sweet love words and subjected her to little, nibbling kisses, as lovers will once the heat and fury of lust is over.

Flora finally left him, a fully satisfied woman. He had treated her with a respect that was rare among casual partners, and she positively glowed, her step light and springy as she hurried to the café.

'Ah, there you, Mrs Smythe,' Fabian said, his brows drawn down in a frown. 'We almost gave you up for lost. We must hurry to the hotel, for there is a ball tonight. You will come along, of course, in your capacity as Lady Emma's duenna.'

So, before very long, Flora was once again in Giacomo's company, but studiously ignoring him as she sat with the young ladies. However, as she gave him her hand when leaving the gondola at the Hotel Danieli's steps he squeezed it, and gave her a meaningful look.

'Tonight,' she whispered very low. 'I'll meet you while the others are engaged at the ball.'

Guard Lady Emma indeed! All Flora's sense of responsibility had flown away like chaff in the wind under the Latin charm and expert lovemaking of Giacomo.

Chapter Five

'How delightful they are! Thank you for encouraging them to accept my invitation, baroness,' exclaimed Henri, as they stood on an indoor balcony looking down on the newly arrived English couples who were unaware of being scrutinised.

'Do you mean the splendid young men or the girls?' Esmeralda asked with a quirky smile, admiring them from this vantage point.

'Both, darling,' Henri answered, his eyes glinting with wicked mirth. 'I'll concentrate on Lady Emma and Lady Candice, while Bianca will give of her best to Lord Clive and Lord Fabian, with, no doubt, a little help from yourself.'

'Ah, but comte, how are you to achieve your purpose? Bianca and I may make free with the men, but have you forgotten that the young ladies are chaperoned?' Esmeralda reminded, nestling her bare arm against his brocade-covered one as they leaned on the marble balustrade like a pair of wily conspirators plotting a Medici prince's downfall.

'My dear baroness,' he responded, with a curl of his thin lips. 'I have come to the conclusion that all men are venal... women, too. I've never yet met a chaperon who couldn't be bribed with gold.'

'Or if not, offered a tempting alternative?' she suggested, nodding to where Flora and Gwenda stood at the back of the spacious reception hall.

Though they wore evening gowns, these were of uncompromising plainness, indicating that while a little above the servant class, they were still employees. It would be their duty to sit on the sidelines and wait their mistresses' pleasure, but also to ensure that gentlemen who asked to add their names to the young ladies' dance-cards were of impeccable lineage. Though tonight their work would be lightened, as the girls were accompanied by fiancés who might demand that they partner them in every waltz, polka or quadrille.

'Chaperons won't foil my plans, Esmeralda,' Henri declared, and lifted a finger to tease one of her nipples that was partly exposed by her daring décolletage, at the same time diving a hand under her skirt and fondling her damp, silky cleft.

Candice was awe struck. Never, in her most extravagant imaginings, had she envisaged a ball such as this.

The Palazzo Barbesi was like a huge, glittering jewel set in the midst of water. The lights from its windows sparkled on the canal where a fleet of gondolas was hitched to posts below a magnificent flight of steps. They bobbed gently after disgorging a deluge of guests. Private craft, their gondoliers would wait patiently till the party was over.

Candice entered the main hall on Clive's arm to be presented to her host and hostess. Countess Bianca was the first to greet them.

'I've been so eager to meet you,' she cried, gliding towards them. 'And how do you like Venice?'

She spoke excellent English with a slight accent, and her voice was low and musical. She was garbed as Cleopatra in a fragile gold tissue skirt, draped in the front and slit to the thigh on each side. This partly concealed the reddish shadow at her fork, though it was evident sometimes as she moved her shapely legs. From beneath her snake-ornamented headdress her hair trailed down her back in a mass of auburn curls.

'Venice is quite remarkable, but we've not seen a quarter of it yet,' Fabian responded as he bowed over her beringed hand, his eyes glued to the curve of her breasts, the nipples proud and stiff, poking through the gold bodice.

'You must allow me to take you on a conducted tour,' Bianca said graciously, her amber eyes going over his body as if he were a stallion at stud, while her fingers played with the long strings of beads that dangled tantalisingly in her cleavage.

'We will be honoured. Thank you, countess,' he murmured. Candice was struck by the sensual current flowing between her brother and this gorgeous lady. It washed over her, too, making her nipples crimp and her nubbin thrum.

Then all other thought was banished as an incredibly handsome man passed through the throng, making a beeline for her. Esmeralda was with him, but Candice had no eyes for anyone else. As she dipped into a curtsey she could feel her knees shaking and, when he raised her up and stared into her eyes, the room seemed to sway.

Was it *him*? Could this possibly be her dream lover?

He was dark-haired and distinguished, with icy grey eyes and a high-bridged, patrician nose. There was an underlying hint of danger about him that made her quiver with delicious, wanton anticipation. Sparks shot up her arm to her cortex at his touch, despite the barrier of her kid glove. That frisson of excitement did not diminish, even when he introduced himself as Comte Henri Merlion.

Candice was possessed of the crying need to ask him – what? Have you dreamed of me? Did we make ecstatic love in some weird, celestial realm?

How could she possible say that? He would think her a silly, imaginative schoolgirl and she could not bear it if he rejected her.

The room suddenly seemed unbearably hot. The scent of flowers was almost overpowering. There were jardinières full of white blooms, spilling over and adding their strident odour to that of blood-red roses, frilly pink carnations and exotic purple-spotted orchids.

The light was subdued, and a curious green-blue as if one walked under water. It shone from opaline globes set in gold wall-brackets or from large, petal-shaped trumpets held aloft by statues of naked men. Their genitalia were sculpted in minute detail – each curling pubic hair, every vein knotting the phalli, each plump net holding the ripe fruit of their testicles.

The shadow of a smile crossed Henri's lips as he saw Candice staring at these realistic statues, then, 'Shall we go in?' he said, gesturing to a lofty arched doorway.

His tone was so intimate that Candice was sure he was speaking to her alone. He cupped her elbow and she trembled as they crossed the threshold of a salon were guests in fantastic masquerade costumes drifted, chattering and admiring each other's outfits. She could see further doorways leading to grottoes decorated with greenery which turned them into dimly lit forests.

Somewhere a boy was singing a madrigal, his voice high-pitched and sweet.

Candice wished she had had time to find fancy-dress. She felt out of place, though her cream satin gown was fashionable, the skirt clinging revealingly to her rounded hips, outlining the deep divide between her buttocks before gushing out in flounces. The bodice was trimmed with artificial silk roses, so low-cut that the upper half of her breasts swelled over the lace. Diamonds flashed at her neck and earlobes and she had felt confident in her appearance, but not any more.

Some guests were masked, some not. The men were disguised as troubadours, cardinals, Egyptian gods and satyrs, pirates and cavaliers, and the ladies displayed a good deal of flesh as they took on the personas of harem girls, courtesans or Grecian nymphs.

Though this appeared to be a decorous gathering, Candice was aware of darker undertones, sure that all was not as it seemed. She was surprised to see angular, mincing figures whom she recognised as male, though they wore flowing wigs and skirts and high heels, and a few women dressed as soldiers, swaggering around in form-hugging buckskin breeches and thigh-length boots.

Henri conducted her to a room draped in autumnal hued silk, caught up here and there by gem-encrusted clasps. It opened out into a conservatory filled with tropical plants where, on an oval pond surrounded by palms in terracotta pots, a stately white swan floated.

The room was furnished with carved divans upholstered in green damask, small, ebonised chairs and low buhl tables supported on squat legs ending in lions' paws. The air was warm and humid, its almost narcotic atmosphere inducing a curious kind of lethargy.

Henri clapped his hands and servants appeared, placing trays of fruit and little confections on the tables, with chilled champagne served in slender flutes.

Candice glanced at them, then looked away, blushing. The men's liveries were formal but their breeches were exceedingly tight, exposing the hard muscles of their buttocks, the hollows at their flanks and the long boughs of their cocks trapped against their inner thighs.

The females had on very short, full skirts that reached the apex of their legs, displaying transparent knickers through which their hairy mounds could be seen. Their waists were restricted by tightly laced stays that finished under the bust, leaving their breasts and nipples bare.

Candice gulped at the sight, but told herself that she was now in the centre of Venetian high society and must expect to be astonished, maybe even shocked.

The boy's voice had been replaced by the sound of an orchestra playing a waltz and, through the opened double doors leading into the salon, couples could be seen, twirling like colourful toys on the polished floor.

Seated next to Emma on one of the divans, her knees pressed tightly together, arms clasped about her body defensively, Candice peeped at Henri through her eyelashes. He lounged back, a glass in one hand, making expansive gestures with the other as he talked to Fabian. She did not take in what they were saying, too engrossed in trying to make head or tail of this worldly company in which she now found herself.

Henri was devastatingly attractive, enough to turn the head of any hot-arsed female, and Candice was discovering that this described her with alarming accuracy. She was boiling with unfulfilled passion, and had even considered going to Clive's bedroom one night and offering herself to him. Her fingers, or Emma's, no longer satisfied her.

The enchantment of Venice, the languorous atmosphere, the heady perfumes, the wonderful light like no other on earth, the gondolas riding the canals steered by handsome boatmen, were all conspiring to rob her of her virtue.

And those two women – the baroness and the countess – she was perfectly certain they did not go around with wet love channels aching to be filled. No, they would do something about it. She watched them surreptitiously, wishing she could be so bold.

Where Esmeralda was lush-bodied, Bianca was sleek, with a piquant, kitten-shaped face and eyes that tilted upwards at the outer corners. She reminded Candice of a cat – a pampered feline who yet retained its untamed instincts. Of aristocratic birth though they undoubtedly were, neither she nor Esmeralda gave thought to modesty in their choice of garments. They were out to lure lovers into their webs – male, female, it didn't much matter.

But Candice wanted a man – needing to experience the force of a male organ thrusting into her, to feel his hands cupping her breasts, his thumbs rolling her nipples but, above all, the thrust, thrust, thrust of his penis.

'Have another glass of wine, Lady Candice,' said Henri, leaning towards her from his chair and holding one out.

'Thank you, sir,' she answered shyly, while taking in his wide-shouldered body in the elaborate eighteenth century coat with large turned-back cuffs.

He wore this over a lavishly embroidered yellow waistcoat, with Mechlin lace foaming at his throat and wrists. His hair, with those shining silver wings, was drawn back into a queue and tied with a black ribbon, and he carried a tricorne hat. But it was his legs in those cream breeches that drew her eye constantly, athletic thighs, strong calves but, most of all, a burgeoning fullness at the crotch. She burned to run her fingernails up and down it.

She had nearly finished the second wineglass, and was feeling tipsy. The champagne was stronger than she had imagined. It was becoming harder and harder to resist the impulse to touch Henri's bulge.

Full of alcoholic *savoir-faire* she beckoned to him and, with a smile, he dropped to his knee before the couch and said, 'What is it, Lady Candice?'

'Were... were you in my dream, sir?' she stammered, stumbling over her tongue which seemed twice its usual size.

He laughed a rich, low, mocking laugh, and said, 'Not that I'm aware. But what a charming idea. What did we do, Lady Candice, in this dream of yours?'

One of his hands caressed her satin-shod foot, then slid upwards to her ankle, her long skirt concealing his action. Colour flooded her face in a hot tide but it was as nothing compared to the heat laving her delta in love juice. His hand advanced higher, skimming over her knee, a finger inserting itself into the top of her stocking, smoothing the bare skin above and following the line of her thigh to where it disappeared beneath the hem of her wide-legged knickers.

Candice started as that exploitative digit stroked the fair floss coating her mound. She sat upright, her heart beating a wild tattoo against her ribs, her nodule swelling, seeking the pressure of his finger which would rouse it to untold heights of bliss. But, to her disappointment, Henri did no more than gently tug at her maidenhair.

The others were engaged in small talk, but even had the world suddenly become one large ear she would not have been able to prevent herself from saying, 'In my dream, we made love.'

'Did we? And I can't recall it? What a tragedy!' Henri exclaimed, and his eyes cut to Clive, who seemed unaware of what was taking place between the comte and his fiancée, his attention focused on Bianca.

Was Henri the one? Doubts tormented Candice. Though she wanted him with panting, lubricious eagerness, he somehow lacked the magic, the menace, the sheer majesty of her demonic-angelic lover.

'I would like to show you some of our treasures,' Bianca said, her eyes hooded, deviltry playing over her plum-coloured lips. 'Will you come with me, Lord Fabian, and you, Lord Clive? Esmeralda shall accompany us. She knows more about art than I do, and I have some extremely rare and... unusual pieces... I'd like you to see.'

'Thank you,' both men replied as if mesmerised by her words and her body, the shimmering gown undulating over her curves with every sinuous movement.

'But what about Lady Candice and Lady Emma? I don't see the chaperons anywhere,' Fabian protested, but without much conviction.

'Don't worry. I'll take care of them,' Henri promised and, abandoning Candice's aching bud, rose to his feet and smiled down at the girls. 'I'm sure they'd love to see my private collection. I have such interesting things on display.'

Flora had slipped away early with the excuse of needing fresh air, and Gwenda, fuming, had been left alone in that unenviable spot reserved for chaperons. She had the feeling Flora was up to something and hazarded a guess it might involve Giacomo, a cocky young pup, in her opinion, far too full of himself.

'I'll report her behaviour to Lord Fabian,' she vowed to herself, but at that moment she was confronted by a maidservant.

'Please come this way, *signorina*,' the girl said, a pretty, doe-eyed creature whose brief skirt resembled a ballet-dancer's tutu.

'Me?' Gwenda replied, immediately suspicious.

'*Si, signorina*,' the maid answered, smiling and bobbing. 'The countess has ordered it.'

Gwenda was mystified, but intrigued by this olive-skinned beauty whose skirt swirled up as she moved, revealing a patch of sepia fuzz sliced across by an even darker slit. She was naked to the waist, her firm breasts almost consumed by the prominent red nipples. Gwenda's loins lurched and her clitoris pulsed as she feasted her eyes on them, her saliva running as she imagined taking them into her mouth like firm-fleshed strawberries.

She felt the press of warm fingers on hers and was led up some backstairs and into a room which resembled a gymnasium, except that the equipment would never have been seen in such sober establishments.

Gwenda stared round her with growing comprehension, a thick skein of excitement weaving down her spine into her womb.

The floor was of polished wood. The windows were barred. The light shone on whips and paddles, canes and rods, birches and taws, all neatly arranged on hooks screwed into the walls. There was a thing that looked like a vaulting horse, the difference being that it was furnished with chains and handcuffs. By it stood another bench with holes at strategic points – where the mouth or genitals would be if one were bound to it, lying on one's stomach.

The maid closed the door and placed a hand under each of her breasts, bouncing them and playing with the nipples, watching this performance in a large gilt framed mirror positioned on one wall. Then, looking at Gwenda, she murmured, 'The countess told me to do whatever you wanted, *signorina*.'

'What's your name?' Gwenda asked gruffly, hardly able

to speak.

'Maria,' the girl murmured softly. 'Your slave for tonight.'

A red mist formed over Gwenda's sight, and a great surge of longing swept through her. This girl – this toy – given to her for her entertainment!

Gwenda was nobody's fool and she guessed that the countess had a hidden agenda. It might concern the seduction of Lady Candice, but no matter. This was a heaven-sent opportunity that she simply could not afford to miss.

She advanced on Maria who stood there unresisting. Gwenda pinched those strawberry teats that hardened even more, and pushed up the white muslin skirt. The scent of woman filled her nostrils, strong as dittany, sweet as honey, tempting her to wriggle a finger in the pouting sex and encourage it to give forth more ambrosial essence.

She yielded to temptation, opening Maria's cleft and burying her middle finger to the second knuckle in the warm, pulsating vulva.

Maria moaned and pushed upwards to meet this invasion, her nipples standing out hard as stone. Gwenda lowered her head and, still thrusting her finger in and out of that velvety passage, took one of those delicious dugs between her lips and sucked vigorously.

Maria's legs started to shake and she gyrated her pubis against Gwenda's hand. The chaperon stopped fingering her, a cruel, teasing smile on her face as she said, 'You're a lecherous little tart, aren't you, Maria?'

'Yes, mistress,' she whispered, hanging her head in shame.

'You want me to rub your button and bring you off, don't you?'

'Yes, mistress,' Maria sighed, submissive and meek.

'I'm going to beat you for your unclean thoughts,' Gwenda hissed, her lust running like a river in full spate.

She could feel wetness soaking into the crotch of her cotton drawers that rubbed against her swollen lower lips. Her nubbin ached and throbbed, demanding satisfaction, but first she must fuel her fire even more.

'Bend over the horse,' she ordered crisply.

While Maria arranged herself across the padded bench, Gwenda paced along the racks of implements. She was spoilt for choice. What should it be? A flexible cane? A smooth paddle? A many thonged taws which would flick tender flesh in a dozen sensitive places? Or a birch, that bundle of prickly twigs bound to a wooden handle?

She tried one, tested another, then her fingers encountered a leather strap – as simple as a belt, and as effective for meting out punishment. Gwenda was experienced. She had been at the receiving end often enough when her stepfather beat her mercilessly before shafting her anal hole.

Gwenda flicked it against her own thigh experimentally. Then, smiling grimly, she stalked towards Maria.

It was a sight to turn a saint's head, a double vision of heaven mirrored in the large looking-glass – Maria, stretched across the vaulting horse, head hanging down, her long black hair streaming towards the floor. The lovely rotundity of her buttocks was exposed, as plump as sun-ripened melons. Her stockings had wrinkled to below her knees and her calves strained to balance her weight on the high heels of her shoes.

Gwenda did not hurry, savouring every moment of this encounter which fulfilled her every darkest, deepest, most perverted fantasy.

Going round to the far side she jerked Maria's head up by the hair and stared into her wide-spaced, frightened eyes. The girl's breasts swung down and Gwenda pinched the nipples, forcing a gasp from Maria's lips. Then, seizing the metal cuffs hanging from short chains bolted to the wooden sides, she drew Maria's arms apart and snapped the bracelets on each wrist.

She could no longer control the urge to hurry, fingers fumbling as she spread Maria's legs and manacled her ankles. It was impossible not to touch those ripe globes. She passed her hand into the avenue between the bountiful halves of that magnificent rump, rendered open and vulnerable by the tight shackles. She pushed a fingertip against the wrinkled anus, then explored lower. There she found slippery wetness seeping from Maria's vulva.

Just for a moment she permitted herself the joy of working that tell-tale juice over Maria's engorged lower lips and around the stalk of her clitoris, hearing her mew with pleasure. Then she withdrew.

Her bodice was tight and she needed her arms free for action, so unfastened the front and stripped it off, then hung it over the back of a chair. Her skirt and petticoats came next, joining the bodice. Now she stood in her chemise, whale-boned corsets and knickers. She saluted her image in the mirror, then wound the end of the strap round her hand and took a few practice swipes.

It whistled through the air.

Maria whimpered.

This was too much for Gwenda's fading self-control. She raised her arm again and brought the strap down forcefully on Maria's soft hinds. The crack echoed through the room and the girl pulled against her restraints, the imprint of the lash leaving a mark that rapidly turned bright red. Gwenda could feel the sensation running back up the leather into her arm as she watched Maria squirm.

She listened to her gasping, waited for the pain to reach its peak, then laid on another stroke that landed on the fullest part of Maria's buttocks. The figure bound to the bench bucked in anguish, the second welt tracking across her posterior turning the colour of sunset, forming a flaming path just below its fellow. Maria cried out in her extremity and urine splashed to the floor as her bladder betrayed her.

Gwenda watched, the blood drumming in her ears. Then she drew the strap between her own legs, rubbing it briskly over her mound and into the slit of her arse, her clitoris on fire, her knicker seam drawn tight over it, soaked with juice. But she denied herself orgasm.

'Not yet,' she muttered under her breath. 'Not quite yet.'

Balanced on one foot, she lunged with the strap, her weight adding to its velocity. This blow was placed just under the curve of Maria's bottom, the tip of the lash catching the purse of cloven, hair-fringed flesh that protruded between.

Maria arched like a bow, opened her mouth and screamed. This was like the sweetest music to Gwenda's ears. She wielded the strap with renewed vigour till Maria lay there like a stranded fish, shaking with sobs, begging for mercy, her buttocks marked by a ladder of red stripes.

'This is for your eyes only,' Henri said, taking Candice and Emma by the hand and leading them to a large window set in the wall of his bedchamber.

'Good gracious! It's Miss Turner!' Candice cried, staring at the astounding spectacle of her chaperon, in corsets and drawers, beating a girl bound helpless to a leather upholstered bench.

'How can this be?' Emma asked, grasping the side of the window and staring as if she could not believe the evidence of her own eyes. 'Can't she see us?'

Henri shook his head, smiling at their bewilderment. 'It's a trick window, my dears, giving me the pleasure of witnessing all that takes place in my punishment room without the occupants being aware. On their side, it appears to be an ordinary mirror.'

'What a diabolical device!' Candice shouted, backing away from him. 'You spy on people!'

'That's no sin,' he expostulated. 'Can you honestly say you've never wanted to watch others indulge their base desires?'

'I have,' Emma piped up, her cheeks pink with excitement. 'I confess to be eaten up with curiosity, comte,' and she could not take her eyes from the tableau in the window, adding, 'Why is Miss Turner beating that girl? And look what she's doing now! Oh, dear me!'

103

All three stared through the glass as Gwenda stood in front of her victim. She pushed down her knickers and exposed her coarse pubic bush and the scarlet line dividing her mound, the swollen lips parted. She stretched them wide, two fleshy pairs of wings, then began to rub the prominent nub at the top of her cleft.

'Esmeralda was right,' Henri mused, his hand dropping to where his breeches were distended over his tumescent organ. 'She judged your duenna to a nicety, Lady Candice. By her appearance and mien, she guessed she lusted after women, not men, and enjoyed handing out corporal punishment.'

'And where is my chaperon?' Emma asked. 'It's not fair if Candice can be free of hers, whereas mine may come nosing around at any moment.'

'She won't,' Henri said. 'My informants tell me she is even now fornicating with Giacomo.'

'The gondolier?' Candice cried, experiencing a sharp stab of jealousy, for she had been convinced he wanted to bury his weapon in her virgin sheath.

'The very same... a vigorous man, hung like a donkey by all accounts,' said Henri, and he and Emma shared a smile as if the situation was amusing.

'It's disgraceful. As for Miss Turner, it's her duty to care for me. Why is she with that maidservant?' Candice asked indignantly. 'I could have her dismissed for this.'

'But you won't,' Henri said softly, and taking her hand he guided it down to the solid mass in his groin. 'Slip off your glove, my dear, and see what viewing her does to me. Aren't you aroused, too? Doesn't the sight of the lash disturb you in a strange way? And that bounteous bottom of Maria's – like a grape about to burst with flavoursome juice. Don't you long to strike it?'

'No, sir...' she lied, but worked her fingers out of her kid glove nonetheless, his action reminding her of Clive's on the ferry-boat when he desired her to handle his masculine part. 'As for enjoying the strap... Miss Turner has caned me in the past.'

'And you enjoyed it?' he murmured, his eyes slitting as her fingers examined his mighty rod concealed by the cream satin.

'On the last occasion... perhaps,' she admitted, aware of Emma's surprised, questioning gaze.

'You didn't tell me,' she accused. 'I thought we'd agreed to share everything.'

'I was too ashamed,' Candice confessed, feeling Henri's cock stir in her hand like an awakening serpent.

'But why?' Emma demanded.

'I know why,' Henri answered, and slid an arm round Emma's waist. 'I'll wager it was because she reached her crisis, if not under the rod, then shortly after. Isn't this so, Candice?'

How shameful to have to admit to this, she thought. How humiliating, but his steely eyes bored into hers, forcing the truth from her, while the feel of his cock in her hand melted her resistance.

'I did. She brought me to it, just as she's now doing to that wretched servant,' she admitted, unable to stop watching as Gwenda reached a convulsing climax and then released Maria, laying her down on the floor and delving into her most private niche, making her writhe and shudder.

'There's nothing to be ashamed of,' he assured her, and his penis was harder and hotter than before, its dampness penetrating his breeches. 'It's natural to seek release. Don't let anyone convince you otherwise. Pain and pleasure can intermingle. To submit oneself to another's will... to reach depths or heights for which one is not responsible. Ah, my darling young ladies, will you submit to me? Let me teach you. Accept me as your master.'

'I think not, sir,' Candice replied, drawing her hand away. 'No man shall be my master.'

'Oh, come along, Candice. Don't be such a spoil-sport!'

Emma admonished. 'It's only a game. I'm willing to play.'

She was panting, eager, her eyes bright, her ample breasts rising and falling in a way familiar to Candice. All those lovely memories of their lovemaking returned to torment her. Yes, she admitted to herself, watching Gwenda had roused her to fever pitch. Why not join in? There could be no harm in it, providing it did not go too far.

'We are both engaged to be married, sir,' she said sharply. 'And must therefore retain our maidenheads.'

He fetched a sigh, but moved towards the massive bed that dominated the beautiful room. Candles burned in sconces on either side of it, shining on the beaten silver that adorned its headboard, the mirror set in its tester, the velvet curtains that draped it.

Such a sensual, voluptuous setting, filled with rare and priceless ornaments – paintings in massive frames, the subjects arousing in the extreme – naked men and women in the throes of passion. There were statues, too, and tapestries depicting hunting parties in dark woodlands, with baying hounds and bleeding stags and gentlemen in hot pursuit of their hapless prey, mounted on horses with rolling eyes and tossing manes.

Henri removed his jacket and waistcoat, then tore off his cravat, his shirt open over a sunkissed chest, while Candice watched him, as helpless as a cornered deer. She heard Emma take a sharp breath and saw that she, too, was unable to do other than feast her eyes on him. He was so masculine, so dominating – a master indeed.

'Virgins, eh?' he said with a slow, thoughtful smile. 'You shall keep that precious gift.'

He's wicked, Candice thought, but I can't but admire him. What is there about evil that appeals to me so much?

Now he took hold of Emma's hands and she yielded eagerly as he captured her mouth with his, bending her over his arm and kissing her deeply. Candice clasped her hands against her breasts, consumed with envy. She wanted to feel his lips, to taste his tongue, to be devoured and absorb him in return.

He raised his head and smiled at her, then opened Emma's bodice and released her breasts to his hands. Emma hung in his arms, unresisting, her eyes closed, a rapturous smile on her face.

'You want this, don't you?' he said to Candice, flicking over Emma's nipples which stiffened immediately.

'No,' Candice lied, feeling her body stir and flare.

'That's not true,' he retorted with a deep-throated chuckle. 'You're wet for me, wanting me... longing for me to caress you.'

His expression changed to fury and he flung Emma aside. She cried out in protest, grovelling at his feet, but he strode over to Candice and yanked her up against him.

'You lie. Why deny it? You're too proud, an independent English miss, but I will make you beg me to take you, never mind your confounded virginity.'

He hauled her towards the bed while she kicked and struggled. There he flung her across it and rolled her over on to her face. Cold air struck her as he yanked up her skirts and pulled down her knickers. In the next, appalled instant, she screamed aloud as his hard hand descended on her bare bottom.

The blow smarted, and she threshed under the hand that was holding her firmly, yet the smart warmed into something else – a dart of pleasure that penetrated her epicentre.

'No! Don't! Please...' she yelled, and tears sprang into her eyes.

Henri ignored her, and his hand slapped down brutally again, once, twice, landing on each of her buttocks in turn. He had slim, strong hands with callused palms, used to handling a sword or schooling horses. She could smell his sweat, overlaid with pungent perfume, and could hear his rapid breathing.

Emma stood close by, and she had a hand under her skirt,

and was stimulating her clitoris, giving vent to gasping sounds of pleasure.

This is insane! Candice thought, then was caught up in the madness of it as Henri went on smacking her viciously. Her bottom stung and burned. She yelled and whimpered, hating her wayward bud that was stinging and burning too, urgently demanding relief.

'You want it! Say it, you stubborn bitch! Say it!' he hissed in her ear, and his hand plunged between her legs, dabbling in the wetness there, pushing into her vagina and meeting the resistance of her membrane.

'I don't!' she moaned, refusing to submit. 'Let me go!'

For answer, he smeared her juice over her clitoris, rubbing the hardened gem till her moans turned to ones of ecstasy. She heard him laugh as his finger left her nubbin and spread her dew up the crack of her arse. Shrinking and gasping, she felt him touch her nether hole. Not even Emma had tampered with this forbidden place, but Henri was not only touching it – he was invading it – pushing a finger into her cringing anus – in and in till she felt as if she was being impaled.

'Stop! You're hurting me!' she screamed.

'You have to be stretched, my dear. There are more ways than one of skinning a cat,' he said, breathing heavily, and worming his finger in and out, forcing her sphincter to relax.

'I can't... please,' she wailed, yet her loins were responding to this unnatural invasion.

'That's better. You're loosening up nicely,' he muttered, and for a blessed instant, left her tortured anus.

She looked round over her shoulder and was aghast to see him unbuttoning his breeches. Horror flooded her, but this changed as he drew out his penis. It was awe-inspiring, a huge fleshy spear rearing up from a forest of wiry hair. She fell silent, her emotions in turmoil, her lust urging her to touch it, take it in her mouth, run her tongue up its mighty shaft and suckle at the acorn-shaped glans.

He smiled as if reading her thoughts, and ran his hand up and down its length, making it grow even bigger. Then he pressed close between her spread legs, ran a hand under her belly and lifted her hips. Too late, she realised his intention – unable to do other than accept as he took his cock and pressed the swollen purple head against the portal of her rectum.

She shrieked, consumed with pain, though he did no more than insert the tip, but this was enough to convince her he was about to offer her an agonising experience. He pressed in, then withdrew a little, easing his organ up and down between her sore bottom cheeks.

Candice sprawled there as if dead, her clitoris aching, her rump a stinging sea of pain. Then she felt him rise. The bed shook with his frantic movements as he worked his phallus in his hand.

He gave a sharp bark of satisfaction, and shot a stream of warm, milky libation over her buttocks.

It could have been hours or little time at all, when Candice found herself in the ballroom. She had fled Henri's bedchamber, leaving Emma to his tender mercies.

After he had spurted over her, she had struggled to her feet and run away, passing through corridors and lofty rooms, coming across guests engaged in copulation, no longer disgusted or shocked or even surprised. Henri had cured that.

In one grotto she had found a pair of diminutive oriental girls chained to a block while men whipped them or mounted them like cattle, bending those wonderfully supple bodies to their lusts. Further on, young male slaves were pleasuring men, offering their arses in abject submission. Whips sang and paddles whacked down on firm flesh while voices were raised in pain or exultation.

Candice ran on, her feet skimming the ground, seeking her brother or Clive – needing someone – she was not sure who, tears threatening to overwhelm her with the disappointment of finding Henri falling far short of her ideal.

The ballroom was full of whirling dancers, the music now soft and sweet, now loud and compelling. Candice stood on the edge of the floor, searching for a familiar face. Though surrounded by people she had rarely felt more isolated. No one noticed her. It was as if she had become invisible.

Then something, an intuition, a gut feeling, made her look over to where a flight of marble stairs curved down into the room.

The breath caught in her throat and she was transfixed.

He was there!

Moving slowly, almost gliding, was the man who had taken possession of her in her dream. This time there was no mistake. She recognised him by the singing in her soul, the yearning of her body and the rushing heat of her blood – like calling to like.

Chapter Six

Even as Candice registered his presence, so he materialised in front of her as if spawned from the heart of darkness.

He was clothed entirely in black, and stared down at her from his immense height. She was helpless under the penetrating glare of his hungry green eyes. Images of icebergs and the Polar wastes flashed across her brain, of snow stretching an unconscionable distant, of frozen plains and glaciers and, in the midst of this untrodden purity, a red ember, growing and glowing, drawing her into the fiery realms his pupils.

He did not appear to move, but she felt him take her hand, felt herself rising effortlessly, floating upwards with him, hovering over the ballroom, nearly touching its stained glass dome.

An eerie blue-white light blasted the scene, the dancers locked in time, posing like living statues in exactly the same positions as when he appeared. The musicians, bows poised over fiddle strings, flutes raised to lips, hands lifted over piano-keys, were suspended mid-play. The servants, too, were motionless. All were like the occupants of Sleeping Beauty's Palace when the princess pricked her finger on the spinning wheel and everyone fell victim to the wicked godmother's spell. A hundred years of sleep!

Candice was bewitched, impervious to what happened to her or anyone else, dancing in the ether with her prince, that giant, magnificent lover who might be an angel or a devil. She half expected to see her physical self standing below, but through some unimaginably mysterious process she was really with him, in body as well as spirit.

He caught her in his arms, and she felt the tremendous

power and force of him, and paralysing danger and a need within herself that demanded instant satisfaction. She reached up and wound her fingers in his raven hair, dragging his face down to hers.

'Make love to me,' she sighed, her core liquid with desire.

'Not yet,' he answered, his accent strong, rendering the deep cadence of his voice even more devastating.

Its timbre scraped down her spine into her secret depths, finding that sensitive spot which communicated with her clitoris, setting up a painful throbbing. Her nipples peaked under her bodice, and his hands were there, a perfect cradle for her breasts, his long, strong fingers pinching the ardent little crests.

'I want you,' she sobbed, staring at his face that was fashioned with an unearthly beauty.

That smooth skin, corpse-pale except for the colour flushing his high cheekbones, the nose that gave him a hawk-like appearance, and his mouth... the upper lip finely cut with an arrogant curl, the lower sensually full.

He drew a pointed fingernail lightly down her hot cheek, then kissed the crook of her elbow, parting his lips to lay his teeth against the blue vein that throbbed beneath the soft skin.

'I shall have you, never fear,' he murmured, his breath raising the fine down all over her limbs.

Waves of music billowed around Candice. Not that of the players beneath her, but the sound of a symphony orchestra. Sonorous chords resonated through the atmosphere, poignant and sad, and she wept as she danced with him. It was not the waltz or any other step she knew – but wider, wilder – free and abandoned.

And the song was old as time, as new as tomorrow: she had found him, they were as one, but nothing was for sure.

Her tears spilled over and he licked them from her face, his tongue a barbed icicle. She stared deep into the age-old mysteries of his eyes and struggled to speak. He silenced her with his mouth, his lips bruising and hard, forcing hers apart, teeth gnawing with animalistic pleasure, tongue jabbing against her palate.

As in her dream she heard the rustle of wings, glimpsed them rising from his back. They were metallic black, melding with the surrounding star-scattered darkness of the sky as she shot into infinity, clasped to his mighty chest.

She tried to hold him, but though he seemed solid, her hands went through him like water. Then she felt him grasp her between the thighs, fingers pressing against her aching clitoris. A fierce, lighting bolt of sensation seared her. Without warning, a terrifying orgasm exploded within her. She screamed and lost consciousness.

'I hope you're broad-minded, gentlemen,' Bianca said, her arms linked through Clive's on the right and Fabian's on the left.

'We're not stuffy, if that's what you think,' Fabian retorted quickly, his cock reacting to her body like steel to magnet.

'I'm glad to hear it,' she returned with a musing smile, and pressed her breast against his arm as they walked towards her apartments.

Fabian had always been greedy: he liked money and he liked power. As the Fortescue heir he stood to gain it all, and his parents were more than generous in his allowance. But now his eyes glinted covetously as he was led through the private quarters of the Palazzo Barbesi. Though owned by Henri Merlion, the mansion was also Bianca's stamping ground and she was rich in her own right.

On every side was evidence of great wealth and influence. The comte was a connoisseur of all things beautiful, and his mark was everywhere. Fabian knew that Bianca fancied him and beside relishing the possession of her gorgeous body, he guessed she would be generous to her paramours. Would Henri mind her sharing her favours with others? Fabian thought not, already deducing that theirs was an open relationship.

Bianca flung back a superb pair of cedarwood doors and stepped into a room which surpassed anything yet seen. It had an eastern ambience, not only apparent in the silken drapes and incense-sweet air but by the naked slaves, male and female, chained to pillars or crouched subserviently on the floor. Each one was a paragon of beauty, nubile and desirable.

Fabian's cock sprang to full stretch, the swollen head chafing against his underwear.

He glanced at Clive, wondering if he was experiencing the same thrill, then smiled as he saw the front of his friend's trousers pushed out of shape by the swelling behind the fly. He looked extremely embarrassed, his face flushed beneath his beard, his eyes darting uneasily from side to side, but unable to avoid the blatant display of nude bodies.

Esmeralda saw it too, and reached out to stroke that awkward looking protuberance. The tip of her tongue wetted her carmined lips and she exchanged a mischievous glance with Bianca.

They've planned this! Fabian thought, excitement coursing along his veins. I'm sure they are hell-bent on our seduction. And what has Henri in mind for Candice and Emma? Somehow, this did not bother him. He was able to concentrate on nothing but the overwhelming urge to drive his penis into a slippery orifice and work it frantically till he discharged his semen.

The sound of Bianca's palms clapping together roused him from his lustful reverie. A slave girl shuffled over to her, walking made difficult by the chains confining her ankles. She stood with her hands clasped above her head and her eyes cast down. With a sharp stab of lust that almost tipped him over the edge, Fabian saw that little gold rings pierced her nipples, with thin links looped between them.

Lissom and lovely, her timidity delighted him. He wanted to tug on the rings, to hurt her, to make tears fall from those almond-shaped eyes, to force her to her knees and stick his cock in her mouth.

'Her name is Nina. You like her?' Bianca whispered. 'You approve of the pretty ornaments in her nipples? She has more. Spread those gorgeous legs, girl,' she commanded, with a brisk slap across the pierced orbs. 'Let the master look at you.'

Nina's breasts wobbled under the blow and the skin flushed. Her feet slid apart, and her fork was revealed. It was nude of hair and Fabian's fascinated gaze fell on more rings fastened into her labia majora.

He advanced a hand and his fingers turned the golden hoops passing through those plump wings. Wonderingly, he inserted his middle digit into her crack. It was hot and wet, shameful desire making her juices flow. Her bud rose to his touch, a firm sliver of flesh seeking his caress.

Fabian was too much of a gentleman to refuse a lady's request, and frigged her vigorously. Nina quivered and moaned, and Bianca said firmly, 'Don't let her climax, my lord. I suggest you give her a good thrashing first, then when you enter that sweet cleft she'll be more than ready for you.'

It was on the edge of Fabian's tongue to confess that he had never before beaten a woman, only the boy who had fagged for him at boarding school, but the challenge in Bianca's eyes stopped him. She slapped a pliable rubber paddle against her open palm, then handed it to him.

He was the centre of attention, the tethered slaves, Clive and the ladies all waiting breathlessly for his performance. Nina did not look up. She simply sobbed quietly.

'Aren't you forgetting your manners?' Bianca asked her sharply.

'I'm sorry, mistress,' Nina snivelled, and went down on her knees and kissed the toe of Fabian's black shoe and the paddle hanging from his hand.

He was intrigued by the way her breasts swung forward, the chain dangling between them, her long golden hair hiding her face. He could smell her, the scent of cinnamon mingling with that of the honeydew escaping from the smoothly shaven delta.

It was too much for mortal man to bear. Fabian could feel his stomach knotting and his pulse racing. His penis swelled. He lifted his arm and whacked the paddle down across that perfect rump.

'Bravo!' cried Bianca, leaning against a bronzed young slave, sliding her hands up and down his erect cock as he stood upright and immobile, staring straight ahead.

Now Nina's backside was marked by a crimson patch the exact shape of the paddle. She bit her lip, sobbing, but trying to stifle the noise.

Fabian was enjoying himself, the veneer of the civilised, upper-class Englishman stripped away. He remembered getting an erection when he flogged young Brentford Minor in the dorm after dark. He had brought himself off under the bedclothes when the punishment sessions were over or, better still, had the unfortunate fag satisfy him with fellatio.

The paddle slammed into Nina again, and she screamed. Tears ran down her face as she quivered under a further assault.

'Nina! I'm ashamed of you! Stop that caterwauling!' Bianca shouted.

'I'm... s-s-sorry, mistress,' Nina stuttered.

'So I should think. Such an exhibition is a slur on my disciplinary measures. Accept six more strokes and then suck the gentleman's part.'

Fabian delivered these enthusiastically, laying them on hard. Now both of Nina's buttocks were glowing, and the meaty underhang and the tops of her thighs. A trickle of moisture escaped between the pursed lips of her sex.

Fabian unbuttoned, exposing his throbbing weapon, iron-hard and more than ready. He could hardly contain himself, forgetful of everything in his need to release his pent-up lust.

Nina knelt between his feet, her crimsoned bottom raised, her face so close to his genitals that the feel of her breath made his testicles crimp. His prick was vastly swollen, the foreskin pushed back by the emergence of the helm, the tiny slit glistening with jism.

'Lick it,' he commanded, his voice unusually gruff. 'If you don't do it properly I'll use a whip on your arse... and on your tits, and that hot wet quim of yours.'

He was talking like a foul-mouthed East End stevedore, every vestige of sophistication stripped away. He had not even behaved so crudely in Madame Carenza's bordello. It was Nina's meek compliance that fired him, bringing out the bully. Some men might have been moved to cherish her: he wanted to abuse and shame her further.

Whimpering, she reached up to take his cock in one hand. This light caress was not enough. With an oath Fabian pushed his pubis into her face, getting a stranglehold on her yellow hair. His penis leapt, jabbing against her mouth. Steeling herself, she opened up, stretching her lips to encompass the glistening purplish glans.

'That's it!' Bianca exclaimed, her voice shrill with excitement as she left the slave and came closer. 'Make her suck you, but don't lose your spunk. I want it in me!'

He nodded and grinned vacantly, surrendering to the divine feeling as Nina rocked her head, her mouth taking him in to the full, her tongue licking and stroking, rolling and fondling till he groaned. She was gasping and panting, stopping briefly to gulp in air, then returning to her task, her fingers brushing the hairy sac of his cods.

His crisis was almost upon him. His fingers dug into her scalp, holding her to his crotch. He could feel the need surging in his testicles, mounting to his shaft. Release was a breath away.

'Stop!' Bianca commanded and he dragged his cock from Nina's mouth, swinging round to where the countess sprawled on a heap of cushions.

Hardly aware of anything save the heavily veined rod swaying stiffly from his underbelly, he registered her naked thighs, naked fork, the gash of her opened sex lying between the fox-red bush. Her skirts were up, her breasts exposed, and as she pulled at the pink stalks of her nipples and rubbed her swollen clitoris, so she watched with heavy-lidded eyes as his prick advanced towards her.

Fabian positioned himself between those magnificent thighs and his savage column of flesh found its way unerringly into her slippery haven. As he powered it with his hips, burying it deep within her, so it soared and spasmed in a consuming orgasm.

Candice was on the ballroom floor, surrounded by other dancers, the sad, lovely, passionate music replaced by a prosaic waltz tune. Limp as a rag-doll she clung to her partner, her feet automatically following the steps.

The music stopped. There was a spattering of applause and Bianca was there, holding out her hands and crying, 'Prince Dimitri! How charming of you to accept my invitation. And where are your sisters?'

He smiled sardonically and bowed, an aristocrat in a superbly cut evening suit worn with a black shirt and black cravat.

'Your servant, countess,' he rejoined with old-world courtesy. 'They are here.'

Three extraordinarily lovely women stood at his side. Each was splendidly gowned, bejewelled and coiffured to perfection, but Candice shivered at the sight of their chalky skins, vulpine eyes and blood-red lips lifted back from their teeth in predatory smiles.

'Lady Candice, may I introduce you to my sisters?' he said solemnly. 'Princess Medea.'

'So delightful to meet you,' the raven-haired charmer said, slanting Candice a black-eyed glance.

'Princess Madelon,' he continued.

118

'My pleasure,' lisped the small blonde, her pale blue eyes holding a depth of wisdom that was frightening in its intensity.

'And Princess Allegra,' Dimitri concluded, his voice warmed by pride in his remarkably beautiful siblings.

'I hope we shall become friends, very close friends,' pronounced the one whose hair flamed about her handsome head, vying in brightness with her jewelled tiara and amethyst eyes.

'I see you have already made the acquaintance of Lady Candice, prince,' Bianca remarked.

'I have had that honour, madame,' he replied, and his hand tightened on Candice's arm.

'But I don't remember,' she protested, half smiling, half afraid, completely confused. 'Were we introduced? How did I come to be dancing with you?'

Bianca laughed, and so did the princesses. 'My dear, perhaps you've had a little too much to drink?' she suggested.

'I don't know. I can recall being with Emma and the comte... then nothing more till you spoke.'

'Then perhaps you've not had enough,' Bianca said gaily and signalled to a passing footman who balanced a tray of wineglasses. 'You'll drink a toast with me, prince, and you too, princesses?' she continued. 'Here's to England, birthplace of Lady Candice. Italy, my own homeland and... where is yours, Prince Dimitri?'

'Transylvania,' he replied seriously. '"*The Land Beyond the Forest*", where my ancestors founded a dynasty a thousand years ago.'

He bowed again and his sisters curtsied like mechanical dolls. They accepted the wine, but did not drink, merely placing their lips to the rims of the crystal goblets.

Transylvania! Mountains, rugged terrain, fertile valleys and cascading torrents, a castle on a crag. Images passed before Candice's inner eye like slides at a magic-lantern show. Who was projecting these visions? Was Prince Dimitri

119

trying to control her?

Breathtakingly handsome though he was, the idea was faintly repugnant. She wanted to be in control of herself – her life – her destiny.

This was just possible, as long as she did not meet his eyes – or touch him – or allow him to touch her.

So this was the mysterious Prince Dimitri, the man Giacomo had made the sign of the cross on naming. And the princesses? Who were they and what part were they playing in this game?

She was feeling totally disoriented. Was he the one with whom she had mated in her dreams, or was it nothing more than a fantasy on her part? Suddenly she could not tell what was real – what up and what down. To add to her dismay, there was a hot tingling in her centre, a wetness between her legs and what were nothing more nor less than the fading spasms of orgasm rippling through her groin.

She wanted Emma to comfort her, her heart beating fast, her body shaking with fear.

Fabian strolled through the door, white-gloved and bandbox fresh. Candice stared as the princesses undulated round him, as insubstantial as smoke at one moment and solid the next. She dismissed this as a trick of the light.

More introductions and Fabian smiling at Bianca in an intimate way. 'Prince Dimitri,' he said, nodding and shaking hands. 'I've heard so much about your country. Spectacular scenery, I understand.'

'And splendid hunting,' Allegra butted in, looking at him boldly. 'Do you like to hunt, my lord?'

'Certainly. I ride to hounds at home, chasing foxes and deer.'

'I love to hunt,' Allegra almost crooned, her black velvet gown fitting her like a sheath before flaring out below the knee. 'It's so thrilling. Don't you think so, my dear sir?'

'Absolutely,' Fabian agreed.

Bianca's auburn locks seemed to grow dull and lose their

colour compared with Allegra's flaming mane. As she moved with sinuous, snake-like grace, her shoulders and the curves of her breasts rose from the velvet, as smooth, cold and white as alabaster.

'Would you care to dance?' he asked, and he wore a fixed expression, unable to take his eyes from her.

'Oh, yes. Next to hunting, dancing is what I like best,' she said, in that melodious foreign voice.

'One moment, Lord Fortescue,' Dimitri interrupted. 'My sisters and I must leave now, but come to dinner tomorrow evening. We can talk further about my country... you and your other companions.'

'Oh yes, do come,' the princesses chimed, laughing with throats arched and teeth flashing. 'We'd adore to have you for dinner.'

'Thank you, prince,' Fabian replied gravely. 'We will be pleased to accept.'

'And you will be there, Lady Candice?' Dimitri said in a way that brooked no refusal.

She inclined her head, unable to speak.

'I'll send my gondola to fetch you at eight o'clock.'

He turned to Bianca who was gazing at him with naked lust in her eyes. 'Now if you will excuse me, countess, I must be going.'

'So soon, prince?' she pouted, and placed a detaining hand on his arm, then gasped and withdrew it as if scalded.

'At once,' he said crisply, his face set in haughty lines. 'Good night, madame.'

Candice blinked and when next she looked there was no sign of him or his sisters. They seemed to have vanished into thin air.

'I should go and find Candice,' Emma sighed from her place on Henri's lap.

'Not at all,' he answered, teasing her left nipple through the slippery satin of her bodice. 'I want you here, with me.'

121

His lips fastened on hers, tongue delicately tasting and teasing, and this, coupled with his attention to her breasts, made a bubble of excitement gather in her belly. Candice had kissed and fondled her, but this was different. He was harsher, harder, more demanding, and Emma's flesh responded joyously.

Seated on his lap, she could feel the heat of his organ pressing against her hip. He had not fastened up after Candice's departure, and his swollen rod protruded. Emma ventured down, found this staunch part and fondled it.

Hot, hard, it jerked under her fingers and she could not resist closing her palm round its thickness. He gasped into her wide open mouth and pushed down her bodice, teasing and tweaking the buds that rose from the crimped areolae. His lips followed suit, and as his mouth closed over one teat, sucking it strongly, Emma's whole body arched, catlike, to meet that exquisite pleasure.

Moving to the other, leaving the first wet and aching, he lipped it thoroughly, then pushed up her skirt and tenderly stroked the bare thighs above her garters until he touched the crisp hair at the apex. He lifted her knickers aside and opened her secret lips with his fingertips. Emma cried out but did not resist as he went further, exploring the juice running from her and inserting a digit into the ripe virginal opening.

'You are ready, my pet,' he muttered, and his cock released a tiny trickle of pre-come, wetting her hand.

Emma was beyond thought or reason as he eased her from his lap and part led, part carried her to the bed. With the tiny bead of her clitoris throbbing with want, her breasts throbbing from his touch, she would have liked to have had him undress her, wanting to be stark naked, impatient with the restrictions of corset and petticoats and the satin gown.

He smelt wonderful, of male sweat and expensive cologne, and held her away from him just long enough to lift both breasts above the ridge of her stays and push aside the low-cut bodice. Her breasts jutted out proudly, squeezed together by this restraint, large globes of flesh crowned by rosebud nipples at which he feasted, sucking and licking till she wanted to scream with frustration.

Although in the throes of carnal heat and wanting to be stripped naked, Emma was nervous. In her dreams of wedding-night completion she had welcomed her bridegroom in the dark, concealed by bedclothes. Henri was staring at her openly, assessing her charms as a buyer might when purchasing a slave at an auction.

But his fingers rolling her nipples formed a direct link with her clitoris, bringing forth the eager dew of anticipation. Shyly, she stared down at his phallus. It was huge, rearing up aggressively, its clubbed head pointing towards her.

Would it be possible to take a thing that size inside her? She had watched as he pushed the tip into Candice's anus, and had shivered in sympathy for her friend's anguish. And now he intended to insert it into her maiden hole. She wanted this so much, but could she bear it?

'To add to the pleasure, I'm going to bind your wrists and ankles with these silk cords,' Henri murmured. 'Take off your knickers.'

In a ferment of arousal she hesitated for an instant, then untied the ribbon drawstring, let them drop and kicked them aside.

Henri arranged the bed with the pillows positioned so that when she had bunched up her skirts and laid over them, her bare buttocks were high in the air and her thighs stretched open. Her feelings alternated between shame and elation. Her secrets were revealed, her hair-fringed furrow, the lips of her sex, the opening to her vagina and the tightly closed aperture of her rectum.

Henri opened her arms and slipped a cord over one wrist, securing the other end to the bedpost. Emma, head turned to one side, watched him with scared eyes. He smiled and caressed her buttocks lingeringly, then dipped into the fissure between, finding the pool at her vulva and spreading the fragrant liquid over her clitoris. She hardly noticed when he tethered her other wrist.

Next he bound the cords around her ankles and tied them to the carved posts at the foot of the bed. Now she appreciated how that servant girl must have felt when manacled to the bench and beaten by Gwenda. So helpless, so open... so aroused. And Candice too, when Henri put her across his knee and spanked her.

She could not see what he was doing, only hear his breathing and stealthy movements. Then she felt something teasing its way down between her bottom cheeks and along her crease. It was soft, tickling and exciting – a feather!

'Oh... ooh,' she gasped, wriggling back against this gentle invasion. 'What are you doing to me?'

'Putting my quill pen to a novel use,' he replied, his voice filled with wicked humour. 'Just the tip, not the point. Do you like that?'

'Yes. Do it harder,' she pleaded, her clit on fire to feel more of that strange sensation.

The quill slid along her labial folds, flicking and tormenting, then stroking the stem of her love-bud. Emma tensed, hovering on the brink of orgasm but needing something firmer to bring her off. She moaned in disappointment as the feather was removed.

'Don't stop,' she begged.

'No?' Henri whispered. 'You want more?'

'Yes! Yes!'

For answer, he replaced it with a harder toy, smooth-tipped, bigger, wetting the tip in her dew and rubbing it across the swollen lips and taut bud. 'You like this perhaps? It's a lingam, a mock phallus. D'you want to see it?'

Emma lay with her right cheek pressed against the pillow and now Henri let her look at the article with which he had been stimulating her. It was large and black, the ebony carved to represent a penis. Polished, wet with her essences, it had the split glans and long curving shaft of a man's erect organ.

'I'll let you feel it inside you, once I've opened your love-channel with my own weapon,' he promised, and ran the lingam across her lips. It tasted of her own salty juices. 'But now for something else,' he added and withdrew from her sight.

What now? Her heart was racing. She struggled to look round but her bonds prevented this. She tried to hear, but sounds gave no clue. What was he doing?

Her nipples seemed to be on fire, chafing against the embroidered quilt. Her clitoris was a throbbing point. There were ripples of excitement in her belly and tension in her loins. She tugged against her bonds, but even the feel of silk cords restraining her added to the discomfort and arousal. She was unable to do anything to help herself. Her pleasure, her release, was entirely dependent on Henri.

'Are you beginning to understand?' he whispered in the region of her ear. 'I shall be your mentor and master. Will you call me that?'

'If you wish.'

'I do. Let me hear you say it.'

'Master,' Emma faltered.

'Good girl. I can teach you so much, initiate you into the contrast between agony and desire. Each adds to the other.'

'I don't understand,' Emma whispered, longing only for the feel of his hands on her clitoris, bringing her sweet relief.

'You will, darling. You're going to be an apt pupil. Think of the pleasure my touch brings you. Can you imagine how much more it will be enjoyed after suffering a little pain?'

As he spoke, Henri slid a finger into her cleft, working the tiny button up and down, but holding off before bringing her to orgasm. He kept her in a state of intense arousal, but refused to apply the right pressure needed to hurl her into the abyss of release.

'Master... master...' she whimpered, wriggling frantically in pursuit of that tantalising fingertip.

'You like what I'm doing?' he asked in those dark, silken tones.

'Oh, yes... yes... but I'm desperate...'

'Then I must do something about it, mustn't I?'

To her plunging disappointment, he removed his hand altogether.

Nothing happened for what seemed a racking eternity. Then without warning, something small, hard and smooth was drawn over her crack. A handle perhaps? The top of a cane? Before she had time to get used to this, it was sharply lifted.

Emma heard a swish and in the next second bucked and screamed as a band of fire seared across her buttocks. Before she had time to recover another scalding blow fell just below the first. As the pain of this shot through her hinds, so she writhed and bucked under a third assault on her naked flesh.

She braced herself, expecting more, a tethered animal in the throes of agony, but instead she felt Henri's finger rubbing her clitoris with sure, deft strokes, the heat of her stripes somehow communicating with it.

'You see what I mean,' he whispered huskily. 'It's such a contrast, isn't it? Extreme pain and extreme pleasure. It excites me to see the red kisses left by my riding crop, contrasting so beautifully with your white skin. I'll show you later.'

He knelt beside her, and she was buried in his crotch, in velvet and hairy underbelly and that huge, throbbing cock which he thrust between her lips, rocking there for a moment, then withdrawing.

'Don't leave me like this!' she cried, tears trickling to the pillow beneath her cheek. 'Beat me... whip me... but give me release!'

'Am I your master?'

'Yes, master, yes!'

The crop whooshed. She jerked and screamed as it fell. The heat from her whipped derriere spread into her loins,

126

into her breasts, into her epicentre. Each blow was slightly overlapped, catching the fullness of her rump, the lower part too, and the plumpness of her thighs.

She writhed and strained at her bonds, hurting her wrists and ankles, and pressed her pubis against the quilt, frantically seeking some friction that would bring about her orgasm.

'Master! Master! Take me... possess me!' she yelled in a frenzy.

She felt his hand beneath her, felt those cool fingers pinching her clit. Immediately she convulsed in a powerful, wrenching climax that flooded through every nerve and burned in the welts left by the crop.

Half fainting, shuddering from that shattering experience, she was dimly aware of Henri untying her and rolling her on to her back. She yelped, pain bringing her to her senses. He muttered something she could not catch, then knelt between her slack thighs. Agony shot up and through her as he thrust with his swollen penis.

There was a moment's resistance, and then she shrieked as he succeeded in vanquishing her hymen. He was in her, pushing strongly, her virgin muscles relaxing to take him, and the pain gave way to pleasure.

She moved her hips to the rhythm of his, feeling that spear penetrating her very vitals, and she clutched him as a wave of new sensation rushed like a torrent through her body. He hung above her and she looked into his face, seeing the tense expression as he drove his phallus in and out, intent, obsessed, seeking his own satisfaction.

It was a feeling like no other. She was a woman at last, a passionate being who could control men by their lusts. Even Henri, who liked her to call him master, was as nothing in that moment when he was buried in her plushy sheath. She was the powerful one.

She folded her legs about him, crossing them at his waist, her arms clenched around his neck as he pumped and plunged while she drew him into the darkness of her womb.

I must tell Candice, she thought, and smiled secretly as Henri jerked suddenly and cried out in mighty flurry of climax.

Chapter Seven

Candice relaxed in a padded deck-chair aboard the ferry bearing passengers to the Lido. The day was glorious, a gentle wind drawing little puffs of cloud across a heavenly blue sky, with the bright sea running before it.

Her heart ached with a queer sort of happiness mixed with trepidation as she anticipated the evening when she would be with Dimitri again.

'Isn't the view perfect, my dear?' Clive said, occupying a canvas seat near by, his Panama hat canted over his eyes. 'I'm glad we decided to come here and not go on an excursion to the Venetian Glass Works on the Grand Canal. Though we must pay it a visit. I hope to purchase a piece to adorn our drawing room, when we're married. In fact, I was wondering if we might return here on our honeymoon.'

Mention of this jarred and Candice could only summon up a weak smile, her mind filled with Dimitri. He frightened her, intrigued her, tormented her with passionate longings. She was like a woman possessed and could think of nothing else.

It occurred to her that Esmeralda had seemed over-friendly to her fiancé on their return to the ball, but this did not trouble her. She had no interest in what he did or with whom. Since the episode on the steamer he had never again made a sexual advance, as if ashamed of what he had done.

It was a short trip and soon she was on the landing stage and strolling along the broad-walk towards the yellow sand and azure water. A cooling breeze from the Adriatic Sea stirred the veil of her wide-brimmed hat and rippled the Valenciennes lace on her white lawn dress.

A tanned, barefoot man in linen trousers and striped jersey, showed them to the beach hut. Smartly painted, with a veranda, it stood with several others, this part of the Lido rented by the Hotel Danieli for the exclusive use of its guests.

Within a very short time the man had dragged out reclining chairs and set them up. Then, after Fabian had tipped him, he summoned vendors who came across with fruit, sweetmeats and cakes for sale.

'Well, here we are then, Lady Candice,' puffed Gwenda, humping a basket containing her mistress's bathing-dress and towels. Little beads of perspiration stood out on her upper lip. The warm climate did nothing to improve her temper.

White was almost *de rigeur* among the ladies and most of the men as well, but she insisted on wearing dark clothing. On the surface, she loudly disapproved of what she termed "foreignness", which included holiday-makers, locals, food, manners and mores alike, but inside she was thinking of Maria and itching to see her again. Or wondering about the possibility of Countess Bianca needing other servants punished.

'How lovely it is,' breathed Flora, a complete opposite to Gwenda. Her flirtatious eyes roamed over the well-to-do taking their ease, and lingered on the muscular, sun-browned boatmen on the lookout for trade and pretty women.

Gwenda snorted and stomped into the cabin, returning with her arms heaped with rugs and cushions. She commenced spreading these in the shade of a rust-coloured awning.

'Who wants the hut first?' Fabian enquired briskly. 'I can't wait to change and get into the sea.'

It was decided that he and Clive should use it, while the girls wandered along where wavelets lapped the shore, hems lifted from the damp sand, parasols unfurled.

'Thank goodness for a moment's privacy,' Emma exclaimed, eyes sparkling and a blush staining her creamy complexion. 'I'm dying to tell you. Oh, Candice... I've done it.'

'Done what?' Candice was not attending, searching the beach where children waded in the shallows, and families converged under silken tenting or on cabin verandas and gentlemen in garish bathrobes marched up and down after invigorating dips.

Would *he* be visiting the Lido that day?

'*It*, stupid!' Emma hissed impatiently. 'I've done it... had carnal knowledge of a man... rogered him... made love with him... call it what you will.'

This had the desired affect. Candice stopped, rooted to the spot. 'You've lost your virginity?' she exclaimed, different emotions chasing through her: disbelief, shock, horror, curiosity – and envy.

'Yes. I've been deflowered,' said Emma with a superior smirk.

'By whom? What was it like? Will you do it again?' the questions tumbled from Candice's lips.

Sure of her captive audience, Emma now took her time in the telling. 'I did it with the comte,' she said, giving Candice a slanting glance. 'It was strange...wonderful... very exciting. I'm not sure if it's always like this, because he beat me with a riding-crop first. I'll show you the marks when we undress. But yes... oh yes... I want to do it again.' Her limpid, hazel eyes became dreamy and she sighed deeply and added, 'I call him master.'

'Oh, Emma, what have you done?' Candice cried, trembling as she took her friend's hand in hers. 'What of your betrothal to Fabian?'

'Fabian?' Emma announced scornfully. 'He, my dear innocent, was pleasuring himself with Bianca the while, so Henri told me. And Clive was fornicating with Esmeralda. I don't think we need worry about being faithful to them, do you? Henri wants you, too. He has asked me to ask you if you'll come with me next time I go to him.'

'I'm not sure about that,' Candice replied. 'I didn't like what he did to me. At first, I thought he might be the one, but now know he is not.'

'How can you be so sure?' Emma asked, fingers playing nervously with the fringe of her parasol.

'I'm sure,' Candice replied firmly.

All around them were normal things; the privileged class chattering and hobnobbing; servants in attendance; nursery-maids parading little children while their mothers idled on cushions gossiping with their friends and their fathers swam or lounged indolently. Sandcastles were under constructions, and there were small blue and red rowing boats bobbing on the waves.

What has this to do with dark sexual encounters where strange desires are explored? Candice mused. More than this: what has it to do with Prince Dimitri and his mysterious hold over me?

'I, too, have something to relate,' she said as they started back to the cabin. 'Last night I met my dream-lover. He appeared in the ballroom. We danced, but not on the ground. It was in the air. He kissed me, and it was no earthly kiss. He brought me to pleasure's crisis, and it was like those times when I thought I was dreaming. Then we were back in reality and Bianca was introducing us. His sisters were there. Oh, Emma, they are not like mortal women... fairies, enchantresses, maybe witches. But I love him. I need to go to him. I shall see him tonight and you, too, will meet him at his palazzo. I'm mad with love... sick with it. I can't live without him!'

Emma stared at her, eyes wide with worried concern. 'You speak so wildly,' she said, and paused to put an arm round her. 'Who is this man? Where does he come from?'

'Transylvania, a remote region of Europe, not far from Russia, I believe. But what does it matter? He's here, Emma, and he wants me.'

'Take care, my love,' Emma warned, and it was as if a giant hand had passed in front of the sun, the sky grey, the sea sluggish. 'I have a premonition about this.'

'I don't care what happens. I love him and I'm going to have him,' Candice declared rashly, and the scene righted itself, brilliant once more.

A little later, Emma stripped off her clothes in the privacy of the cabin and displayed the pattern of bluish bruises lacing her backside. 'You see,' she said, on a note of pride. 'I daren't undress when Mrs Smythe is about. This is the master's handiwork. I was helpless to protest. He tied me to the bedposts with silk scarves. What price your stranger prince now?'

She ran her fingertips almost lovingly over the welts, and Candice stepped closer to examine them. Emma winced as she touched a particularly inflamed stripe, and Candice had an instant picture of her tethered to the bed, her exposed sex swollen with blatant desire, while Henri belaboured her rump.

It caused a furore in Candice. Her bare breasts tingled and the nipples peaked, while honeydew inched from her vulva to trail down her inner thigh. She wanted Dimitri so much that her heart was like an open wound within her. Her buttocks echoed the glow of Emma's and her clitoris rose from its tiny hood as she imagined Dimitri's hand slashing down on her tender, quivering hinds, as Henri's had done.

Her master? Oh, yes, she would call *him* master.

'It hurts, but sets me on fire,' Emma whispered, her ivory skin pink about the breasts and neck.

One hand stroked the welted cheeks of her bottom, the other reached down to fondle the fleecy mound at her fork. Rays filtered through the slats, dappling her body with highlights and mauve shadows.

Candice, seated on a stool to roll off her silk stockings, looked across at her, admiring such perfection. Even the weals added to Emma's attraction, a reminder of her sinful behaviour with Henri. She must have bathed before coming out, but Candice was sure she could smell the heady odour of their mingled juices emanating from Emma's secret delta.

133

Her own essence dampened her pubic floss and she thought of Dimitri's phallus as she had known it in her sleep. Would he take her tonight? Would she soon know the secret, as Emma now did?

'Come to me,' Emma sighed, standing in front of her, mons veneris on a level with Candice's mouth. 'I need your soft fingers inside me. Henri was so rough and impetuous. His huge penis hurt me. I'm still sore there. See?'

She thrust her pubis forward and stretched the labia open, displaying her deep pink crack with the kernel of her clitoris swelling at the top.

'Poor darling,' Candice murmured, and ran a soothing finger up the stem of that ardent bud.

Emma's response was immediate. She quivered and caressed her breasts fervently, first the crinkled areolae, then the pointed nipples. As Candice watched, her own dew seeped between the closed lips of her pudenda tightly pressed into the wicker seat of the chair.

Sounds reached her from outside; the laughter and voices of children, the deeper tones of adults, the shrill calls of the sea gulls that wheeled and dived overhead. But she and Emma were caught in that sensual web which only women can spin, concentrating entirely on pleasuring one another.

She massaged Emma's nubbin in slow circles, feeling the moisture gathering, the sliver of flesh slippery with juice. Still keeping up the pressure, she eased her other hand below Emma's mound, her middle finger finding the entrance to her womb. She ventured further, pushing in gently whilst still playing with the clitoris. Her finger slid inside, the velvety walls closing round it, sucking it in. Before, she had never been able to penetrate far without meeting the obstruction of a membrane. Henri had removed that.

Now she could go deep into the dark inner chamber – slide out and push in again, aping the action of a penis. Emma moaned and arched her back as the twofold rhythmical movements brought her to an inevitable conclusion.

Her juices swamped Candice's hand and her vagina convulsed around her finger as she shuddered in violent orgasm. She sighed deeply and collapsed against Candice's shoulder, giving her a loving, satisfied smile and saying, 'What of you, my love? Do you want me to rub you?'

Candice was ablaze, but somehow she wanted to hold on to this liquid fire, clasp it close in her holy chalice and only let it pour forth when she was in Dimitri's arms again.

'Better not,' she said, and reached for her bathing-costume. 'They'll be wondering why we're taking so long.'

The azure sky deepened gradually through twilight into night. The stars shone out of its indigo depths with a diamond bright, though cold effulgence, reflected in the waters that flowed in quiet stillness on every side.

Candice's nerves jangled with impatience. She had been ready for what seemed hours, bad-tempered and tetchy. Her maid had helped her bathe, sponging away the salt water of the Lido, then towelling her dry, dusting her all over with jasmine scented talcum powder and assisting her into delicate underwear and her evening gown.

'I can understand why gentlemen drink whisky and smoke cigarettes,' she complained to Emma as they waited in the foyer. 'It must steady the nerves. I'd like to try it.'

'Really! The things you say,' Emma remonstrated with a laugh.

Both were wearing pastel silks, their waists clinched to doll size, their bosoms rising over the daring necklines, their shoulders and arms bare, except kid gloves that reached above their elbows.

As if to bear witness to Candice's statement, Clive and Fabian strolled from the smoking room, smelling very high of Havana cigars, finest malt and eau de Cologne.

At that moment a pageboy came through the main door, announcing, 'A gondola waits for Milor Fortescue.'

Candice leapt up, grabbed her sapphire blue cape and beaded bag and almost ran for the entrance.

'Such unseemly haste,' Fabian chided as he caught up with her, his cloak over one shoulder, top-hat jammed on his head. 'What ails you, Candice?'

'Nothing,' she lied, though her heart skipped a beat as she saw the sinister looking craft moored at the bottom of the landing stairs.

Its boatman was angular and ugly, sombrely garbed to match his boat, and his face glimmered like wax in the light of the flares.

He addressed Fabian in a gravelly voice, 'Lord Fortescue? I am Carl. Prince Dimitri has sent me to convey you to the Palazzo Tassinari.'

He reached out a bony hand and gripped Candice, helping her aboard. She ducked her head and entered the canopied mid-section where a chair awaited her, painted in black and upholstered in the same coffin colour.

The others settled beside her, and a heavy silence descended. Even Emma ceased chattering as the gondola glided swiftly along canals and into side waterways, until it came to a standstill at the steps of a palazzo that towered above them into the darkness.

'Gloomy old pile,' Clive ventured, in an attempt to lighten the atmosphere. 'Must be centuries old.'

By some strange trick, almost a sleight of hand, Carl was at the door, acting the butler and ushering them into a paved patio. A series of windows faced inwards, each with an iron grill, and the palace had a forlorn, unlived-in air. A fountain trickled fitfully over the bronze statue of a mermaid, with flowing hair and coiled tail. The surface of the pool was green, slimy and stagnant smelling.

The lower walls of the building were covered in vines and creepers that sprawled unchecked. Huge plants that might have hailed from a tropical rain forest spread their sickly green leaves wide. Hectic-hued blossoms wavered like the tentacles of sea anemones.

'They are insectivorous,' Carl explained and snatching a fly from the air in one hand, he placed it on the sticky surface of a petal. The flower snapped shut over its wriggling victim.

'Ugh!' Emma said in disgust.

'All things have to feed, my lady,' Carl observed, and darted in front of them. 'Come this way, please. The master is waiting.'

They followed him along a shadowy cloistered walk. Life-sized statues in alcoves turned blank blind eyes on them as they passed. Their feet clattered loudly, awakening the echoes. Soon they reached a massive doorway.

Candice shuddered, suddenly ice-cold. It resembled the entrance to a mausoleum.

It was forcefully opened from within and a form stood there in silhouette. Candice stopped dead, her heart fluttering in her chest like a bird trying to escape a cage.

'Good evening, and welcome to my house,' said Dimitri. The tension broke.

He stepped back so that they might enter. They went from darkness into a blaze of light.

'Ye gods!' Emma breathed into Candice's ear. 'I can see what you mean! What a man!'

It was indeed Dimitri, but never as Candice had seen him. He wore an outlandish, exotic costume that accentuated his distinctly foreign looks.

A coarse white linen shirt lay open over his chest where a crisp mat of black hair curled. Lavishly embroidered at cuffs and hem, it was hip-length and drawn in at his narrow waist by a leather belt with a silver buckle. He wore it over full crimson trousers tucked into the tops of supple red leather boots.

He smiled, picking up on Candice's thoughts and saying, 'This is what the peasants wear in my beautiful land. Soon you will see it for yourself.'

It suited him, emphasising the fact that he was descended

from savage tribesmen who had fought their way up to become bloodthirsty warlords.

She looked into his supremely haughty face, and that lubricious, melting feeling swept over her, banishing all coherent thought and making her loins throb. She wanted to press against him, surrender her mouth to his, grind her pubis against the baton of his phallus which she could see resting against his thigh. Nothing else mattered – neither modesty nor decorum.

The door closed behind them with a thud that reverberated under the vaulted roof of the vestibule. After Carl had taken their cloaks, Dimitri conducted them into a banqueting hall, the grandeur of which brought admiring cries to their lips.

He introduced his sisters to Clive and Emma who goggled, momentarily stunned and forgetting their manners.

The princesses dazzled the eye and bewitched the senses. Madelon's lint-white hair was topped by a flowered head dress, a brief velvet bodice was tightly laced under her pert breasts and a filmy blouse revealed the points of her dark red nipples. A flaring, part-transparent skirt undulated round her legs, sometimes hiding, sometimes revealing the shape of her mound.

'What beautiful workmanship. Such lovely embroidery,' Emma said shakily, as dumbstruck as Clive.

'A traditional costume for feast days,' Madelon explained with a demure nod, then added, teeth flashing, 'And this, my dear young English lady, is surely a time for feasting.'

'And your attire?' Emma persisted, eyeing Allegra and Medea uneasily.

'Is Turkish,' Allegra answered, giving her an oblique glance, her wide scarlet mouth curved in a mocking smile.

'The Turks invaded the area, but our ancestors vanquished them after a bitter struggle that soaked the land in blood. They left their influence behind,' Dimitri put in, lips set in a grim line.

'The ladies of the harem would have worn garments such

as these,' Medea murmured, focusing on Clive and Fabian, her shining dark eyes emphasised by a thin line of kohl drawn close under the blackened lashes. 'Do you like it, sirs?'

'Who couldn't fail to be impressed?' Fabian answered, with a catch in his breath.

The princesses laughed, the sound high and musical and chilling, sexual allure in their every movement. Their bold eyes assessed, admired and bewitched him, then slid back to Clive.

As Allegra closed in on Fabian an aroma wafted around her. It seemed to breathe out from her skin as if she had been steeped in attar of roses. Yet there was a subtle additive, like the drop of bitter distillate in a perfume, a faintly rotten undertone as of game left to hang a little too long.

'You show excellent taste, my lord,' she whispered, her lilac eyes glittering under lids sparkling with silver shadow.

Her fiery hair flowed to her waist, and her fingers decorated with intricate patterns in red henna, brushed casually across his fly in so swift a gesture that it might have been imagined.

Like Medea's, her loose chemise was open, showing the chasm between her perfect, cloud-white breasts. The nipples protruded, hard as rubies, inviting lips to suck and hands to stroke them. The curve of her belly, the dimple in her navel and the darkness of her fork showed through her tiffany pantaloons.

Adorned with Eastern jewellery, the three posed gracefully, arms around each other's waists and shoulders, fingers encountering nipples and buttocks, shamelessly wanton in their display. Every movement they made was alluring, each practised, provocative sway of their hips calculated to make men's cocks rise, hard with lust.

Dimitri shot them a warning glare and, 'Carl!' he thundered, 'Serve dinner now!'

Candice found herself seated next to Dimitri who occupied the carver at the top of the table. It stretched into the distance, lost in the dimness of the hall, the diners gathered around him at one end.

He leaned across and filled Candice's goblet from an antique decanter. 'You must try Tokay,' he said, his mesmerising voice playing havoc with her senses and making her skin crawl. 'The glorious wine of Hungary.' He lifted his own glass and the light of the candles shone through it. His voice held a wistful note as he went on, 'What a colour! It's like the golden glow of the sun, and reminds me of the long, dry autumn weather during which the grapes are harvested.'

'You have been there, in the vineyards?' she asked, nervous of him. His moods changed mercurially, and now he seemed almost sad.

'When I was a boy I often helped with the harvest on the hilly slopes above the River Tisza. But that was long ago – almost another lifetime.'

'But you're not old, prince,' Candice protested, evoking giggles from his sisters who were perched on their chairs like gorgeous Morpho butterflies, blatantly flirting with Clive, Fabian and even Emma.

'Older than you think,' he murmured.

She could feel the heat mounting from her core to her cheeks as he looked at her over the rim of his glass. Her clitoris thickened as she saw the slumbering fire in his eyes, reading there messages which challenged and excited her. He held his glass without drinking, but she sipped hers, the sweet liquid sliding down her throat and settling like fire her belly.

Though his lips did not move she distinctly heard him say in a clear authoritative tone, 'Keep your knees apart so I may touch you when I want.'

Candice clutched her glass as if it were a lifeline, darting a glance around her, but no one had heard, save perhaps the princesses. By the way they were slyly peering at her she had the awful feeling that they, too, found mental communication easy.

Sitting there numbly, she wondered how long it would be before she felt his fingers on her silk-covered knee.

The soul of courtesy, he addressed her brother, saying, 'I hope you will pardon us for not partaking. We satisfied our appetites earlier.'

'Oh, really? You should not have gone to so much trouble on our account,' Fabian answered, not really attending, unable to keep his eyes off the princesses.

'Not at all. It gives me pleasure to ensure that my guests are entirely satisfied,' Dimitri rejoined, with a sardonic twist to his lips.

'You must take full advantage of our hospitality or we shall be mortally offended,' said Medea playfully, and dug her long nails into Carl's crotch as he passed by her chair. 'He's such an amazing chef. Aren't you, Carl?'

'I do my best to please, lady,' he replied in his guttural accent.

He waited at table, one superbly cooked course following hard on another, each served with its accompanying wine. There were fish dishes with aromatic sauces; game swimming in rich gravy; new potatoes, peas, carrots and asparagus; desserts of mouthwatering decadence, heaped with chocolate and cream and almonds.

Great pyramids of fruit adorned the board; strawberries bursting with juice, velvet skinned peaches as smooth as a young girl's pubis, luscious grapes, piquant olives and tangy oranges redolent of the heat and passion of Spain.

Candice merely picked at her food, her mind wandering as she listened to the conversation flowing round the table, trying to nod and smile in the right places.

Dimitri brooded, slumped low on his spine, his long legs stretched out before him, sinewy fingers toying with the stem of his wineglass. Candice trembled with need, her thighs apart under the damask tablecloth, waiting for him to begin his secret caress, praying that he would.

He did not move, but she suddenly felt his hand brushing

141

across her garter and the silky flesh above it, settling between her thighs to comb gently through her pubic bush. The pearly gem of her clitoris hardened, and his fingertip circled it, then caressed the throbbing head.

She felt his touch on her spirit as well as her body – that finer, insubstantial part of her that she inhabited in dreams, and the pleasure was doubled, the tension building, sweeping her towards a powerful eruption.

She clung to her self-control, making no movement, as stiff as a board in her chair. Fabian was still holding forth, trying to impress the princesses, but Emma was sensitive to her distress, asking, 'Are you feeling unwell, Candice? You've turned very pale.'

'It's little hot... and the wine is strong,' she managed to gasp, gripping the arms of her chair so hard that her knuckles shone as white as her rolled back gloves.

Dimitri's invisible fingers stroked her tingling bud, and she heard him say, 'Don't worry, my love. Just enjoy.'

She peered at his implacable profile with her human eyes, and saw an aristocratic nobleman entertaining his guests, one hand round his glass, the other resting on the table. But even as she watched, so she felt one of his fingers probing the entrance to her vagina, dabbling in her honeydew. He slipped it inside her and stimulated the hidden, virgin nook, making her want to wriggle and get it in further.

'What a delicious secret garden you have, Candice,' he whispered in her brain. 'I long to enjoy every single one of its treasures. Your petals that fold back at my touch. Your tiny pistil that rises to greet me from your sex lips. I want to taste you, sup off you – eat you. And I will.'

Candice bit back a moan and her eyes met Allegra's across the table. That bizarre beauty smiled slowly and knowingly and, fixing her with her freezing stare, bared her teeth and ran the tip of her fleshy tongue over her crimson lips.

Candice tried to look away, but could not. Dread seized her, even as Dimitri continued to stimulate her bud and heavy, insidious waves of pleasure carried her towards the peak.

What game was he and his weird sisters playing? And why had he singled her out for attention?

But he had found the core of her, his touch like slippery satin, and she surrendered to the feeling, all negative thoughts banished. The force was too strong to resist, sweeping her to the top of the arc. Spasms of impending orgasm tightened her belly, and she fought to retain her outward composure, pinned upright to her chair as she reached her zenith.

His eyes became huge, boring into her own – blotting out the room. She saw herself reflected in them – then nothing else – borne away on a tide of darkness.

Candice opened her eyes and stared up into the face of a sombre, orange-red moon hanging above her like a severed head.

Too languid to question this, she burrowed into the nest of luxuriant furs that covered her. The cold knifed her lungs. She could hear the swish of runners on crisp snow and the slither of horses' hooves and the jingle of harness. All around her was thick, black forest.

She ventured a hand down, fingers encountering the velvet nap of a cloak, the harshness of thick gold embroidery, the edge of a furry jacket. The cloak's hood was lined with sable. It was drawn close around her head. On wriggling her toes she discovered that they were encased in fur-lined boots. Heavy rings circled her fingers, wide bracelets banded her wrists and many thin chains were fastened round her throat, each with a jewelled pendant.

Where was she?

'On the way to my castle in the mountains,' Dimitri said from his perch on the driving seat.

She could make out the shape of his broad shoulders – his shaggy wolf-skin coat and hat. The carriage whip in his gauntleted hand curled back and cracked loudly, startling the six black, foam-flecked horses. They leaned into the traces, the troika flying along, hardly touching the ground.

Night, deep night – eerie gloom where snow glistened and gaunt pines loomed on every side like foe waiting in ambush, and overhead that unnatural moon and star spears stabbing the dark, frosty vault of heaven. Steam misted the air, rising from the hides of the sweating horses.

She became aware of a dog howling somewhere. This was joined by another, and another. Not dogs, she realised with a jolt. Wolves.

She sat up sharply. 'We shall be killed!' she cried, every storybook legend she had ever heard about the savagery of these ferocious animals rushing back to torment her.

He laughed, a wild sound that somehow complemented the wolves' baying. 'They are my children, come to escort us home,' he said. 'I love the company of wolves... run with them... become one of them when it suits my purpose.'

'What an odd thing to say,' she murmured, a strange melancholy stealing over her, one which she almost enjoyed, this sad state of mind alluring and sweet.

Now she could see sleek shapes keeping pace with the sleigh. Mouths salivated and tongues lolled in the light of the carriage lamps. Eyes gleamed, phospherant green then red, and teeth curled back over fangs, reminding her of the princesses.

Dimitri's companions? A bolt of superstitious terror made her quake. She clutched the furs around her, wanting to duck her head under them and hide, but she could not move, petrified by those fierce escorts, and by the circles of blue fire through which the sleigh now glided.

'Take no heed of it,' Dimitri said. 'The flames burn on certain nights of the year, over the spots where treasure is hidden.'

'Don't you want to dig for it?' she gasped.

He laughed again, a great wave of buffeting laughter, and the wolves raised their voices in chorus. 'I have no need,' he chuckled.

'You're very rich?'

'Indeed. I'll show you some of my wealth, only a portion, you understand. There is much more stored in various parts of the world, and at different times in its history.'

'You talk in riddles.'

His lips were warm, caressing her cold cheek, but he had not moved. 'All is illusion,' he said. 'Smoky mirrors.'

They stood in a stone-walled chamber deep below ground. The walls glowed, and she stared in amazement. Gold coins cascaded like a river bursting its banks, flowing from decaying trunks and worm-eaten chests. Jewels spewed from caskets, diamonds like frozen waterfalls, rubies the size of pigeons' eggs, the wicked flash of snake-eyed emeralds, ropes of gleaming pearls.

There were golden candlesticks filched from churches, chalices, altar pieces, goblets and plate, icons depicting Byzantine Madonnas and the Christ Child. Gem-studded crosses, gilded armour, swords with jewelled hilts, paintings by famous artists, silks in dazzling array from every quarter of the globe and rugs that had graced a Mogul emperor's palace.

Dimitri took up handfuls of precious stones and bejewelled her till her whole body and limbs were covered in a shining mass of necklaces, scintillating bracelets, earrings and anklets. Then he propelled her to a pier-glass that threw back her reflection. She was transfigured, now a pagan goddess, fantastic and awe-inspiring or – and the thought brought a prickle of dread – a sacrificial victim before the throat was cut and blood flowed down to fertilise the earth.

She was in the sleigh again. The way grew darker and narrower, winding through a pass between monumental crags, with a chasm yawning into the darkness on one side. Water thundered far below. Dimitri whipped up the horses. They squealed in protest as they increased speed, ascending steeply towards a grim, turreted castle that loomed against the sky, clinging to the jutting rocks malevolently, like a grotesque fungus.

As if in answer to the dread that paralysed Candice, a jagged fork of lightning split the heavens and thunder shook the mountains. The noise of water became deafening as they breasted the last rise, coming out in a clearing before the sheer walls of the fortress.

Hooves drummed on frozen planks, the sleigh flying over the drawbridge. Flares set in iron rings sent out a sullen glare. The shadow of a portcullis engulfed them as they passed beneath a gateway.

The courtyard burst into light and activity. People came running, surrounding the troika, smiling, full of greetings, peasants and servants and men-at-arms, Dimitri's own personal army. A man detached himself from the others, a dandyish fellow in a splendid military uniform.

He stared at Candice intently as Dimitri scowled and said, 'What are you doing here, Belphegor?'

'How unfriendly,' the man chided, never taking his eyes from her. 'Aren't you going to present me to your *amoret*?'

'You already know her, though not through me,' Dimitri said angrily. 'I closed my mind to you.'

'Your sisters told me,' Belphegor replied smoothly, twirling the waxed moustache adorning his upper lip. 'They are such gossips... can't stop prattling.'

'You will not touch her,' Dimitri shouted and, lifting him by the lapels of his jacket, bore him aloft and pinned him high against the wall, both of them suspended in space.

'I won't. I promise,' Belphegor spluttered.

'Ha! Much good is that!' Dimitri snarled, and dropped him. He landed in a heap in the snowy yard.

'Tut, tut... such a temper,' he reprimanded, brushing particles of ice from his clothing. 'So ungrateful, Dimitri, after all I've done for you. But you are still my adored prince... and you bring a rival here... most tactless of you, my dear.'

Dimitri stood on the ramparts twenty feet above, hands

on hips, legs spread as he glared down.

The courtyard disappeared. Now Candice found herself in a massive hall within the fortress. Fires blazed at either end in wide hearths with carved stone canopies that rose towards the beamed ceiling. A feast had been prepared, the long oaken tables groaning beneath the weight of laden dishes. Peasants and gypsies in gala costume thronged the hall, cheering and laughing, drinking toasts to their ruler.

The cry went up again and again, 'Prince Dimitri! Master! Lord!'

Candice was bewildered by the noise and confusion. Gypsy violins throbbed passionately, mingling with the weird rippling notes of the cimbalom and the high-pitched call of a flute. The wine flowed. The dancing became abandoned. Virile young men took the floor, stamping their way through the intricate steps of the *hora*. The girls whirled, tambourines vibrating in their hands, their skirts flying out, showing slender brown legs, buttocks and bellies and dewy, feathery mounds.

'Such a superabundance of youth and beauty. Makes me hungry, my dear fellow. Pity I've already glutted myself this evening. I have no room for more,' observed Belphegor, swaggering over to where Dimitri lounged in a high-backed chair, encrusted with carving and ivory inlay.

Candice, crouched at the prince's feet, looked up at his swashbuckling, somehow alarming friend. Belphegor wore a Hussar uniform; a short blue jacket frogged with silver braid, a fur-trimmed dolman slung carelessly over one shoulder and highly polished boots.

His matching blue trousers were thick with braid down the outer seam and so tight they seemed moulded to him. Thighs, bottom cheeks, and the substantial ridge of a finely developed penis were all clearly outlined.

Even as the desire to touch it flashed through her mind, so she found her hand encompassing that hard, hot member, feeling it through the material.

He smiled down at her, the chain strap of his tall fur kalpac fitting under his jaw, his hair in a pigtail at the back, with little plaits falling each side of his finely chiselled face. A long sabre knocked against his left thigh as he moved.

'Ah, so she reads mind commands without hesitation, and has such a pleasurable touch. Humm, do that some more, sweetheart,' he mused, sneaking a glance at Dimitri's brooding face and asking, 'Does she know what you are? Have you told her yet?'

'No,' he growled.

'You hesitate? Aren't you sure of her reaction? Ah, of course, you're remembering Mariella's silly reticence. I recall it as if it were yesterday. She was so indignant. So saintly. So fearful of offending God!'

'Her upbringing, her religion... Candice will not repeat this,' Dimitri answered sharply, and the blazing anger in his eyes should have withered Belphegor where he stood.

'You're sure?' he mocked, and Candice marvelled at his courage in the face of such fury.

'She will obey me in everything,' Dimitri averred.

'Are you certain she hasn't already found a master?' questioned Belphegor in his sneering, insidious way.

'Who?' Dimitri demanded.

'Comte Henri.'

'What! That mincing popinjay. Is this true, Candice?'

'No. He spanked me... tried to enter my forbidden place...'

'And you enjoyed it?'

'No... yes... I can't tell you...' she sobbed.

'I'll show you who is your master!' he shouted, his voice resonating like the Last Trump.

His serfs stopped dancing, riveted in fearful silence, then fell to their knees, foreheads pressed to the floor, chanting, 'Master! Master! Be merciful to your vassals!'

Some rent their garments, bloody strips appearing on arms, breasts and thighs as their nails ripped into the skin. Others leapt up, seized hold of whips and lashed themselves or those

148

nearest to them, beating genitals, breasts, any portion of anatomy offered to them. The sound of cries, moans and whistling thongs echoed under the rafters.

A horrifying sense of evil possessed Candice. A deep, primordial fear that went beyond terror. It dazed her mind and distorted her vision so the hall seemed to be filled with the dead: skeletal figures, rotting faces, eyeless, grinning at her, plucking at her – wanting to make her into such as they.

Dimitri seized her. Gone was the velvet cloak. Now she wore nothing but a robe of so fine a material that it resembled smoke drifting around her. Dark with desire, pointed with fear, her nipples poked through it, and her legs were silhouetted against the glaring torch-light.

With his followers chanting and drawing closer he hauled her up against him, lowering his head to suck her aching tips through the silk, leaving great wet circles which showed them even more. He growled low in his throat, and the wolves howled in unison, snarling and circling, their red eyes blazing, teeth bared.

He gripped the neck of her robe and tore it from her in one stroke. It dripped, melted, vanished. His hand thrust between her thighs, parting her sex, forcing his fingers into her quickly and easily. She felt her feet leaving the ground, borne upwards by the pressure of his hand in her most intimate parts as he rose, streaking over the diabolical company.

The next thing she knew was being bound, face pressed against a wooden stake, naked breasts chafed by its rough surface. Fingers fastened chains around her wrists and raised her arms high above her head, securing them to an iron ring. She fought for a foothold, but found none, her arm muscles forced to take her weight, agony screaming through them. Her ankles were seized, legs pulled apart and shackled to the base. Now she was prepared, helpless to do other than accept Dimitri's will.

But somewhere, in the eye of the storm, she knew a strange sort of peace. She was no longer responsible for her actions, and that dark skein of sexuality was about to be satisfied in a way she had never dared even think about. Her nipples tingled, the tender tips abraded by the wood, and she embraced the stake, driving her pubis against it, seeking friction for her throbbing clitoris.

Dimitri circled her like one of his wolves. Then, midst the wails and cries of the assembly, he unwound a whip from his narrow waist and held it before her eyes. He smiled, his wet red lips parted over teeth that had grown longer, sharper, deadly weapons in that sinisterly handsome face.

'I shall mark you so that no man will ever dare touch you again,' he promised. 'You belong to me, and will learn to obey me.'

The whip became a snake, swaying, hissing, tongue forking along her cheek. Then it was leather again. He flourished it, its short handle fitted with a metal joint to allow the lash full play. It was a heavy, rawhide plait, razor-edged and iron-tipped.

Before she had time to react he sent it whistling through the air. It landed across her buttocks with a crack.

Numbness. Shock. A slice of searing agony. Candice screamed, bucking against her bonds. He gave her no pause, the next blow cutting into her white shoulders, leaving a crimson trail. The dark lash did not relent, rising and falling, rending her flesh with appalling agony. Her piteous cries spurred him on, the force of his blows unremitting, till her back and haunches were laddered with stripes and she hung, fainting, in her restraints.

His hand was under her, fingertip grinding on her clitoris, forcing it back against her pubic bone and she orgasmed in a splintering rush. She felt herself crushed against the stake as he slid his hugely erect phallus into her, strangely icy in contrast to her red-hot cunt. He rode her in deep bursts, while she lifted her hips for him, offering herself to his lust.

His frantic thrusts skewered her to the post, his breathing harsh on the back of her neck, his teeth nipping like a stallion mounting a mare. She screamed out her joy, pain and terror, as his freezing tribute burst inside her.

'Mariella,' he groaned, his husky voice buried in her hair. 'Candice... beloved bride.'

Chapter Eight

It was too hot to wear a nightshirt, a sultry, unhealthy heat, suggestive of malaria and typhoid and other nasty life-threatening diseases never found in temperate England.

Fabian dismissed his valet and stretched outside the covers of his canopied bed. The netting quivered as he moved, looped back because it was not yet the mosquito season, yet sufficiently draped to give the room a misty aspect from where he lay.

His hand roamed over his naked body, feeling the light sheen of sweat, pleased with his musculature. There was not an inch of fat on him anywhere. He was in prime condition, and so aroused by his own touch that he would not be able to resist self-relief. Holding his lust at bay in order to exacerbate the need, he dwelt on the evening just passed at the Palazzo Tassinari.

Jesus Christ! Those princesses! And his penis jumped at the thought.

Esmeralda and Bianca had been a revelation, lecherous and immoral, but the sisters! They reeked of unspeakable sins, summoning up visions of debauchery as yet unknown to him, even though he had frequented brothels since he was sixteen. Where had they received their training? In some sacred temple dedicated to sexual deviations?

They had not revealed anything about their backgrounds. Neither had the prince, now Fabian came to think about it. In fact, he could remember little of the dinner party, except that the food had been superb, the wine strong, they had been conveyed there in a black gondola and later returned to their hotel. Only the sisters shone like dark comets in his memory.

His hand strayed to his crotch where his rigid member pointed towards the ceiling. His fist closed round it and he pulled back the pliable skin, exposing the shiny head. It glistened in the lamplight, expelling a drop of pre-come juice. Fabian breathed deeply and parted his thighs, reaching down to cup his spongy balls in their wrinkled sac.

Then, through the muslin curtains, he saw them – Allegra, Medea and Madelon, rising from the darkness and moonlight.

They undulated like smoke, their corpse-pale breasts and limbs now veiled, now nude. Jewels sent out flashes of sullen fire, mingling with their flowing hair.

They stood there whispering together and then, 'He's mine,' Allegra hissed.

Her white teeth shone against her voluptuous scarlet lips, her flaming hair a mass of vipers writhing round her shapely head, then turning into ringlets.

Leaning over him she laid the palm of one hand to his cheek, and probed the curve of his throat with a dagger-sharp fingernail. Her touch was an ice-cool stream flowing over his skin, and a frisson shot through his chest to his cock as she flicked the point of his left nipple.

'Don't be so selfish, sister,' Medea reproved, black eyes snapping. 'There's plenty for all. He's young and lusty. Look at the fullness of his testicles, a pair of plums gravid with juice. Note the size of his organ. See how it twitches eagerly. We can each take our fill of kisses and caresses and sustenance.'

'How did you get into my room?' he spluttered, unable to move, his leaden limbs pressed into the quilt.

'Do you want us here?' they questioned, teasing and lovely and ready for action.

'Yes,' he gasped, feeling he would die if they left.

They laughed, the sound as nerve jarring as when a finger is drawn round the rim of a wineglass. Whirling like dervishes before his dazed eyes, they were everywhere at once, beside the bed, at foot and head, over and above him, till he was enveloped in fragrant flesh, as cold and smooth as marble.

'Ah, such firm muscles, such pulsing blue veins,' Madelon sighed, and her silken curtain of flaxen tresses smothered him.

She sucked at his lips and tongue fiercely, crossing the boundaries of pleasure into pain. He tasted the honey of her saliva, coupled with another acrid flavour as his own blood filled his mouth.

It was then that he knew fear, a freezing spasm running the length of his body, yet heating him to passion's boiling point.

There were hands on his ankles, forcing his legs apart. He stared down in alarmed fascination, seeing his phallus erect as never before, throbbing and ramrod hard. Allegra crept toward him from the foot of the bed, her body low and reptilian. His skin crimped as her curly mane brushed his thighs. She slithered up between them, her mouth open in a hungry smile as her nails dug determinably into the base of his lust-hardened cock.

Medea lay beside him, stroking his belly, her mouth clamped to his wrist. He was hardly aware of the stabbing pain as her fangs pierced the skin, only a sense of floating weakness. She crawled up over his chest, pushing Madelon aside, falling on his lips like a ravenous beast, the dark, rich scent of blood emanating from deep in her throat.

Allegra licked his cock from base to tip. Her tongue was rough, feline and pointed. Terrified but aroused beyond reckoning, he waited breathlessly for the blessing of her mouth taking it in till the glans butted the back of her throat. She hung over his, eyes sparkling, then wormed that agile tongue tip into the slit, opening it, lapping at his juice.

'Ah... ah...' he moaned, wanting to writhe but paralysed.

They laughed again, low, musical, wickedly amused laughter that trilled down his spine, leaving filaments of ice behind.

'He's a virgin for us,' observed Madelon, her voice ringing uncannily. 'No one has drunk from him before. Belphegor will be eaten up with jealousy. There's nothing he likes more than a fresh young man.'

'But not Dimitri,' Allegra murmured, smacking her lips as she tasted Fabian's jism. 'He's besotted, and can see no one but Candice.'

My sister? What do you mean you hell-whores? Fabian wanted to shout, but the sound was strangled.

'Be silent!' Medea grated. 'You can't hide your thoughts from us. Candice wishes it. She's his slave. Soon she'll belong to him for all time.' She threw back her head and gales of savage laughter rocked the room. 'The devil's concubine! There's nothing you can do to stop it.'

'What are you? For God's sake tell me!' Fabian cried while they swarmed over him, fingering his crotch, his nipples, his lips and anal ring, mouths fastening on his throat, his wrists, at every point where the blood pulsed strongly.

'Don't mention God,' Allegra snarled, eyes flashing viciously. 'God and angels have nothing to do with us. Haven't you guessed what we are? We're vampires. *Nosferatu*. Citizens of the Dark Kingdom of the Undead.'

'Vampires don't exist,' he started to protest, then moaned as Allegra clamped her teeth round his glans, bit down then left it quivering. She lifted his arms above his head and crossed his wrists together.

'Oh, but they do. Our numbers are legion the world over,' she said, gloating on his helplessness.

'We have the strength of twenty men, can juggle with our molecules, becoming fog, bats, wolves, anything we like, passing through keyholes and under doors,' Medea added triumphantly.

'We can explore other dimensions, go back and forth in time,' Madelon cut in.

'We're almost indestructible, though we do have enemies,'

Allegra crooned, fingering that sensitive spot between his balls and his anus. 'But not you, my precious. You appreciate us, don't you? You'll not deny us the surging fountain of your warmth and youth, in return for blissful pleasure.'

Still doubting, unable to credit the things they were saying, he felt Allegra deftly binding his hands, though he could not see any cords or straps, but grunted as she yanked the invisible knots painfully tight. It was true: she was unnaturally powerful for a woman.

Then she knelt over his face, clenching his head between her ivory thighs, the fleshy wetness of her cunt bearing down, enveloping him in her pungent, female odour. Rivulets of juice dripped from the pulpy ripeness of her vulva. Ravished by this total engulfment, Fabian rolled his tongue over the head of her pleasure nugget while she groaned and gyrated, mashing it against him.

Hands were pinching his nipples, and Medea was poised over his cock, allowing a mere inch to penetrate her vagina. Allegra gave vent to a banshee screech, her clitoris spasming. He could breathe again, no longer in the clutch of those iron thighs. She slid to one side in a shimmering, incandescent glow, her sharp fangs flashing blue in the half light. Then her luscious mouth came closer and closer, and her teeth fastened on his throat. He moaned in a combination of revulsion and bliss.

In one thrust Medea took his rod into her depths, driving streams of ecstatic sensation through his loins. She pumped up and down, riding him, driving her clitoris against his pubic bone. The sensation was exquisite. As was that of Madelon kneading his arsehole, prodding and sliding within it, pushing past the tight ring and landing unerringly on the gland inside.

Allegra raised her head from his neck, her eyes unfocused and blazing, blood running down her chin. In one lithe movement she was between Madelon's thighs, her hand parting the dewy frills of her labia, her long-taloned fingers stroking the rabid clitoris.

Fabian's breath came in short gasps. His cock pulsed and kicked, desperate to relieve itself in Medea's freezing passage. The demonic trio radiated a rainbow luminescence. He was drowning in plump breasts and juicy cunts and curving buttocks. The air was thick with the cloying aroma of female arousal, of sandalwood and incense and animal rankness. He was drenched in sweat, lacquered with his own blood, his tormented phallus about to explode.

The sisters were singing, a wordless liturgy, wailing and eerie, a siren call of invitation and enticement. Fabian's cries turned into screams of suffering, ecstasy and agony as his spunk was wrested from him, the vampires drinking it as avidly as they had drunk his blood, mouths wide open, teeth dripping, tongues outstretched.

Waves of light streamed through his consciousness and he seemed to be falling, hearing only the sisters' voices, beautiful, howling, fading…

'What was the matter with you last night? You hardly said a word all evening,' asked Emma, as she and Candice sat on the hotel's terrace after breakfast, waiting the arrival of Fabian and Clive.

'What did you think of him?' Candice said, turning defence into attack, still stunned by the extraordinary adventure orchestrated by Dimitri. This time she knew it was no dream, remembering everything with razor-sharp clarity.

'He's very handsome,' Emma conceded slowly, staring unseeingly at the finely dressed hotel guests parading up and down while waiting for gondolas to bear them away to see the sights.

'Is that all?' Candice challenged, disappointed by this tepid reaction. 'Don't you think him the finest, most magnificent of men?'

'Oh yes, he's all these things, but…'

'You don't like him. Is that it?'

'Not exactly. He's suave, cultured, extremely polite. He entertained us royally, but to tell the truth, I find him somewhat sinister,' Emma replied, touching a hand to her slender throat which was banded by a velvet ribbon with a central cameo brooch.

'He's different, that's all. Was born far from civilisation,' Candice exclaimed, rushing to protect him from criticism.

Emma reached across and took her hand, saying, 'I dare say I'm wrong. But you've alarmed me with your talk of nightmares and him being a part of them. It's unnatural, Candice. If I really believed it, then I would begin to doubt your sanity... and mine.'

'And the princesses? Do you also hold a poor opinion of them?' she answered frostily, pulling away from her friend.

Emma rolled up her eyes in exasperation, saying crossly, 'They're the strangest females I've ever met. They're supposed to be royal, yet act like harlots, so bold and immodest.'

'But confess that they fascinated you. Fabian and Clive could hardly contain themselves. Did you see what was happening below their waists?'

'I did. That's what I mean. No real ladies would have behaved in a manner calculated to arouse gentlemen's basest instincts. It was quite shocking.'

Candice cast her an annoyed glance, adding, 'And you? Can you honestly tell me that you didn't want to touch them, kiss them, wrap your limbs about them and make love?'

Emma shifted uncomfortably as if the seat beneath her was tickling her anus and causing irritation in her lower lips. 'Ah, well, if you put it like that. Yes, they attracted me in a weird, unwholesome way. I found my thoughts confused and filled with dreadful images... of blood and death and things too ghastly to put into words.'

'Oh, Emma, that's not so, I'm sure,' Candice exclaimed hotly. 'They may be an unusual family, but you must admit that our horizons have been sadly limited up till now. You don't find Baroness Esmeralda and Countess Bianca and Comte Henri awful, do you? They adopt an odd lifestyle, you must admit. All those slaves, and the comte's interest in punishment. I notice you don't condemn that.'

'It's entirely different,' Emma returned, her eyes wet with tears. 'I'm sorry, Candice, but I simply can't share your enthusiasm for your new friends. Oh, my dear, be cautious in your dealings with them, I beg of you.'

Clive listened silently to Fabian's story, his brown eyes narrowed thoughtfully.

'Are you quite certain it wasn't the result of too much Tokay?' he asked when Fabian had talked himself to a standstill. 'I must confess, I find it very hard to believe. The princesses and Prince Dimitri vampires? You're raving, man.'

They had left the ladies in St Mark's Square, sipping coffee and enjoying ices at Florian's, a renowned café. Fabian had taken Clive off on the pretext of browsing in the bookshops and antique emporiums in which the resort abounded. While they walked he had recounted his visit from the princesses.

'I can hardly believe it myself,' he replied mournfully. 'When I woke this morning there were marks on my throat and body and I stank of blood and sexual emissions, but by the time I had bathed and my valet had finished shaving me, they had faded. There's nothing left, old chap... nothing except a fearful lassitude.'

'There you are then,' Clive said confidently. 'You're suffering from an overindulgence in wine.'

He peered into Fabian's face, and had to admit that he showed a pallor beneath his tan. 'They told you they were vampires?' he questioned slowly. 'This is preposterous. No such creatures exist outside legend or tales of mystery and imagination. I've read about them of course, fictional works such as Sheridan Le Fanu's *Carmilla*, and others in the Gothic tradition. But as for thinking they are real, that's the purest nonsense.'

'How can you be so sure?' Fabian gloomed as they entered the dusty interior of a book-lined shop. 'Would our forebears have believed in electricity, or the railway train or combustion engine? And what about gunpowder and the way it has revolutionised warfare? As Shakespeare had Hamlet say, "There are more things in heaven and earth, Horatio, than are dreamt of in your philosophy."'

'You'd like to think it true,' Clive said with a quirky grin, aware of a stirring in his groin. 'To find yourself helpless and completely in the power of three lovely women! What more could any man ask?'

'In normal circumstances it would be delightful,' Fabian agreed, unwontedly serious. 'But not like that, I can assure you. They fed off my blood, Clive. Not only that, they sucked out my spunk. They possessed me, drained me dry, mocked and tormented me, were concerned only for their own gratification, not mine.'

'But you were gratified, nonetheless?'

'Oh God, yes... never have I known anything like it.'

'Then why this depression? Perhaps you felt it an affront to your manhood because, somehow, the princesses had gained access to your room and had their wicked way with you. It turns the tables, does it not? Men like to think of themselves as predators.'

'It was more than that... much, much more,' Fabian replied, and lowered himself on to a stool as if too weak to stand any longer. 'They talked of Candice, said Prince Dimitri had singled her out, mocked my inability to do anything to stop this.'

'Candice?' Clive said sharply, and a great hand seemed to squeeze his heart. 'You think she's in danger?'

'I fear so,' Fabian sighed, with so deep a conviction that some of Clive's disbelief gave way to apprehension.

'He may be a skilled seducer,' he put forward sensibly, though suddenly chilled to the marrow. 'But a vampire? It's

160

ludicrous.'

'I don't think so. If you had been there in my room last night, you too would have been convinced,' Fabian answered, shaking his head.

Clive came to decision, thinking Fabian slightly deranged, 'Look here,' he said briskly. 'I'll ask the bookseller if he has anything on the subject. We'll read up about vampires and you'll change you mind, recognising that the princesses were having a joke at your expense.'

The shopkeeper seemed reluctant to produce any relevant material, but relented when offered a substantial amount of lire. He spoke a modicum of English, muttering as he disappeared into a back room, 'Vampires, demons, monsters... *si signor*, I find you something.'

He returned with two leather-bound tomes, translated from the German. After haggling Clive bought them for half of what the bookseller had first asked, had them wrapped in brown paper and left the shop with the parcel under one arm. He did not wish to alarm the ladies by letting them peruse such frightening literature. It was something he and Fabian must study in private.

They strolled back across the square where visitors and locals enjoyed the sunshine. Dignified dames clad in Parisian outfits paraded, feathers rippling in their huge Gainsborough hats as they chatted with their elegant escorts. Meanwhile their nursery maids, in quaint silver headdresses with streaming ribbons, showed pride in the plump dark-eyed babies in their charge.

In the adjoining piazzetta boats were awaiting the tourists' pleasure, and the voices of their owners could be heard shouting, '*Gon*-dola! *Gon*-dola!'

Candice looked up to smile at Clive as he approached and he thought what a perfect picture she made, with her gleaming curls under an absurd little bonnet, her high, firm breasts covered by a lacy bodice, and those clear blue eyes. Flocks of soft-plumed, ever hungry pigeons circled, and one perched on her wrist, pecking up the grain she held on the flat of her palm.

It was so delightful a scene that Fabian's tale of succubi and demons seemed even more ridiculous. They would read the books and soon be laughing at what proved no more than an alcohol induced dream.

At that moment a flower seller sidled up, an old woman of gypsyish aspect. She was about to present her bouquet for sale when she suddenly stopped, stared hard at Candice, shot a glance at Fabian and retreated, muttering an incantation, holding out her closed fist with the thumb poking between gnarled first and second fingers.

'What ails her?' Candice asked, puzzlement in her eyes.

Clive watched the woman as, still backing off with her arm outstretched, she vanished in the crowd. 'It's odd,' he said slowly, aware of shivers trailing down his spine. 'I've seen this during my travels in Morocco. It's a sign against the evil eye.'

'We went to the Palazzo Tassinari last night,' Flora said as she started to take off her clothes. 'It was creepy, with this one peculiar manservant who seemed to do everything,'

'Was his name Carl?' Giacomo asked, laying on his bed, hands locked behind his dark head as he watched her curvaceous body emerge till she wore little but her pink satin stays.

Flora posed in front of him, arms akimbo. 'It was,' she said, the feathers in her round white hat nodding in agreement. 'Gwenda and me sat in an antechamber while the others had dinner and Carl came in from time to time. He gave us queerish looks, like he wanted to fuck us, but was sort of starving, too. I couldn't understand it 'cause there was lashings of grub about. Didn't seem like anyone else was eating apart from our young people, and Lady Candice was only picking at her food. Such a waste.'

She heaved an exaggerated sigh and her breasts bulged

like watermelons above the whaleboned corset. Below that nipped-in waist her rounded belly and hips were laid bare, appearing to be even larger in contrast.

A triangle of crisp brown fluff covered her pubis, making her thighs seem paler. Flora was proud of her legs, admiring her dimpled knees, shapely calves and gracefully arched insteps. She had made these even more alluring by the addition of white silk stockings, cerise satin garters and tiny shoes with high Louis heels. Flora was even more proud of her feet, and with justification.

Giacomo adored them, liking to strip her of stockings and shoes and slurp at each toe as if it were a fat clitoris. It afforded Flora almost as much pleasure as when he went down on the real thing.

'I not enter the devil prince's palazzo, Floria *mia*,' he said firmly. 'Not should you pay me a million lire. Once over that door step, and who knows?' He lifted hands and shoulders in a dramatic gesture.

'What are you afraid of?' she enquired teasingly, pinching her nipples into hard cones, feeling deliriously wanton, her hat still pinned to her brassy hair and a polka-dot veil shading her eyes.

'I fear nothing,' he exclaimed, swarthy features and melting dark eyes expressing indignation. 'No man, that is. But Prince Dimitri? They say he not human. And those women, his sisters! *Diabolico!*'

'I can't speak Italian, but I imagine you don't think well of them,' Flora ventured, with a coquettish smile.

'They bad,' he announced. 'We not go near them... the workers, that is. The rich? Maybe. Some admire evil. It heat their passions. But why we waste time speaking of bad things?'

'Why indeed?' Flora sighed, already dewy between the thighs.

She crossed the floor, thrilled by this assignation in his shabby room on the second storey of an old house that bordered a grass-grown, rubbish-strewn square. It was quiet there. Siesta time, when all who could rested in the shade. The vaulted windows opened on a balcony, its ironwork adorned by a little Venetian lion. This was a part of the city seldom visited by holiday-makers.

Flora's afternoon off, and his also. The first tryst where they could occupy a spring-squeaking double bed.

Looking at her beneath heavy eyelids, Giacomo unbuttoned his fly and released his awakening serpent. Flora watched it emerge, her heart beating so hard it made her breasts shake. So perfect a pleasure tool, so tireless in endeavour. She was sure it would spit at her not once, but several times during the course of the afternoon.

Giacomo reached for her, pulled her down beside him and, propping himself on one elbow, bent over her, his unshaven cheek rasping her breasts as he drew one brownish-pink dug into his mouth.

Her hand groped in his crotch and found the upright bulge she sought. 'Let's take our clothes off,' she begged, exploring him as if she could see with her fingertips. 'We've never done that.'

He rumbled with laughter, and reminded, 'We only do it two times, and in the gondola. Yes, I want to see all of you, every little piece. First... your so soft stockings.'

'No. Your trousers,' she pouted.

'*Si signora*,' he replied with mock humility.

She did not want to let him go, not even for a second, but he rose and ripped off his white shirt. His body was tanned and muscular, with a dark pelt covering arms and chest. It scrawled past his navel and disappeared in a pencil-thin line into his waistband.

Next he undid his belt and let his trousers drop. He wore nothing underneath, and once he had kicked the garment away and slipped off his shoes, he stood before Flora in all his naked glory.

The upraised tribute of his cock faced towards her, and

she slid from the bed, fell to her knees and worshipped at this strange altar. Her tongue found the twin lobes at the head. Slurping and sucking, she rocked there, taking him deeper, his hands buried in her hair, holding her to him as he murmured words she could not understand but knew to be dirty.

He started to seesaw, hips falling into a steady rhythm, his fully extended cock buried in her mouth, but not quite all. She choked, gasped, said, 'My God! You're so big!' then continued to bring him to the peak, her cheeks bulging as she sucked vigorously, succeeding in enveloping the length, her face buried in his hairy groin.

His knees buckled. She felt the surge as his penis twitched, swelled that last little bit, then discharged a flood into her throat. Flora took it all, that spicy tasting cream, savouring and swallowing it. Greedily she licked up the droplets that had escaped to coat her lips. She caught a trickle on her finger and transferred it to her mouth as he withdrew his softening but still semi-erect member.

'Ah, you so lovely English lady,' he whispered, raising her and holding her against his heart, its beat slowing as orgasm's rapture faded. 'All woman. We do it again. *Si*? And you come, too.'

'It's no good arguing, Candice. My mind is made up,' Fabian said loftily, her guardian and brother who controlled her unreservedly while they were away from their parents.

'But, Fabian... I promised,' she pleaded, heart-clutchingly lovely in a lilac satin evening gown, sequinned in fuchsia.

'You had no business promising anything until you had consulted me,' he said coldly, drawing on his cigar as they stood on the terrace, gaily lit by coloured paper lanterns. 'You will simply have to send the prince a note of apology. No, better still, I'll write. You shouldn't be corresponding with another man. Are you forgetting your betrothal to Clive? You're behaviour is, I regret to say, rather unseemly.'

'I didn't know you had already agreed we should visit Comte Henri again,' she muttered, her mouth dropping sullenly.

'You were in such an abstracted state last night, I doubt you were aware of much,' Fabian answered, unable to communicate his worries to her and resorting to being unhelpfully bossy. 'There's nothing more to be said, Candice. We're expected at the Palazzo Barbesi at eight o'clock.'

He had spent an hour before dinner with Clive and the matters disclosed by those factual books had left a sickening taste in his mouth and horror in his soul. If only half of what was printed there was true, and could be applied to Dimitri and those wild females, then he must do his utmost to save his sister from them.

As for himself? Oh, his resolution was strong while in Clive's company. But what would happen if those harpies appeared to him as they had done last night?

'We'll take precautions,' Clive had insisted, consulting one of the volumes. 'It says here that vampires don't like garlic. We must go to the market in the morning and buy some, then rub it round the doors and windows. In the meantime, I will sleep in your room tonight and if they come, I'll defy them. Have you a crucifix? There must be one somewhere about? Some vampires fear them, and the Communion wafer and holy water, but not all.'

During dinner Fabian had sat in the splendid restaurant, under the eye of that master-of-ceremonies, the head waiter, surrounded by people who were going about their normal occupations, eating and drinking and enjoying themselves. He had been quite unable to get to grips with what he and Clive contemplated doing. It was the height of folly, surely? Had the heat gone to their heads? Were they suffering from sunstroke? They weren't seriously preparing to ward off vampires, were they?

Yet when he had looked at Candice, and seen that innocent face which contrasted so vividly with the fierce countenances of those terrible women, and heard her prattling about going to visit the prince again, he had known he must keep his resolve. She must be protected until they left Venice. He had even thought about curtailing the trip, though this would be inconvenient. How should he explain it to Mama and Papa? Oh yes, that would go down well he was sure! He would be told off for being flippant, and he would get the blame for spoiling the holiday.

It was almost time to leave for the comte's palace, but Candice had managed to escape for a moment, running up to her room.

It was a wonderful dark blue night, and the throbbing of her blood, the pulsing in her sex, urged her to go to Dimitri.

Despite his threat, there had been no stripes on her buttocks, though her ethereal body tingled. When she had examined her vagina early that morning she had found her hymen undamaged and this was a mystery as she so clearly and thrillingly recalled his phallus penetrating deep into her heartland. And how she had come to be in that wintry place, amidst wolves and peasants and that weird orgy, she had no idea.

Dimitri must be a sorcerer, a magician, a skilled mesmerist, but it was not important. He had called her his beloved, and she yearned for him, her vagina aching, her labia swollen and her clitoris pulsing with need. He had whipped her cruelly, proving himself her master, but this had done nothing but increase her desire. How could she endure being parted from him?

'I wonder how you would feel if you really knew what he was?' whispered a silky voice behind her.

Candice spun round from the window and looked straight into Belphegor's whimsical face. 'You?' she quavered, hand flying to her breast.

'Your servant, ma'am,' he said, with a sweeping bow, elegant as ever though he was wearing tight blue cotton trousers and a roll-neck sweater. 'I've just popped back from the late twentieth century to remonstrate with you. Rather a bore, as it is quite my most favourite period of history. The things one can do, my dear. You'd never believe.'

'But you were at the castle last night?'

'True, but this is one of the bonuses of being a vampire,' he explained with a cryptic smile. 'One can be here, there and everywhere.'

Candice sank down on the stool in front of the dressing table, staring at the dapper figure who now leaned against the bedpost, crossed his legs at the ankles, folded his arms over his chest and continued to fix her unblinkingly.

'Did I hear you correctly?' she breathed, while alarm bells clanged in her brain. 'Did you say you were a vampire?'

'That's right.'

'Do you take me for a complete moron?' she asked levelly.

'On the contrary, my dear. I think you're a lady of exceptional intelligence.'

'And you seriously expect me to believe you?'

'No, but I'll give you a demonstration. Dimitri is also one of us.'

'Dimitri?' Her heart jumped madly and horror quivered along her nerves. It wasn't true, of course. Belphegor was teasing her. He had to be, didn't he?

'That's what I came to say. I made him, you see, so I feel somewhat proprietorial about him. You might say I love him,' Belphegor answered, beside her now, but though she was reflected in the mirror, he was not.

She swivelled round and he stood solidly at her side. Glancing back at the looking-glass she saw herself, the lamp-lit room, the big bed, the armoires, the drapes, but no Belphegor.

Her spirit plummeted like a stone.

A voracious reader, she had secretly thrilled to romances considered to be utterly unsuitable for genteel young ladies, in which these mythical creatures appeared in villainous roles, but had never seriously thought they were anything other than fiction.

'You say he's a vampire?' she asked, pressing her hands to her breasts in search of comfort and remembrance of his touch there, and the devastation it had created in her damp and fragrant delta.

'That's right. He was made so by me in sixteen seventy-two. He is immortal, and remains as he was on the day his body "died". The princesses are our kind, too. He made them, as a vampire has the power to do.'

'And yourself?'

'Oh, I'm very old indeed, and was transformed by my own maker in medieval times. I won't bore you with the details now.'

'Why is Dimitri interested in me?' she whispered on a sob.

'He wants to imbibe your blood and have you drink his in return. This will make you into a creature such as he. Then you will be his bride and remain with him throughout eternity.'

'How monstrous! He would deny me heaven?'

Belphegor inclined his head, gazing at her through slitted lids. 'Indeed. You would never again walk in the daylight, becoming a child of darkness, and you would be compelled to drain the blood of the living in order to survive.'

She sprang up, her face as white as his. 'You lie! It's not true. It can't be. Dimitri isn't a vampire.'

'I can prove it. Will you come with me?' he said slowly, and held out his hand.

Candice took it.

Chapter Nine

Dimitri awoke, his ravenous hunger telling him it was time. The sun had slipped below the horizon, great fans of colour meeting purple night clouds, that golden glow reflected in the sea, but where he lay it was black as the River Styx.

Reaching up he slid back the stone lid of the sarcophagus that stood, with three others, in a cellar under the palazzo. It was damp down there, below water level. As he threw a leg over the side and climbed out, so Allegra, Medea and Madelon left their resting places, too.

'Good evening, brother,' they said in unison, yawning widely and flexing their limbs.

'Did you sleep well?' he asked, kissing each in turn.

'Oh yes, very well. A deep, dreamless sleep,' Allegra said, winding her arms round him. 'Like death, perhaps. I wonder what it's like to die.'

'You know,' he said with an indulgent smile. 'You went through the process when we exchanged blood.'

'So I did. It was painful,' she averred, remembering.

'I didn't care for it at all. Being a corpse was tiresomely unpleasant,' remarked Madelon, smoothing down her silk skirts and patting her shimmering hair. 'I hope I'll never be one in actual fact.'

'You won't, unless some bumbling do-gooder decides to catch you asleep, drive a stake through your body, chop off your head and burn your heart,' teased Allegra waspishly.

'Stop it!' Madelon said, flouncing away from her. 'You do say horrid things sometimes. Tell her to be quiet, Dimitri.'

He shrugged and did not reply, knowing this was a possibility. Or being tied down in direct sunlight, which would reduce an undead to ashes in minutes. They were not happy with flowing water either, needing to cross not enter it. These weaknesses were known to the professional vampire hunter, but fortunately there were not many brave enough to take up such an occupation.

'I was simply thankful for a second chance,' Medea butted in, then glided up the crumbling steps that wound aloft. 'I don't know about you, but I'm ready to feed.'

'The sweet Fabian?' asked Allegra with a knowing grin, fingers combing through her tangled mane.

'Perhaps, later.'

'What have you been up to?' Dimitri demanded suspiciously.

'Nothing,' they trilled, sweetly innocent.

He did not trust them, but before he could form a reply they had vanished on their nocturnal hunt.

Should he give in to his ferocious hunger for Candice, draw the vitality from her, the sheer exuberant life? He wondered, throat parched, loins aching. Her blood would be like potent wine as it slipped over his palate, of so strong a consistency that it would give him energy and a feeling of euphoria like no other.

The temptation was awful, yet he wanted more than that: her promise that she would accompany him on his immortal journey, and to give of his blood after he had drained hers. She would die physically, yet in a little while be resurrected, born again but into darkness.

He rarely emptied his victims till they expired. And even should he do so they would not become *nosferatu* unless he chose to bequeath the dark gift by allowing them to drink his blood. And for this he must first obtain their consent. No vampire was made unwillingly, or by chance.

In his baroque bedchamber he put on superbly tailored evening clothes, a swirling black cloak lined with red silk, and a top hat.

Thinking of Candice had whetted his appetite even more. It was full dark outside now and he willed himself to be part of it, choosing a back alley, linked by little squares and canals. Old houses, once grand but now decaying, surrounded him. He could hear raucous singing from a café, shadows passing against lamplight and flung on the frosted glass panels, his nostrils flaring at the smell of warm blood.

Dimitri waited. The noise swelled as the door opened, wafting odours of alcohol and cigar smoke and sweat, then crashed shut again. With his preternatural sensitivity, the sounds, sights and smells were exaggerated to an almost painful degree.

When he was first initiated by Belphegor he had shrunk from taking human life, but that ancient vampire had trained him, sometimes cruelly starving him of the more humble warm-blooded mammals till he was screaming with need. Over the years he had become as cynical as his mentor. His scruples had disappeared, as had his reluctance to study the shady side of magic.

He had perfected the deviations he had learned with Madame de Montespan. He was a master, subduing his female victims with whips and bonds before taking his astral fill of them, as he had done with Candice at the castle. Sometimes, at daybreak and twilight when he was at his most vulnerable yet could function as a man, he had penetrated them with his hugely empowered sexual part, but not her – not yet. This was his ultimate ambition.

A man stumbled from the wine shop, leaning on the shoulder of a straggle-haired young whore. Dimitri's lip curled as he scornfully remembered the coarse vulgarity, cunning and low-grade lust of the average *Homo sapiens*. Vampires and ghouls, spectres and werewolves were not the only monsters walking abroad in the world.

His prey was of medium height, stocky, stout and short-legged, with a red face and watery eyes, wide nostrils and slack lips. A local businessman, a pillar of the community and fervent church-goer, but a womaniser nonetheless, constantly unfaithful to his downtrodden wife. His time was up, and he was about to meet his Nemesis.

Dimitri stepped under the gas lamp, deliberately showing himself. He closed one hand in a vice-like grip on the man's fat neck, instantly freezing him. The whore stood bemused, held rigid by his spell.

The man's face was suffused with colour, sharpening Dimitri's hunger to frenzy. A silent scream struggled to escape from the lips of his prey as he stared, boggle-eyed, at the pointed fangs emerging from Dimitri's mouth.

He sank his teeth into the jugular vein and ecstasy poured through him as he fed on liquid energy. He drank and drank, as if his ferocious thirst would never be quenched, bending over the man, his cloak spread wide like the wings of some monstrous eagle.

And Candice saw him as she stood with Belphegor, looking on to the street scene as if through the two-way mirror in the comte's chamber in which she had watched Gwenda flogging the maidservant.

It was horrible, a grisly nightmare. Dimitri lifted his face from the man's torn, gaping throat, alert, listening, aware of her presence perhaps or that of another super-being. His eyes gleamed green-yellow, wolf's eyes, demon's eyes, his mouth running with gouts of blood that trickled down his shirt-front, and dripped from his hands.

He tossed away the empty husk of bloated flesh. It hit the wall with a sickening thud and slithered down to lie on the paving stones. At his command the young whore woke and he bent her across his arm while she gazed, hypnotised, into his eyes. When his teeth touched her throat she wailed with pleasure and her body jerked up to meet his as she erupted into orgasm.

'I don't want to see more. Take me back!' Candice cried in that whirling, storm-racked space which owed nothing to reality.

'Now do you believe?' came Belphegor's sibilant voice.

'Yes! Yes! How could I have imagined that I loved such a

173

fiend? Emma's right. I've been insane... stark, staring mad!'

The bath house was built on classical lines, the brilliant prismatic light of chandeliers sparking off blue mosaic tiles, Islamic arches and pillars with carved impish faces peering through stone foliage.

A mixture of architectural styles had been employed to adorn Henri's hammam, and crowned by a multifaceted cupola.

When Candice entered through the tropically lush conservatory, she found her host clad in an East India robe, his bare feet dangling in the water, playfully tickling Bianca's toes. She sat beside him, shoes and stockings discarded, black taffeta skirts pulled high, revealing a flash of russet maidenhair at the apex of her thighs.

She was giggling into her champagne flute at something he had just said. He was leering at Candice and she guessed his remark had been a lewd one concerning herself.

She stared at them defiantly.

What did it matter any more? She might as well join in their licentious games as Emma had done. Why dream of princes? Why hanker after the meeting of true minds? She had allowed herself to be seduced by evil, falling in love with a blood-drinking monster.

After a headlong flight through the starry darkness over Venice, Belphegor had returned her to her hotel room, then disappeared. In a state of shock that had encased her in ice, she had not even been able to cry. That deadness remained, and she had locked her mind to Dimitri.

She knew she should warn Fabian and Clive about the princesses, but feared their mockery. They might dismiss it as fanciful nonsense, or worse still call in a doctor, thinking her hysterical.

'I say, how perfectly splendid!' carolled Esmeralda, already immersed in the oval pool. 'I hope you'll pardon the informality. We don't stand on ceremony when with our intimates.'

Faint wisps of steam rose around her, but the water was transparent, rippling over her voluptuous naked body. Her large breasts rose as she waved, the nipples puckered and coffee-brown. A short while ago Candice would have been embarrassed by this display, but her brief sojourn in Venice had changed all that. She had known passion and horror in quick succession, and felt immensely old and world-weary.

'I'm going to suggest that you undress and join us,' Bianca added, rubbing her bare foot up Henri's leg and under the edge of his robe till it connected with his heavy balls and erect penis.

She ran her tongue over her lips, looked at him with smoky amber eyes and twiddled those impudent toes. Then she withdrew her foot and clapped her hands.

At once a quartet of beautiful slaves appeared, two male, two female. Candice recognised Maria, but the others were strangers. They were all naked apart from black leather thongs that crossed their bodies, linked to the hoops in their nipples and down to clip on rings through their pierced genitalia. Their faces were painted in brilliant designs, their hair plaited and braided with ribbons and beads. The men were hugely aroused, their pricks standing up stiffly.

As they moved humbly, with bowed heads, the most wonderful spicy scents breathed out from their oiled skins, coupled with oceanic female juices and the sharper tones of semen.

'Shall we take our clothes off and swim?' Emma asked, her eyes going to Fabian. 'I must admit to a curiosity concerning nude bathing.'

'Why not? I can't see any harm in it,' he answered, and the swelling behind his trouser closure became more pronounced as he looked at the blonde girl, Nina, and recalled the feel of her lips around his cock.

'Is it proper?' Clive demurred, a stickler for etiquette.

Fabian stared him straight in the eye and murmured,

'Wouldn't you rather we were here than in my bedroom, waiting the arrival of unusual guests?'

'I suppose so,' Clive replied, glancing round him uneasily. 'But I was thinking of Candice and Emma. Should we subject them to a scene such as this?'

'You worry too much, Lord Clive,' Bianca called across, then rose from the blue tiled edge of the pool, and one of the slaves pattered over and began unhooking the back of her bodice, then letting her skirt fall.

Now she wore nothing but a thonged black leather bustier that exaggerated her wasp-waist, ended in a frill at her hip-bones and sent her breasts swelling like ripe apples over the edge of the half cups.

'Antonio! You clumsy oaf!' she shouted as the slave dropped a garment to the wet tiling.

He was a lovely, chestnut haired youth, and now stood with his head bowed in contrition, hands clasped at the back of his neck.

'Davide... the birch!'

Bianca signalled to the other young man, who selected the instrument from several other rods and canes standing amidst silken flowers, grasses and peacock feathers in an Oriental urn. He salaamed and handed it to her.

'Bend over,' she commanded, and Antonio obeyed, reaching down and clasping his ankles.

Candice felt a flutter of fear, longing and pity. How humiliating to be punished so ignominiously. Why did he endure it? What hold did Bianca have over him? And, stronger than all else – what would it feel like to have the countess lay about her own hindquarters with the birch?

Antonio made no sound as the bundle of prickly twigs lashed his muscular back and fast reddening buttocks. His tight balls were exposed as he leaned over, and the deep crease of his bottom and the tiny brown mouth of his anus. His cock was ramrod stiff, its head touching his navel.

Bianca saw his arousal, paused for a moment in her

birching, and said to Maria, 'This wretched slave can't control his organ. Slap it. Play with it. I want to see how long he'll last before he disgraces himself in front of everyone.'

Maria came forward, never lifting her head or showing any discomfiture, apart from the blush staining her cheeks. To the swishing accompaniment of the birch meeting flesh and the stifled sobs of its victim, her hand struck smartly across Antonio's phallus. It jerked. He flinched. She struck again. The penis swelled harder still, pulsed and discharged its load, spattering Maria's hand, arms and breasts.

'Filthy beast!' Bianca roared as he fell to his knees and kissed her bare feet. 'How dare you defile the bath house till I say you may?'

'I'm sorry, mistress,' he whimpered.

'Lick it up, every last disgusting drop,' she cried, and aimed a kick at his crotch.

He began with the floor, then worked over Maria's fingers, throat and breasts. She moaned and thrust her nipples towards his lips, but he avoided them, obeying his mistress to the letter.

Then he was permitted to straighten, taking up his submissive pose again, his buttocks red and patchy. His cock was alert, as hard as before, rearing from the thicket of hair between his legs.

Candice could not stop looking at it, or at his beaten rump and brown-skinned balls. To her everlasting shame she had to admit that since she had seen Dimitri with his victims, witnessed his bloody feast and recognised him for what he was, her desire had spiralled, upwards and upwards. Her sex throbbed with longing and juice seeped from her gateway.

Watching Bianca beating Antonio had added to this. Her labia swelled and her buttocks stung. She needed to be severely punished for so desperately desiring carnal knowledge of her devil prince. No wonder the flower seller had made the sign of the evil eye. Candice felt herself already tainted.

She did not realise how tightly she had been gripping Clive's arm until he said, looking down at her in concern, 'Shall we leave, my dear? We don't have to remain, you know.'

'We can't go back to the hotel alone,' she reminded with false modesty. 'Fabian dispensed with the chaperons tonight, so we four should stay together or our reputations may suffer.'

This sounded ridiculous under the circumstances but Candice was ready to make any excuse to stay. Her breasts throbbed hotly under her sequinned bodice, her bottom was on fire with remembered chastisement, while her nubbin was so ready that she was sure the smallest flick across its tender head would precipitate a powerful climax.

She wanted Henri with a need beyond all reason. Wanted a *real* man with a *real* penis, not some fiend who had deceived her with his perfidious lies.

Emma had said Henri lusted for her. Now she was more than ready to comply.

'Oh, you mustn't leave,' Esmeralda cried, rising dripping from the pool. Davide handed her a thin silk robe that clung wetly to every curve and hollow of that well preserved, pampered body. 'This is nothing, my dears. Merely sport between Bianca and her servants which all enjoy.'

'Let them prepare you,' Bianca urged, slipping an arm round Candice's waist, and running a hand down to press into the line of her arse under the satin skirt. 'No thick serge bathing-dresses here, my dear.'

'A massage first, I think,' Esmeralda suggested, and led the way to a series of small curtained cubicles that ringed the pool.

She encouraged Clive to enter one, and disappeared within. Nina followed Fabian into the next and Emma went into a third with Antonio. Henri sauntered away in the direction of his apartment.

Candice stood lost and lonely, wondering what was

expected of her. Then Maria tugged gently at her sleeve, saying, 'If you will permit, *signorina*?'

The cubicle was decorated in deepest rose, with a tiled floor and rococo gilt mirror. A glass shelf contained unguents and little phials of oil. When Maria lifted the stopper from one of these the scent of summer flowers poured out.

'May I, *signorina*?' she asked, and when Candice nodded, proceeded to undress her, hanging each garment on a hook.

Candice could not help remembering this dark-haired beauty helpless under Gwenda's blows, and said, 'Do you recall Miss Turner?'

'*Si*, I remember her very well,' Maria answered, smiling. 'She is a most vigorous lady. Not lovely, like you... but her arm is strong and she knows how to pleasure members of her own sex.'

'She's my chaperon,' Candice replied, and wondered if they had met since.

'I know,' Maria answered softly.

It was strange to be attended by this lissom creature, whose every movement brought some part of that olive-hued body into contact with Candice. She found herself wanting to touch the tightly bunched nipples, and stroke the crisp black hair between Maria's thighs.

She could not wait to be naked herself, and hurriedly pulled her chemise off over her head and pushed down her silk drawers, wriggling out of them. Sitting on the massage table she waited in breathless heat as Maria, kneeling, took off her shoes, carefully rolled down her stockings and hung them with the rest of the things.

The air struck Candice, but it was warm not cold.

'Lie down, my lady,' Maria coaxed. 'Allow me to soothe away your cares.'

Her kind, accented voice stole over Candice's senses like a caress and she found tears scalding her eyes as she thought of Dimitri and grieved for his infamy. She wondered if she could trust Belphegor and why had he chosen to betray

Dimitri. Was it to save her? She doubted this somehow, and tried to find another motive. Maybe she had been naïve to believe him, but the evidence of her own eyes was damning. She was no green girl liable to give credence to any sensational story, but an intelligent, well-read young lady. Yet it was impossible not to accept such aberrations as vampires after all she had experienced.

Now she allowed her thoughts to drift, every baffling question pushed to the perimeter of her mind as she enjoyed the sybaritic pleasure of Maria's oiled hands. She lay on her stomach on snowy towels, the pale mounds of her buttocks, the crease between and the lines of her slender spine open for inspection. Maria's strong slim fingers kneaded and stroked, pummelled at knots and released tension.

Candice moaned and pressed her pubis down, seeking friction on her clitoris. She parted her thighs a little as Maria reached the overhang of her rump. The slippery fingers worked round the cleft, rubbed the little moue of the anus, slid down to the pursed lower lips then fluttered away like a tormenting moth. Candice could hardly contain her disappointment as Maria circled her calves and ankles and pulled each toe gently.

'Turn over, please,' she said, and Candice rolled on her back.

A dollop of cream landed on her chest, and she closed her eyes and gave in to her feelings as those hands massaged each breast, rubbing and cupping, concentrating especially on the areolae and tense nipples. Candice rotated her pelvis, waves of heat making a film of perspiration break out over her skin, joining the slick layer of perfumed cream.

The hands moved to her shoulders and down her arms, working on each knuckle, each finger, then back to the body, the ribs, the belly, while Candice entered a trancelike state of pleasure and anticipation. Front of legs, over the knees and finally the thighs, Maria parting them, going up, down and around, her hands brushing against the fronds of

Candice's fair bush.

It was as if every hair had its own electric impulse with a wire connecting straight to her clitoris. Unable to stop herself, she slid her thighs apart till her legs dangled over the sides of the couch, her delta completely exposed. She sighed as Maria's gentle fingers applied cream to the swollen tissues of her labia.

Each wing was made slippery, the cream aided by Candice's own lubrication, then the fingers stimulated the creases between, holding the petals back from the clitoris that poked shamelessly from its cowl. Candice forgot everything, where she was and who, in the driving need to feel fingers rubbing steadily over the immensely sensitive head of her pleasure organ.

Maria seemed to read her thoughts, and her thumb settled into just the sliding motion Candice needed, while a skilful finger pushed into the portal of her vulva, caressing the wet interior. It went higher, coated with cream, probing into her anus, then swivelled back to the vaginal entrance, tickling it, in and out, but no more than a quarter inch, respecting the intact hymen.

'Oh, go on... do it... do it...' Candice gasped as she lifted her hips against that expert thumb.

Maria pressed the labial wings further apart, and rubbed with two fingers each side of the engorged clit as she kept up the friction on the slippery head. The feeling was building, wave after wave pouring through Candice till it surged like a great torrent and exploded into a devastating climax.

She opened her eyes, half veiled by their thick, curly lashes and said, 'Thank you, Maria. You did that perfectly.'

The girl flushed at the compliment and replied, 'It is a fable that English ladies are cold. I've found them burning with passion.'

Candice stretched on the couch, too indolent and relaxed to move a muscle, and could not be bothered to protest when Bianca poked her auburn head round the curtain, took one look at her spread legs and wet furrow and said, 'You'd look so sweet shaved. Have you ever removed your pubic hair?'

'Never, countess,' Candice murmured, too comatose to give the matter serious thought.

'I'll send Davide in. He's the comte's barber,' Bianca answered and withdrew.

Maria tucked a towel round Candice and she lay there half asleep to be roused a little later by the covering being removed. Davide was at the foot of the couch, and a small table had been drawn up on which stood a basin of hot water, a bar of soap and a cutthroat razor. He took this up and honed it on a leather strop. The light slanted across the blade. It flashed, blue-white. Candice winced.

'A moment, *signorina*, and it will be over. You'll feel nothing but pleasure, I promise you,' Maria said, enviously. 'It will look so pretty. Nina's pussy is bare, little blonde-haired Nina, but I am not done. The master prefers it like it is... though I wish...'

Davide, of the glossy ebony curls and shining brown eyes, took up his place between Candice's thighs. Maria, leaning over her from one side, held her legs wide open.

He began at the broad top of the wedge, just below Candice's belly, wetting it and using a shaving brush to work up a lather. The fragrance of expensive lavender scented soap combined with that of Candice's honeydew, rose in a heady cloud.

Davide concentrated on his task, the upward curving bar of his naked cock on a level with her body. He stood so close between her legs that a shove of her cunt towards him would have brushed it against that desired pillar of solid flesh. Her excitement soared, though she could see him drawing back.

The wickedly sharp blade gleamed as Davide pressed lightly on her mound, pulling the skin downwards and sweeping across with a sure touch. This put pressure on her nubbin, and it swelled, ready to orgasm again.

'Lie still, *signorina*,' he whispered, and the glint in his eyes told her plainly that he was aware of her need, and reciprocative.

He rinsed the razor in the basin, cleansing it of soap and hair, then repeating his sweeping action on her mound till it was completely denuded, pink and wet. Next Maria lifted Candice's leg and held it at an angle so he could reach the inner side of her groin, and clean off stray hairs on her perineum and round the tightly clenched arsehole. This was repeated on the other side.

By now she was highly aroused, wanting him to caress her naked slit and rub his fingers along the exposed clitoris.

He did neither, a well-schooled slave who must never touch until given his mistress's permission. He sponged the stinging surface of the naked pudenda, and anointed it with a soothing balm, but did not allow his fingers to linger. Candice grew hotter, pushing her pubis against his hand, her eyes straying to his prick that was stiff and uncomfortable looking, a single tear pearling its eye.

With a flourish Davide produced a hand mirror and held it so it reflected Candice's fork. She propped herself up on her elbows and gazed down the length of her body to where the image of her genitals appeared in the looking glass.

Gone was the brownish fluff and her cunt was as she had not seen it for years, the skin rosy and smooth, the crease darker where the edge of the lips met, the button of her clitoris dominating the fascinating cleft.

'How enchanting it looks,' Maria whispered, her breath like a gentle zephyr over the bare, smarting skin. 'Perhaps he will encourage you to have it pierced.'

'Who?' Candice returned smartly, Dimitri still filling her thoughts.

'Comte Henri,' Maria answered with a smile.

'My fiancé lord Clive, would not like that,' Candice said, pulling the towel round her and trying to hide in its folds, suddenly shy.

'No?' Maria made big eyes and jerked her head towards

183

the other cubicles. 'I think he's occupied with the baroness.'

Candice felt nothing but a prurient curiosity to see her betrothed fornicating with the overblown Esmeralda. She had never yet watched a couple doing it, and wanted to see exactly how a man performed. But just for now, she wrapped the towel around her and left the cubicle, venturing towards the deserted pool. Soon she was luxuriating in the novelty of nude bathing.

The sensation was one of unalloyed joy. Candice cleaved through the silken water and scissored her legs. The sparkling substance explored her shaven mound inquisitively, dipping into the delta and washing over her clit. She felt gloriously free – like a naiad – a creature of streams and rivers.

If only a man was there to share it with her, twining his legs with hers, his phallus pressing into her belly, her nipples chafed by his chest hair, flesh to naked flesh. Immersed in exotic fragrance, she kicked lazily in the tepid water, so clear and steeped in light that the little squares of mosaic tiles gleamed on the bottom like pearls seen through blue-tinged gauze.

She swam to the side and, floating on her back, neck supported by the tiled rim, looked down her body, shocked by the sight of her peaked nipples and the bareness of her cloven sex.

She was glad there was no one to see her, or was there? A queer shiver stung her nerves, presaging danger. She stared around. The water gave back an innocent smile, the flowers breathed out their aroma, the bath house like some fantastic stage set depicting harem life.

Her gaze was drawn upwards, compellingly, unwillingly. As her eyes came to rest on the glittering dome, so her attention focused on two spots of green glass. They seemed to grow, to slant, to turn into a pair of fierce eyes glaring down at her.

'No,' she shouted, but could not free her gaze. 'Go away!

184

For God's sake leave me alone!'

Laughter echoed under the cupola, a savage, merciless sound joining the howling of a sudden wind that beat at the shutters and made the chandeliers sway.

'Go back to hell from where you came. I'm finished with you, Dimitri,' Candice screamed, her voice torn away by the blast.

Sudden silence. An unnatural calm. Candice shivered with an icy cold that seemed to stab her vitals. Then she was aware of footsteps and glanced up sharply.

'*Signorina*, the comte wishes you to accompany me,' said Antonio, bowing deferentially.

Knees weak with relief, Candice climbed the curved arc of the water-washed steps and permitted him to wrap her in a towelling robe, then followed him. But no matter where she looked or how hard she tried to dismiss them, the memory of those blazing green eyes seemed branded on her mind, never to be erased.

Antonio pushed open a door and stood back so that Candice could precede him. She recognised the place immediately. It was the gymnasium, where Gwenda had beaten Maria. Yes, there was the gilt-framed mirror, which was really a window into Henri's bedchamber.

It was a large room with a plain wooden floor, a few chairs and a variety of odd-looking pieces – the vaulting horse, which Candice remembered, a whipping post, a rack and several others whose use evaded her. Henri, his paisley-patterned dressing robe girded round his waist, held out his hands and gripped hers, pulling her into the circle of his arms, the heat of his body and the pressure of his cock.

'So, you are ready to submit to me, Lady Candice, you who ran away last time,' he purred, sure of himself.

She jerked free, taking a pace back and shouting, 'Who told you that? I submit to no man!'

But you did, whispered a small sneering voice as if an

imp sat on her shoulder. You submitted to Dimitri and he's a man, isn't he? Or does his vampire status preclude him?

That wasn't real, she argued back. It was a dream, a fantasy, an abomination that should never have taken place. He had whipped her, threatened to mark her, and he had, not on her skin perhaps, but in her soul so that no matter what happened she would never entirely forget him.

Henri snapped his fingers at Antonio who, before she knew it, had slipped a scarf round her eyes, tying it tightly at the back. She was plunged into darkness, crying, 'I don't like this. Take it off.'

'Try it,' Henri said, close to her. 'Give yourself over to me. I promise you wild sensations.'

This is silly, she thought, but had rarely felt more alive, aware of every sound, every touch. And she was wet. She could feel the slippery essence between her legs, and then someone gliding a finger over that wetness, enticing her clitoris to emerge. Other fingers pulled at her nipples and she felt them crimping. Then a tongue caressed her lips from corner to corner. She opened them and tasted a honeyed mouth that pressed hers, now hard, now feathery.

She guessed there were others in the room, not only Henri and Antonio. Being deprived of sight heightened her other senses. She heard rustlings, movement, breathing.

Who was it? Bianca or Esmeralda? Davide or Maria? Nina, perhaps. Her bother and Clive?

How would she ever face them again?

Softness and gentleness vanished. Her robe was stripped off and hands seized her, clapping manacles round her wrists and snapping them shut. The shock made Candice's buttocks jerk back and her breasts jut forward. At once someone grabbed her rounded cheeks and held them against a stiff object that felt like an erect penis. She was shoved forward again and her pubis landed in the palm of a hand. Her outer labia was imprisoned, and a finger trailed along the unfurling folds of the inner, teasing her clitoris.

Now the hands guided her. She was backed up some steps and pushed into something that felt like a chair, except there was no seat, only a rim like a lavatory. Her hands were unlocked, then spread on the arms and fastened securely. Her feet were placed in position and her ankles shackled.

Candice squirmed her bottom experimentally, trying to ascertain what was happening. The rim was warm but her bare crack and arse crease felt cold and exposed. A finger flicked her nipples while another hand cupped and toyed with her swollen sex lips through the hole in the seat.

Someone was standing between her legs. Her nostrils flared. She could smell Henri. She gripped the arms of the chair as he pressed his cock against her lips.

'Suck,' he commanded.

She opened her mouth, ran her tongue over his thickness and took him in deep, tasting the salty tang of his pre-come. He moved his hips steadily, controlled, intent on making the sensation last, and every deep thrust made Candice boil with need. She heard someone beneath her, and then a tongue licked her lower lips, lapping at every fold and cranny. Candice moaned and angled her pelvis so it should not miss her aching nodule. It nuzzled the hot sliver of flesh, then withdrew, leaving it throbbing.

Candice groaned in protest through the pulsating bough in her mouth. At once it was pulled away and Henri left her. For a second she waited in agonised suspense, then gave a startled squeak as a small hard object was pressed against her anus. Slippery with oil, it penetrated her most private recess. Her vagina was unviolated, but a hand was moving the little invasive thing in and out of her rectum, making her gasp for more. Then that, too, was taken away.

She was unshackled and lifted to her feet. Her arms were stretched painfully over her head, the wrists embraced by cold steel. Then they were fastened to a chain and drawn upwards till her toes hardly scraped the floor. She swung there as helpless as a side of beef on a butcher's hook.

'I think you should see your master and thank him for the chastisement you are about to receive,' Henri said, and the scarf was removed.

She blinked to clear her sight, and gazed at her audience. She had been right in her assessment. Antonio and Henri had been joined by Davide and Emma, Esmeralda and the obsequious Gaston.

'Don't worry, pet,' the baroness said, patting her cheek affectionately. 'Your fiancé and brother are swimming. They have been thoroughly satisfied and aren't concerned about you. They trust the comte.'

'You should trust him, too,' Emma said, her cheeks flushed, her body semi-nude as she reached out to toy with Candice's nipples. 'I do. He will give you great pleasure. You'll see.'

'I don't want this,' Candice protested, but she was pulling at her chains, needing more, hot and hungry, her sex aching for completion.

Henri's robe was open, showing his darkly furred chest and the solid spear that protruded through the gap. He strode up to the tethered Candice and ran his hand slightly down her spine, then showed her the silver-handled, slim whip with a flat leather tip.

'It is for the best, my dear,' he said in honeyed accents. 'It will soften you, make you receptive to your husband. I'm doing Lord Clive a favour.'

'How very noble,' Candice snapped, her sarcasm coiling round the room. 'You, I suppose, get nothing out of it.'

'Oh, yes, I do. I'm not noted for philanthropy,' he answered with a lift of one eyebrow and a sardonic smile. 'I shall tame a wayward chit of a girl who has, so far, defied me. Unlike your friend,' and he reached out to stroke Emma's plump mons.

Emma sighed and ground herself against his hand.

Davide sat in a chair with Esmeralda astride him, her ample thighs spread wide as she impaled herself on his cock.

188

Gaston, meanwhile, lay himself across the padded bench, trousers down as he presented his naked rump to Antonio who was already standing between his thighs. He coated his thick cock with cream, took the heavy head in hand and worked it into Gaston's fundament.

Emma sat on the floor directly in front of Candice, her crumpled skirt pushed up as her middle digit rubbed diligently at her love bud.

Candice, strung out between pain, fear and lust, heard the crack of the whip and felt fire explode through her as the first blow landed. It was far worse than when Dimitri had whipped her, for this lash struck her physical flesh and, she was forced to admit it now, she was not in love with Henri.

She yelped as the leather resounded again, catching her on the widest part, flicking round her hip, its tip catching her belly. The pain was atrocious, a red-hot agony that had no time to fade before being joined by another. Her mouth opened and she screamed, unable to bite back the cries. The pull on her wrists was diabolical, the blows making her revolve, every inch of her body seeming to ignite under them.

She sobbed, tears flowing down her face that was half hidden by the fall of her hair. She writhed and struggled and tried to evade the lash, but to no avail. Henri was skilled at whipping. He took a pride in it, and every stroke augmented the last, and the heat of her welted rump communicated itself to Candice's sex, spreading, burning, as she gradually yielded.

Nothing existed except that world of pain and arousal. She was aware of the others seeking to reach climax, and wanted to share it with them. Wanted anything, anyone, who would bring her to the ecstasy of pleasure as acute as the agony she now suffered.

Drifting in a half conscious sea of pain, she was aware that the lash no longer tormented her. Hands took her weight. Others unlocked the bondage straps. She was carried into the next room and laid face down on Henri's bed.

She whimpered in distress, hurting, aching. Was Henri about to satisfy the hunger that scorched her clitoris, or would his cruelty extend to denying her? Perhaps he wanted her to crawl on her knees and beg. And I'll do it, she vowed. I'll kneel to him if only he'll bring me to completion.

Esmeralda stood on one side of her and Maria the other. Cool lotion laved Candice's striped back, taking some of the sting from the weals. A sheet of the finest linen was spread out and she was carefully laid on it, daring to take her weight on her damaged rump.

The room was lit by candles in many sconces, and the giant bed an oasis of peace and safety. Esmeralda brought over a golden goblet, saying, 'Drink this, dearest. Your throat must be dry with all that screaming.'

It caressed her tongue and slipped over her taste buds, deceptively smooth. Sweet as a liqueur, but with a bitter undertone. An aphrodisiac, perhaps?

'Drugging me now, are you?' she spat at Henri who had appeared round the draped bedpost.

'No need for drugs, my sweet,' he said blandly. 'You are more than prepared.'

'Clive. My betrothal vows,' she struggled to say as Esmeralda eased behind her, knees wide open, supporting Candice's upper body against the soft pillows of her breasts.

'You shall keep your virginity,' Henri said, with an ironic twist to his lips. 'I'll not wrest it from you till the day you ask me to.'

'But I need... I want...' Candice sighed, as Esmeralda's hot breath heated that sensitive spot at the nape of her neck.

'I know what you want,' he said quietly, and knelt above her, the palms of his hands laid on each of her thighs, parting them, making him privy to her secrets as he added, 'Ah, so smooth and delicate. These petals are like rosebuds, swelling and opening to the sun's rays.'

Now the baroness's hands slid under Candice's armpits and nestled her breasts, the thumbs rolling and roiling on each nipple. The triple pleasure shot from teats to clit and then returned in a molten stream. Henri dipped his fingers in the wineglass and trickled red droplets over her delta, then bowed his head and licked them up.

His fleshy tongue stroked her clitoris and sucked it from the surrounding membrane. It quivered. Her whole body shook. She twisted her head from side to side against Esmeralda's breasts. Henri increased speed, thrumming on her bud and she was lifted high on billowing waves of ecstasy, attaining the glorious peak and yelling as frantic release hit her.

Henri moved up her body, his thighs embracing her and Esmeralda forced Candice's breasts together, making a channel in which he laid his upright phallus. He moved his hips, his pre-come lubricating the deep groove which now served as a vagina. He watched that long, thick, flushed member sliding up and down, and his eyes were unfocused, his lips smeared with her love juice.

She could smell it, fragrant as sea-washed shells, and looked down to see the glistening head of Henri's weapon appearing and disappearing between the compressed globes of her breasts. His movements became swift. He flung back his head, the cords of his throat standing out as he thrust his cock upwards in a final, convulsive spasm. He shouted aloud as hot semen shot from the eye, spraying Candice's face.

Unable to resist, she parted her lips, drinking in his dew. His prick spasmed again, a second spurt flooding over her hair and cheeks, and creaming the swell of the breasts that embraced it.

Chapter Ten

'Are you sure you don't want me to help you disrobe, miss?' said the lady's maid, after unbuttoning the back of Candice's gown and loosening the stay laces.

'Quite sure, thank you,' she replied. 'Just make certain my jewels are placed in the hotel strongbox.'

'Yes, my lady. I'll bid you goodnight then, my lady,' the maid replied with a bob, giving her an uncertain, sideways glance.

'Goodnight,' Candice nodded and turned to the dressing table, pulling off her kid gloves as she did so.

Oh dear, this is going to prove awkward, she thought. I don't want her to see my bruised backside. Servants gossip and I'll not have her talking about me. Of course, I never strip in front of her, always keeping something round my nakedness, but even so this is tricky.

The scene in Henri's gymnasium and bedchamber had already taken on the quality of an erotic dream. After she had recovered from her whipping and his sexual attentions, she had been helped into her clothes and returned to join her brother and fiancé as if nothing untoward had taken place.

They had gone back to the hotel by gondola, had a nightcap in the restaurant and retired. It was now after midnight and everything fallen into sleep and silence.

Candice's fingers fumbled in her haste to undress. She was eager to see the marks she could feel stinging her flesh beneath her underwear, excited by Henri's mastery. When the last garment was off and she stood before the cheval glass entirely nude, she ran a critical eye over her body from top to toe. The starkness of her bare pudenda gleamed invitingly, the cleft high and clearly defined, and she was sure her breasts were larger, the nipples alert and cherry-red.

Slowly, almost languidly, she squinted over her shoulder at her posterior. Her womb clenched and her pleasure nub twitched as she saw the stripes scoring the spheres of her bottom.

She reached round and ran a finger across one. It smarted. Her vulva spasmed. She wanted to come again. Oh, Henri, she mused, I could love you if it wasn't for that evil spirit who I must put out of my mind. You shall be my master, not he.

She darted a hand between her thighs, rubbing the bare lips. They engorged, opened, allowing her access to the niche where her juices gathered, and up to touch that tiny tyrant who demanded constant attention.

Once again she filled her thoughts with the comte, clinging to the memory of his erect phallus that had spewed its tribute over her. She ran her tongue round her mouth, searching for the smallest remaining trace of his spunk. It should be Henri from now on, till the time came for them to leave Venice and go home to England. Even then, maybe she could meet him sometimes. He was a world traveller – never staying in one place for long and, once married to Clive, she could open her London house to him.

She shut her eyes and concentrated hard, deliberately drawing a veil over the remembrance of Dimitri's face. He would be fearfully angry, she knew, but this did not deter her. It must be done. She could not possibly consort with a vampire.

'Dimitri, go from me,' she cried aloud.

Hardly had the words left her lips when a freezing chill settled round her. Her mouth and throat went dry, and her tongue grated along the inner surface of her teeth. All power of movement had left her limbs. She stared fearfully into the corners where shadows lurked beyond the lamplight.

His anger was already manifesting. A rank smell filled her nostrils and she sensed a stirring in the atmosphere. It became a sound – a low, irritating whine. She strained her ears to catch the direction of the noise, but it was everywhere, joined by a scurrying crepitus.

Rats in the wainscoting, conjured by him to torment her for her defiance?

Icy drops of perspiration crawled down her spine.

The room vibrated. The buzzing and scampering of unseen things rose, booming against her eardrums till it seemed they would split. Then the din stopped as suddenly as it had begun. Complete silence enveloped Candice, terrifying in its density.

She, who avoided church if she could, now tried to pray, the words sticking in her throat, 'Lighten our darkness, O Lord.'

She could not remember how it went – something about the perils of the night. All the time she was feeling around her with fluttering hands as if trying to pluck the words out of the air.

This was Dimitri's doing. He was trying to frighten her and demonstrate his power. 'All right,' she shouted. 'You've made your point, but it won't do any good. I've finished with you. Vampire! Blood-drinker!'

She shivering violently, her nerves jangling, even as her nipples peaked and her vagina ached with his remembered caresses. She felt as if she was tottering on the brink of madness.

Her bladder was full and she almost wet herself with fright as she heard a new, small, insidious noise. It came from the far end of the room where tall windows faced the garden. She listened, hands locked together and pressed to her pounding heart. It was dark down there, and the uncurtained glass glinted like murky water.

It came again, a slight sound as of a dry leaf brushing against the panes. Was it Dimitri? Had he approached her

194

again despite her mind-denial? Or could it be Belphegor, playing spiteful pranks?

She inched forward and the window came nearer, shining like a glacier. She reached a voluminous curtain that draped itself from ceiling to floor. It offered shelter, but she did not bury her face in its folds and hide. Instead, she stared at the glass where once, not so long ago, she had found the view attractive.

The night wore a purple shroud. Someone had doused the moon. She saw her own image flung back as if by a distorting mirror and then, beyond it, a column of much denser darkness.

Dimitri stood there – hung there – suspended metres above the ground. A sudden wind arose, keening round the hotel, beating at the trees that roared like waves gnawing the shore. He remained immovable. No errant gust disturbed his long cloak or pulled at the hood drawn up about his head.

His face was not visible – just a blank of darkness, yet Candice could feel his eyes boring into her – questioning, interrogating – why did you go to the comte? Why let him whip and subjugate you?

Time ceased to exist in this frozen confrontation. Then he slowly raised an arm and put back the hood. His face shone waxen in the dark and his eyes glared. All sense of space and reality dropped away. The walls dissolved and Candice could not tell where she was, drawn into those glowing pits of unappeasable hunger.

'What do you want?' she breathed.

He smiled, the cloak becoming great wings at his back. He glowed – was beautiful – infinitely seductive. His lips were still, but she heard his voice vibrating on her inner ear, in the cavities of her brain, in the depths of her sex.

'Don't shut me out. You belong to me. You've always been mine.'

'No! Go away. You're a monster. I saw you feeding earlier. You drank a man's blood and killed him.'

Rage and pain contorted his features. 'You watched me? How can this be?'

'Belphegor told me you were a vampire,' she shouted through her tears. 'I wouldn't believe it, but he took me to where you were feeding. Now I know. Now I won't, *can't* have anything to do with you. I'll cut you from my heart if I have to use a knife to do it!'

'Belphegor... the traitor!' he growled ominously, and the wind raged harder, banging shutters and making ripples on the canals.

'What he did was right,' she insisted, wet with desire, even now when she knew what Dimitri was.

'No, Candice. What he did was wrong, motivated by jealousy,' Dimitri insisted. 'Listen to me, talk with me, don't shut me out.'

'I must,' she sobbed, tears running unchecked down her face.

'You can't fight it. Your need for me is too great,' he whispered and plunged his hand through the window-glass. It parted like blobs of mercury, then reformed round his arm.

He reached for her, his nails scraping across her nipples. They rose, hard as diamonds, the sensation one of tingling pleasure. Her knees weakened and her thighs opened, pubis lifting towards her darkly smiling lover.

Then she pulled back, crying, 'I refuse you. Leave me. Henri's my master now, not you.'

'It's not true. I've already made you mine. You've given yourself to me in the whirlpool of climax. The marks of my whip are on your soul, never to be removed,' he shouted, his rage awe-inspiring. 'You must hear me out. Let me explain.'

'No! No!'

With a supreme effort of will she broke free, her voice rising from whispered plea to stammering speech, from speech to scream, shrieking the words of the prayer, yelling them like blaspheming as she fled blindly, bumping into furniture which tripped and trapped her, like clawing hands preventing her from reaching the door.

'Let us in. Ah, dear sir, don't deny us.'

The whispered entreaty wove itself into Fabian's dreams, a part of that eldrich country wherein his spirit wandered. He tossed uneasily, and the words were repeated like a persistent pain.

'Let us in. You know you want to. We can give you such pleasure, much, much more than Countess Bianca or Baroness Esmeralda. What do they know about love? We'll kiss you, work our mouths over your cock, tweak your nipples and tickle your scrotum. Let us in... now!'

Now! The word echoed round the bedroom, waking him. Now! Now!

Fabian sat up, sweat pouring off him, and the siren voices kept on and on... cajoling, seducing, imploring.

The windows were open in the humid heat, and he saw them, those three unnatural creatures, hovering at the window. Barbaric jewellery flashed, diaphanous drapes floated. They fixed him with their slanting vulpine eyes – black, ice-blue and violet – their hair twisting and coiling, mingling and parting, raven locks, white-blonde curls, tresses like sun-flares.

They were transparent as mist, unravelling then weaving together again. He could see the balcony rail through them. In the next second they were solid, a complex tangle of female flesh moving in new combinations of slim, bejewelled hands, full breasts, red mouths and rampant, succulent cunts.

His heart beat in heavy measures, like a funeral drum. His phallus rose from its brown thicket between his pale-skinned thighs. It vibrated with need, and the vampire women's deltas seemed to expand and grow – carnivorous flowers rimmed by sword-blades. They sucked in his manhood! They would mangle and destroy him!

And he wanted them, each wicked, wanton fiend – wanted to surrender himself to them, Clive's warnings unheeded.

197

Clive! He suddenly remembered their plan and shot a glance at the couch. He was asleep there. True to his word he had refused to leave Fabian by himself on their return from the Palazzo Barbesi. Pausing only to change from evening clothes to something more practical, he had armed himself with his books and a rosary borrowed from the *maitre d'* and taken up sentry duty. It appeared, however, that sleep had overcome him – or perhaps something more sinister – an hypnotic spell cast by the princesses.

'Fabian, darling, we're cold out here. Won't you invite us in?' the voices insisted. 'We want to rub up against you and warm ourselves on your cock.'

His thoughts were fuzzy, as if his brain was stuffed with cotton-wool. And his penis had taken over, the foreskin rolled back over the flaring rim, a trickle of juice easing down from the narrow slit in the helm. His belly felt hollow with hunger for the smooth, perfumed flesh waiting expectantly on the balcony.

Suddenly fearful and desperate he fought his lust, shouting, 'Clive! They're here! Wake up!'

There was no response, Clive sleeping as if already dead.

Allegra, a foot advanced over the threshold, seemed to be pushing against an invisible wall. 'I can only enter if you want me,' she murmured, and her amethyst eyes held a wealth of longing as she stared at Fabian's prick.

'I want you,' he replied on a sob, resolution crumbling.

At once she was in and wrapping her legs around his waist, impaling herself on his staff in one lithe movement. She bared her teeth in a wide smile and leaned forward to lick a drop of sweat from his forehead.

'You were unkind to keep us waiting,' murmured Madelon, lifting his haunches to accommodate her tiny hand. Her finger pushed past his anal ring and penetrated his nether hole, wriggling and stroking its way to his bowel. It became a fist, clenching and unclenching, taking him to the edge of mind-destroying sensation.

His buttocks tightened, driving him deeper into Allegra's ice-fire sheath. She tossed her head and gyrated her hips wildly, then even as she gripped him with iron inner muscles at the height of her climax, so she threw herself across his chest and sank her teeth into his throat.

Fabian, in the throes of a wrenching, convulsive orgasm, cried aloud. That cry acted as a spark on dynamite. With savage growls, Medea and Madelon pounced. He was absorbed, swallowed whole, drowning in their clefts, smothered by their breasts, drained by their mouths. He was dragged back to the womb, into the tomb – consumed by these powerful, aggressive, insatiable Furies.

Bleeding, sucked dry, his penis limp and useless, he sprawled on his back, and the vampires circled the couch where Clive lay.

Gone was the thin veneer of civilisation. As Fabian turned his head slowly on the pillow and watched them, he saw not women but animals with fiery eyes and bloody teeth bared to rend and tear. He tried to call out a warning, but his tongue cleaved to the roof of his mouth.

The covers of the books on the floor beside Clive flew open with a whoosh. The pages riffled as if by a strong wind. Woodcuts flashed briefly – of vampires with stakes hammered through their hearts, of spells against demons, of quotations and stories, fables, truths and half-truths.

'Oh, look!' Medea exclaimed, unperturbed. 'It's about us!'

Closer they came, stepping on the books contemptuously and touching Clive where the blanket had slipped from his prone form. He wore trousers and a white shirt, and Madelon slipped a long-clawed fingernail into the buttons at the collarless opening.

With a piercing shriek she withdrew it, the tip of her finger smouldering.

'He's wearing a crucifix!' she snarled, shrinking back.

'So what if he is?' Allegra growled.

'It burns me,' Madelon moaned, staring at her blackened

finger.

'That's because you were a Catholic when Dimitri saved you, and still cling to the church's superstitions,' Medea commented scathingly. 'I was an atheist, and Allegra a Jewess, so we're not affected. Why should we fear a piece of wood with a tortured man nailed to it?'

'Then you take him,' Madelon mouthed petulantly, leaving Clive and flashing round the room and up to the ceiling in an incandescent beam of light.

'No one shall take me,' he said sternly, coming awake at once and sitting up. He tangled his fingers in the rosary, then cut to Fabian, saying, 'My God, you're a mess! Couldn't you resist them?'

'They're too strong for me,' Fabian muttered, thoroughly ashamed of his weakness. 'Now do you believe I was telling the truth?'

'There's something going on, but whether it's supernatural or the work of a pack of mad women, I can't tell,' Clive replied and stood up, holding the rosary before him. 'I don't want you. Now get out, vixens,' he continued in that same level voice, facing them without fear.

Hissing and spitting, the princesses gathered into a knot, spiralling smoke-like towards the window. Outside the first grey smudge of dawn was bringing the buildings into prominence and casting a watery pathway across the canal. Perched high on a guttering, a bird started to carol a joyous hymn in praise of the sun.

The room emptied. Only Clive and Fabian remained.

'Bitches! Cheating, disloyal bitches!'

Dimitri filled every corner of the vault with his godlike rage. His voice thundered. His eyes rained fire. He was omnipotent.

'We didn't do anything!' the princesses protested, flattened against the wall by his scorching blast of fury.

'You did. You involved that traitor, Belphegor.'

'Someone talking about me?' With a twirl and shimmer, that self-same traitor appeared, gazing calmly at his livid initiate.

'Why did you do it? Why show Candice the worst side of vampirism, that of a thirst for blood?' Dimitri bellowed.

'Calm down,' Belphegor insisted, ravishingly attired as an early 1800s beau, this decadent period being a favourite of his – an era of gambling, sodomy and hellfire clubs. 'I was just about to attend a soirée at Carlton House, invited by the Prince Regent himself. Then I was buffeted by the waves of your temper tantrum and simply had to come and see what all the fuss was about.'

'I should kill you,' Dimitri threatened dourly.

'That's not likely,' Belphegor said, calmly sniffing at the little dune of snuff balanced at the base of his thumb. 'Care to try some?' he asked placatingly as he held out his silver box.

'You can't get round me. All I want from you are some answers,' Dimitri said, with the blackest scowl ever seen on a face. 'You've been meddling in my affairs, and I warned you not to when I brought Candice to the castle. Now, thanks to you, she has cut herself off from me, wasting her time with Comte Henri.'

'My dear, such a furore. It's for the best,' Belphegor stated blandly. 'We're quite happy as we are, I think. You and me and the princesses. And you were proposing adding another female to our band? Had you thought this through? No, I don't suppose you had. Led by your cock, as always.'

'He's right, brother,' Allegra ventured hesitantly. 'We don't need her.'

'I need her,' Dimitri declared flatly. 'And I'm going to have her. Nothing you can say or do will stop it. It's ordained by fate.'

'Fate, eh? As organised by you?' Belphegor flicked a speck of snuff from his frilled cravat.

'You've always been jealous of me,' Dimitri stated,

towering over him, looking taller than ever in unrelieved black.

'I've always wanted you, beautiful Dimitri, from the very first time I plunged my weapon into your tight butt and allowed myself the indulgence of falling in love with you,' Belphegor said wistfully, his slender hand touching Dimitri's knotted fist.

He snatched it away and turned his back on him, standing with his arms clasped behind his coat tails and his head flung up. 'Selfish as ever,' he snapped, his voice dagger edged. 'I'll never love you, not in the way you want. Candice owns my heart and any trace of goodness left in it. Whatever trick you try, you can't alter that.'

Belphegor gave an exasperated snort, declaring, 'Have it your own way, but don't blame me for the consequences.'

He spun round on the high heel of his boot, and shot back whence he had come.

Dimitri turned the full, vengeful force of his rage and anguish on the princesses.

Hands appeared from the ether. Allegra's clothing was whipped away and she was raised, struggling and screaming threats, to a stone arch that spanned the vault. Here the rope binding her wrists was attached to a metal ring, and her legs pulled straight up so that her ankles could be fixed in the same manner.

Arched like a bow, her head forced between her knees, her furious face, red with rage, showed above her sex. She was fully exposed, her pursed pussy, cleft and amber arsehole available for scrutiny and touching.

'Bastard!' she screeched, bound and impotent. 'You'll pay for this!'

Dimitri smiled and made the smallest possible gesture with his little finger. A goatish smell pervaded the vault. The flagstones moved, heaved and erupted as more of the elementals he had summoned poured from the earth. They were horned, they were winged, they were poisonous blobs of putrefying jelly with waving tentacles, they were bony skeletons, and fat, purple-skinned women.

Madelon yelped as she was strung up in a spider's web of chains and spread-eagled to the ceiling. Medea was clamped into something that resembled the stocks, her ankles thrust through holes in a wooden plank, her wrists fixed to an upper bar. Her shoulders, gracefully curving spine and peachy bare buttocks were vulnerable, her slit spread wide by the enforced angle of her legs.

Trussed up like fowls, the sisters screeched, cursed vilely and spat fire at Dimitri. His hellish cohorts cackled and wheezed, exploring the prisoners' sexual treasures with lecherous fingers and tongues.

Dimitri, having completely stripped the vampires of their powers, now instructed his demons, saying sternly, 'Don't let them orgasm. Bring them to the peak again and again but never satisfy them. I want them on the rack of permanent, agonised lust.'

'Yes, master,' they agreed eagerly.

Squat devil women, all breasts, broad hips, massive labias, and clitoral appendages like those of female hyenas leaped upon the helpless princesses. With gleeful yelps they kneaded their buttocks, dipped thick fingers into their vaginas, plundered their rectums and sucked at their clits.

The air was filled with gibberings, moanings, and the sound of fleshy tongues slurping at genitalia, along with the sisters' angry cries of frustrated passion.

Dimitri snapped his fingers and a black Malacca cane appeared in his right hand. He tested its lightness and pliability, then measured his first stroke against Allegra's taut rump and let fly. Her breath left her with a rush and she jerked against her bonds, swearing profanely.

His second blow followed, catching her on the tops of her thighs where he knew the cut went deepest. He gave her half a dozen lashes till her bottom was embroidered with red stripes. Then he passed on to Madelon. She was positioned high, but this did not pose a problem. He simply elevated himself, his arm as strong in the air as on the ground.

She made a lot of noise, howling and screaming and crying bloody vampire tears. This did nothing but anger him more, and he swung the cane with a smile as hard as his phallus, letting it crack down on her soft skin, slicing her from beneath. He delivered the final blow in such a way that the rod bit into her most intimate part, catching her labial lips where they pouted between her spread thighs.

Medea received the cane's force with dark contempt, biting her lip till the blood ran. She licked it up with relish. The stocks proved an excellent vehicle for punishment. Dimitri fingered her exposed parts, dabbling in her juices and saying, 'How very wet you are, my dear. Such a pity you'll not be able to enjoy copulation.'

He took a large, twin headed black dildo in hand, bent it in the middle and shoved one end into her vagina and the other past her anal muscle. Countless eager demonic tongues probed her upward thrusting clitoris and the hard fruit of her breasts, the bunched nipples ripe for sucking and biting.

Dimitri stood back and the cane changed itself into a python and slithered away.

'You see, my darlings,' he said, staring into each furious face in turn. 'It isn't wise to annoy me. You'll remain here as long as I see fit. Forever, if need be. You'll not be allowed to climax, or enjoy your vampire sleep or feed. You shall experience hunger of the most appalling kind.'

'Dimitri, brother, master... have mercy,' they begged.

He shook his head, left Carl in charge, and vanished.

'So you expect me to believe that he's a vampire,' Emma said, sleepy eyed and yawning. 'Fine thing to wake me up in the middle of the night and tell me.'

'You can't have been asleep long, and it's not night but almost morning,' Candice sobbed, creeping into bed beside her. 'It's so awful. I had to tell someone.'

'There, there, stop crying,' Emma soothed, wrapping her arms around the trembling, naked body. 'Vampires indeed!'

'Why is it so hard to believe?' Candice wailed, snuggling against her like a tired child.

'Because it's so improbable... a fairy tale,' Emma answered firmly.

'It's true,' Candice insisted. 'He's taken me on magical journeys and I've met Belphegor... he's another vampire... who told me what Dimitri was, and then took me to watch him sucking blood from the throats of a man and a woman. The most dreadful part about it is that I still love him. He wants me too, swears he'll never set me free. He was outside my bedroom window just now and I so much wanted to invite him in.'

Emma, ever practical, threw back the quilt and went in search of a sleeping draught in her medical chest. There, among cold cream, smelling-salts and cough medicine, she found a small brown bottle containing tincture of opium. Taking up a spoon and a tumbler, she measured it carefully into water and carried it back to the bed.

'Here, drink up,' she said, her tone of voice brooking no argument, holding the glass to Candice's lips till she had downed every drop.

Emma lay under the sheet beside her, an arm round her protectively, and soon Candice yielded to the narcotic, falling asleep. Emma could not do so, wide awake, watching the dawn breaking over Venice, hearing the church bells and the cries of the gondoliers as they began their early morning task of carrying workers to their destinations.

Though Emma tried to be rational, Candice had been bothering her for days, weeks maybe, if she counted her dream in London. She hated to think that her best friend was suffering from brain fever, but the alternative was ten times worse.

To add to her fears, she recalled a conversation she had had only yesterday with Flora Smythe. The chaperon had come to her in a state, blathering on about something Giacomo had said concerning Prince Dimitri – that he was the personification of evil – perhaps the devil incarnate.

Emma had reprimanded her sharply for spreading malicious rumours concerning her betters but this, coupled with the peculiar behaviour of the flower seller in St Mark's Square, had unnerved her. It was as if a blight had fallen over their holiday.

Oh, Venice smiled – Serenissima indeed, but she was reminded of a time long ago when she had picked a beautiful rose in the garden and, looking into its heart, had found a black maggot squirming there.

I'll speak to Fabian and Clive, she decided. This is too big a burden for me to carry alone. Candice's brother must say what is to be done. Maybe he'll call in a doctor, or make plans to go home. It is up to him.

Candice sighed in her sleep and Emma conjectured fearfully if she was dreaming of the prince. She touched her gently, her breasts, the flat belly with the little indentation of the navel, and admired the smooth, hairless mons. How delighted Henri had been with it, and how much Emma had enjoyed watching her friend being softened by his ruthless hand, brought to extreme pleasure by his tongue and anointed with his seed.

The memory of that scene played out a few hours before was enough to make her own desires burgeon. She had been more than roused by Antonio's massage, excited to molten heat by observing Henri seducing Candice, and later brought to full glory when he plunged his ever active phallus into her own love channel, but Emma always needed more than one orgasm.

She cradled her breasts in her hands, rubbing the nipples in unison. They stiffened, and sent their fiery messages down to her clitoris. To tease it and arouse herself further, she delayed touching it, giving all her attention to her breasts. It was then that she was tempted to wake Candice, needing both teats fondled while she playing with her nubbin, but she did not have the heart to disturb her.

Instead, she turned on her side so that her breasts slid together, full and heavy. She was able to use the fingers and thumb of one hand to stroke and pinch those throbbing tips, and reach down between her thighs to where her slippery gem protruded from between the turgid folds of her labia.

This was heaven. Though experienced with a man now, and having toyed with females for years, she was still convinced that the greatest pleasure was obtained through masturbation. Making love to oneself was intensely satisfying, for who else knew exactly where to rub and when? How to stroke till the peak was almost reached? And the precise moment to hold off, letting the waves die back before they broke, then gradually building them up and up – and up—

Emma gasped as the feeling rushed over her, bearing her to the dizzying crest, hovering there for a split second of bliss, then sweeping her into ecstasy. The little death! she sighed, falling and falling. How aptly named.

Later in the day she succeeded in catching Fabian and Clive without Candice being present, but after explaining her concern she was surprised and shocked to find that they concurred with her friend's wild story.

'I suppose it's only fair to show you these,' Clive said, and thrust two leather bound books under her nose. 'We wanted to shield you, and Candice, but it seems matters have already gone too far.'

'But you can't possibly believe this... can you?' she stammered, and her eyes cut to Fabian.

He lounged in a rattan chair on the terrace and, though handsome as ever with his fair hair falling over his eyes and curling round his ears, she could see he was very pale and listless. Her fiancé of whom she was fond, but not deeply enamoured. Henri and his exciting love-play appealed to her far more.

Now Fabian looked at her under the gold-tipped lashes of his heavy lids and said, softly, 'I have been their victim. Those vampire princesses have already drained my blood and my energy.'

'Oh, Fabian, don't tease!' she cried, annoyed and upset.

'He's speaking the truth, Emma,' Clive put in, his bearded face earnest and little worry lines creasing his eyes. 'I saw them last night. They tried to seduce me too, but one of them balked when she found my rosary, and the others left when I defied them. One has to be willing, you see, and invite them into one's life.'

'Then what is to be done?' she shouted, leaping to her feet in a frou-frou of silken skirts. 'Shall we call a priest? A doctor? Leave at once? What?'

'I think I can handle it,' Clive said confidently. 'We don't want to cause a stir, or people will think, as you did, that poor Candice is unhinged. Now I'm convinced, though I agree with you that it's hard to believe, especially in the broad light of day, there are steps we can take to destroy these foul creatures.'

'Such as?' Trembling Emma paced the terrace, up and down, as if trying to escaped her troubled thoughts.

'We can protect ourselves with garlic, wear crosses... though these are not always effective as we've already proved, be very careful never to invite them into our presence.'

'This is nigh impossible,' Fabian groaned, burying his face in his hands. 'They possess hypnotic powers, you see.'

'And can command the animals and storms, change their shape, appear as mist,' Clive went on.

'Then we stand no chance. I think we should leave right away,' Emma said, coming to a halt by Fabian's chair.

'Dimitri will follow, if he wants Candice as badly as the princesses say he does,' Fabian answered wearily. 'Distance is no hindrance to him. The sisters have fed off me, but don't want to turn me into such as they. But I believe this to be his intention regarding Candice.'

'According to these books,' Clive said, whacking a hand down on them. 'If he persuades her to drink his blood after he has taken hers, then she will go through a form of death and become as he is. *Nosferatu*... one of the undead who will roam the earth forever, feeding on the living... his fiendish bride.'

'So it really is hopeless?' said Emma and, though never devout, she felt the need to find a church, fall to her knees and pray.

'Not necessarily,' Clive said, his voice strong and determined. 'The vampire is all-powerful after dark, but weak during the day. He sleeps then in whatever foul grave he has selected for himself, and rises at sunset to pursue his dread purpose.'

Emma's flesh crawled, but an emotion other than fear tingled through her loins and made her juices well at her vaginal mouth.

In a flash she understood Candice's obsession with that handsome, lost and damned prince. There was something undeniably romantic and appealing about him. Evil was seductive when wearing such a guise. When she remembered everything Candice had said about his tremendous strength and power and the size of his phallus, so her nipples crimped and an ache began, deep in her womb.

She pulled herself together sharply. This was unnatural. Horrible. She should not be thinking this way. It was her duty to help Fabian and Clive find a means of saving Candice.

'She says she wants no further contact with him,' she reminded them.

'How long will she be able to resist?' Fabian said dolefully. 'I yield to the temptation of his sisters every time.'

'But you won't become a vampire?'

'No, simply weakened and falling into this strange melancholy.'

'This will leave him once they have tired of the game and

seek fresh fields and pastures new,' Clive reflected, getting out his notebook in which, always methodical, he had been making jottings. 'I have formulated a plan. It will take courage to do it, but I think the three of us have enough of that between us. We'll visit the Palazzo Tassinari as soon as possible. We've just had luncheon, so this gives us several hours before nightfall in which to carry out our intentions.'

'And what are those?' Emma asked tentatively.

'To find the prince and his sisters where they sleep, take up stakes and drive them through their bodies, then slice off their heads, take out their hearts and consign them to the flames. This is the way to destroy vampires.'

'Oh, my God,' she whispered, the terrace with its flowers, white marble pillars and normality, starting to whirl sickeningly. She sat down, clinging to the table's edge till the faintness passed.

'It's the only way,' Clive averred, his face grave.

'Where shall we obtain these things? Stakes, mallets, cleavers for beheading? To say nothing of knives to cut out hearts and fire to burn them,' asked Fabian, his expression one of deepest gloom.

'Mrs Smythe will help,' was Emma's instant suggestion. 'She's having a love-affair with Giacomo, the gondolier, and he has warned her about Prince Dimitri, convinced he is evil. She'll get him to provide the necessary equipment.'

'Good. Then that's settled. You instruct Mrs Smythe, and as soon as Giacomo has done his part, he shall take us to the Palazzo Tassinari.' Clive's voice was brisk, almost businesslike. He had automatically fallen into the role of leader.

'Don't let Candice know what you're intending to do,' Emma warned, fingers icy as they lay in her lap. 'She'll never let you harm her beloved Dimitri, monster though she knows him to be.'

Chapter Eleven

'Would you like to work for me, Miss Turner?' Bianca murmured, and stretched with sensual feline elegance on the Persian rug, an awning shading her complexion from the sun. No lady worth her salt wanted to become tanned as a gypsy or a woman who worked the land for a living. Heaven forfend! Her skin must remain as white as milk.

She was wearing an ecru muslin dress with a tiny waist and frilled jabot, her perfect breasts outlined by the pin-tucked bodice, her shapely arms, too, under leg-o'-mutton sleeves. Her high-arched feet were crossed, the ankles covered in taut cream silk, the rest in dainty, heeled pumps peeping from beneath the flounces of her skirt and petticoat.

Gwenda could not tear her eyes from this stunningly beautiful, auburn-headed aristocrat who had the morals of an alley-cat and, moreover, encouraged corporal punishment.

'Me, countess? You're asking me to leave my young lady and take employment with you?' she stuttered, lost for words.

'That's right,' Bianca answered calmly, staring towards the sea where Candice was sporting in the waves with Henri. 'The comte watched you chastising Maria.'

'He did? How?'

'A trick mirror,' Bianca replied, dimpling at her, tongue licking her cushiony carmined lips. 'We have several dotted about our establishments. He was impressed. We need disciplinarians like you in our employ. You enjoy such work, don't you?'

She turned her dark-lashed amber eyes to Gwenda, who had the urge to prostrate herself on the sand. 'I do, countess,' she replied, her hands clenched into fists. 'I like to see things running smoothly, with everyone knowing their place.'

'My sentiments exactly, and the comte's,' Bianca murmured meaningfully. 'Have you ever taken the rod to Lady Candice's derrière?'

'Yes, madame,' Gwenda confessed, standing respectfully near the beach cabin, gazing down at the opulent nest of pillows and rugs that covered this portion of the Lido rented by the comte.

'And she liked it, I fancy, if her response to Comte Henri is anything to go by,' Bianca mused, stirring the warm air with a round straw fan.

'I don't know about that, my lady. She cried a lot, but when I fingered her I found her soaking wet, and it took but a touch to bring her to bliss... if you know what I mean,' Gwenda blurted out, feeling hot and heavy between the legs.

'I can imagine. She has responded in the very same way to the comte,' Bianca informed her, face flushed with excitement.

'She has, madame?' Gwenda was thunderstruck.

'Oh, yes. Didn't you know?'

'She never said...'

'Well, she wouldn't, would she? You're supposed to be the guardian of her morals.' There was a slight hint of irritation in Bianca's honey-sweet voice. 'Well, what do you say? I'll shortly need a replacement for my secretary and aide. My present one is leaving to get married.'

'And my duties will be...?'

'Writing invitations to parties, answering those sent to me, with excuses or acceptances. Checking with my bank manager, lawyers and suchlike boring individuals, booking berths on ships or seats on trains, probably sleepers... one meets such fascinating travelling companions. Oh, and dealing with nuisances like customs officials,' Bianca answered, ticking off each item on her slender, pink-nailed fingers, then adding slyly, 'And I may request that you punish me sometimes. You have strong hands, Miss Turner. The very sight of them makes my bottom tingle.'

'I'll do whatever you command, my lady,' Gwenda said, *sotto voce*, and dared place one of those broad-palmed hands on her new mistress's hip. 'It will be our secret, our little game, but shall I never see England again?' she went on, still not reconciled to unfamiliar foreign climes.

'Of course you will,' Bianca trilled, wriggling her rump under Gwenda's touch.

'The comte and I own residences all over the world... New York, Vienna, St Petersburg, Ireland and London.' She tipped her head to one side, looking up at Gwenda archly from the shadow of her cartwheel hat.

'I'll change your appearance,' she continued, eyeing her up and down with bright, lustful eyes. 'I visualise you in leather... a black leather suit, I think, cut like a man's. And your hair must be short, but not too short so that when you wear the neat uniform I'll provide for ordinary occasions, you'll appear to be the perfect secretary.'

'Madame... countess... you are too kind,' Gwenda said, her heart soaring on the wings of promotion and ambition. She had always longed to hold a position of power in the servant hierarchy, as a housekeeper perhaps, but this was better than she had dreamed possible.

Screened from prying eyes by folds of pale green tenting, Bianca lingeringly unbuttoned the front of her bodice and pushed aside the chiffon chemise, baring her breasts to Gwenda. 'You like what you see?' she whispered.

'Oh, my lady,' Gwenda gasped and dropped down beside her.

'You may touch my nipples,' the countess said huskily.

'My lady!'

Gwenda felt her hands were too large and clumsy to handle those delicate white breasts and tightly crimped tips. But she soon lost her hesitancy: they felt so warm, the skin as soft as velvet, the nipples rising encouragingly as she gently stroked over them.

Bianca sighed, took off her hat and lay back amongst the

tapestry cushions, drawing Gwenda with her. 'Kiss them,' she whispered, and closed her eyes.

In that moment, Gwenda knew she had found her forte. Bright visions floated in her brain. She would control and manipulate the countess, and coerce and pander to the comte. In no time at all she would be the most important, sought-after member of his household.

The countess is but a woman like the rest of us, she thought suddenly, and nudged her knee between Bianca's, her conclusion confirmed when she felt the answering pressure of a pudenda so ripe with lust that its heat and dampness penetrated the thin cream skirt.

She thinks I'll be her servant, Gwenda reflected as she took her mouth to Bianca's tit, sucking it in and wetting it with her tongue, but this rich, privileged whore is misled. The roles will soon be reversed.

I shall become as essential to her as breathing. She'll be my slave. As for the comte? So, he's already taught Lady Candice a thing or two, has he? If the countess is submissive to him, then she'll get double the enjoyment when he and I combine our skills on her willing, wanton flesh. And Maria will be my playmate, that little black-haired harlot with whom I'll slake my passion whenever I feel the urge.

The Palazzo Tassinari was as silent as the grave. Deserted it stood in the somnolent heat of afternoon. Giacomo moored the gondola to the post and heaved the heavy canvas bag ashore, then retreated hastily.

'I'll wait here for the *signori*,' he muttered, rolling his dark eyes at the grim façade, and shuddering.

'Thank you, Giacomo,' Clive said, and handed over a purse that clinked invitingly. 'You've been of great help. I trust you'll be discreet.'

'I do it because *Signora* Smythe ask,' Giacomo averred earnestly, but took the purse anyway. He seemed frightened for their safety, wishing to delay them, continuing, 'I think

214

you are right to do this. I speak to my grandmother about the prince and she cross herself and shake her head, not mentioning what she think he is, but I know, *signor*... I guess he be a thing that cannot die. When Flora ask me for these certain tools, then I know I am right. You will kill him, and make it so he never rise again, or those whores he calls sisters. Forgive the so crude speech.'

'We shall do our best to destroy them,' Clive answered and shook him solemnly by the hand.

As Emma listened to this exchange she trembled like an aspen leaf. Clive and Fabian had tried to persuade her to stay at the hotel but she refused. She was already in deep and may as well see this dire business to its ultimate conclusion. Now was the moment to strike, while Candice was out of the way, visiting the Lido with the countess and Comte Henri.

During the inevitable delay while Flora sought out Giacomo, she had sat in her bedroom and studied Clive's books, her heart sinking like a stone as she devoured every page. And now they were here in the prince's lair, about to perform an act of insanity or, if they were right, one of mercy in which four souls would be released to face a judgement higher than that of mortal man.

The water lapped the stone steps. The building was sliced with bright light and deepest shadow. The little bridge spanning the canal was deserted. This was siesta time, when the sensible kept to cool patios and shuttered rooms, dozing or making love, bed being the best place to be.

Not us, Emma thought with something akin to bitterness. We, intrepid English that we are, must needs go a-hunting... vampires, if you please! Small wonder our race is considered eccentric by the rest of the world.

'What happens now?' she asked, voice shrill with fear. 'Do we ring the bell and leave our calling-cards?'

'There's no need to be sarcastic,' Fabian reproved, and she realised sharply how little she wanted to marry him. 'I

215

doubt there's anyone in... not anyone human, that is.'

'I'll try the door,' Clive said, and seized the heavy brass handle shaped like a lion's head.

It turned with an agonised squeal and the door opened on its rusty hinges.

'I want to go to the lavatory,' Emma complained, aware of a sudden need to relieve herself.

'You should have thought of that before,' Fabian snapped, his pale face shiny with sweat. 'Either shut up, or stay in the gondola.'

She was too scared to do other than press close behind as he and Clive passed under the frowning portal. She jumped and clung to Fabian as a figure moved out of the gloom and barred their way.

'You can't come in,' Carl announced, facing them determinedly, his head gleaming, bare and ivory smooth.

'Get out of the way,' Clive ordered crisply, drawing a pistol from an inner pocket.

'Prince Dimitri has given instructions not to be disturbed,' Carl answered stubbornly, large and immovable.

'I said, stand aside!' Clive repeated and he and Fabian rushed Carl, the pistol cracking down on his head. He dropped to the paving stones and lay there groaning.

'Where to?' Fabian shouted as they stormed through reception rooms and along corridors.

'The cellars? There must be wine-vaults. He'll need somewhere dark,' Clive declared, sweating with exertion.

Emma wished, not for the first time, that she could wear trousers instead of skirts that tangled her feet and made action difficult. It was not fair to be so tightly laced and hampered by yards of material.

Behind her she could hear the thump of Carl's feet and his croaking voice telling them to stop. The rashness of this mission overwhelmed her. At the very least he could send for the police and have them arrested for trespassing.

Ahead an archway yawned like a cave mouth. Stairs wound

down as if dropping into a well. Clive opened the bag and produced a bundle wrapped in oilskin. The pungent fumes of paraffin stung their eyes as he uncovered a wooden club with rag wrapped round one end. Fabian struck a match with unsteady fingers and the flare caught, smoking and sputtering in the draught. They began their shaky progress down the worn, treacherous and slippery stone steps.

Clive has thought of everything, Emma mused admiringly as she kept close to him, touching the slimy wall to keep from stumbling. Not Fabian. He has proved to be spineless, an easy victim of the vampire women, a sensualist willing, even eager, to be possessed by them.

The flare gave off an unsteady, yellowish light that threw their shadows into grotesque relief. The steps ended in a passage with a door at the end.

'Nearly there. I'm sure this is it. Bring the bag, Fabian,' Clive said, striding forward, holding the torch high. 'With any luck we'll use those stakes and mallets soon, ending this nightmare for good.'

Spine chilling noises issued from the direction of the door – maniacal shrieks, yells, hideous laughter and women screaming. Emma hung back terrified, wanting to turn and flee, but Clive grabbed her hand and rushed ahead.

The door was made of solid cedarwood deeply carved with patterns of acanthus leaves. As Emma stepped up to it she met a resistance, neither hard nor soft but totally impenetrable. She staggered, almost fell. She reached a hand out carefully, fingers spread, and the air rejected them, held them pressed as if against glass.

'But it's not glass,' she exclaimed as Clive looked at her and frowned, his own hands finding no way through. 'It's horrible. The force stopping us is as resilient as flesh... cold as the damp air.'

'It is, in fact, the air itself,' he concluded, his eyes bewildered in his bearded face.

'Let me try,' said Fabian, setting down the bag and shoving

against the obstruction with all his strength.

The transparent barrier remained, as innocent as light yet unyielding as granite. It could not be felt or penetrated. Fabian, losing control, threw up his arms and pounded against that glass wall. It was useless.

'The master has forbidden entrance,' Carl's hollow voice declaimed from somewhere behind them. 'Leave now, before I send for the police.'

Clive turned on him, thrusting the flaming torch into his cadaverous face and shouting, 'Tell Prince Dimitri this isn't the end. I shall be back with reinforcements!'

Dimitri's instincts told him it was evening, though there was no change in the density of the darkness that enfolded the crypt in which he had fallen into vampire sleep.

Infuriated, he had taken himself off to the island of San Michele situated in the lagoon. It had a church and was used as a cemetery for Venetian dead. The antique building was superb but melancholy, an emotion that exactly suited his mood. He had been betrayed; not by enemies but by those closest to him. It was an injury he would never forgive.

This was a very old and abandoned tomb, now an ossarium. Dimitri rose from the lid of the crumbling, lop-sided stone coffin on which he had laid himself to rest, and stared at the heaps of stark white bones and skulls laid in rows on shelves carved from the walls. At least such a fate would never befall him. There were definite advantages to being *nosferatu*.

And those blundering English fools thought they could vanquish him? He smiled sardonically as he dispatched himself to the Palazzo Tassinari and, totally invisible to human eyes, witnessed their defeat.

When they had gone, he passed through the heavy wooden door and examined the state of his scheming sisters. It was satisfying to see how much they had already suffered. The demons had them hanging by their wrists each end of a triple crossbar, thrashing them with plaited leather thongs tipped with lead, the contraption so designed that it turned with each blow. Sometimes the whips fell on backs and buttocks, at others it lashed their breasts, bellies and vaginal openings. The sisters gave vent to screams of pain and high-pitched howls of rage.

Denied the blood they so desperately craved, they had become hags overnight, faces lined, eyes set in deep brown pits, hair white and teeth missing. They sagged in their bonds, every vestige of their unearthly beauty stripped away.

And still the demons tormented them, conjuring visions of veins pulsing with blood; of gushing streams of it flooding the cellar. And while the princesses twisted in their chains, their other hunger was fanned to scorching flame by the constant titillation of their genitals – without once allowing orgasm.

Smiling still, Dimitri said, 'Well done,' to Carl, and removed himself to his bedchamber, there to take on the persona of a man-about-town.

He fancied a night at the opera, after he had quenched his thirst.

Candice listened seriously as Emma recounted everything that had happened that afternoon. 'You should have told me what you intended to do,' she said.

'You had already gone to the Lido.'

'And if I had not?'

Emma stared at her sorrowfully and shook her sepia curls, saying, 'I should have kept it from you, for I believe you'd be unable to harm the prince.'

Candice leapt up, her heart racing as she cried in anguish, 'You're right. I can't help you destroy him. I simply want him to go away and never come back.'

'Is this true?' Emma gripped her hands and pulled her down on the walnut daybed. 'Will you swear that you hate and despise him?'

All afternoon Candice had been at war with herself,

wanting to fall in love with Henri and forget Dimitri, thinking she had succeeded, then tortured by memories of him which made every other man pale into insignificance.

She bowed her head in her hands and wept. 'I can't swear... I don't know, Emma... I just don't know.'

'Come, darling, don't upset yourself,' Emma soothed. 'Let's bath together and prepare for our visit to the Teatro La Fenice.'

The bathroom was tiled in marble, the tub itself sunk in the floor and big enough for two. Because both of them bore traces of the whip's caress, they dismissed their maids and helped each other disrobe.

A calm scene, the lighting dim and perfume rising on wisps of steam. But there was another odour, too, reminding Candice of walking through the woods on a summer day, stirring up the grasses and wild garlic.

'Clive has rubbed it around the lintels and windows,' Emma explained when they were in the water. She slipped her hands down over Candice's firm buttocks and traced the raised wealds. 'Dimitri won't be able to steal you away tonight.'

'Nothing would stop him once he'd made up his mind,' Candice sighed, easing back so that Emma's finger slipped between the firm, deep crack of her arse and fondled the tight anal opening. 'He will get his way.'

'By fair means or foul... probably foul,' Emma agreed sadly, and continued her exploration of Candice's cleft, parting the wings and idling over the rapidly engorging button.

The water sloshed around them as they lay there, soaping one another and bringing about that singular joy which only they shared, then, later, they donned their underclothing and called in their maids, ready for the finishing touches necessary before they went down to join the gentlemen.

The enchanted starry night was a perfect setting in which to be conveyed by gondola through the canals. Rays of light from the prow lanterns danced across the water. The *calli* were tortuous, insinuating themselves between Renaissance houses with overhanging fronts carved with coats of arms and inscriptions and the ever-present bearded lion.

Romantic Venice, and yet Candice was far from happy, in a ferment of indecision. She longed to see Dimitri, but was very afraid.

There was no escaping him. Despite all her efforts, she could hear him talking to her through her thoughts. Even though she sat by Clive in a black padded chair in Giacomo's gondola, so it seemed the vampire was there, whispering,

'Don't leave me, beloved. You did this once before and I've been seeking you for over two hundred years. Don't you remember?'

She was herself, yet not so. It was night, like the real one, yet oh so different. She was different too, younger, more innocent. Brown haired, not fair. She had been awakened in her narrow convent-school bed by Dimitri's sudden appearance.

'Who let you in, sir?' she cried, dragging the sheet up over her shoulders.

It was dark but he seemed to glow, correct in every detail – plush, gold-laced jacket and flowing cravat, tight breeches and thigh-high riding boots, tumbling black curls and emerald eyes. She was achingly aware of his strong, masculine body that had disturbed her ever since they were introduced, the memory of it impinging on her devotions and racking her with impure thoughts.

'I passed through bricks and mortar to be with you, Mariella. I'm asking you to come with me,' he said, and though not moving, she felt him close beside her on the bed, warm and strong and full of hard male angles and ridges, particularly between the thighs.

She stiffened and shrank away till she could go no further. 'My father has told me to forget you,' she sobbed, truly frightened but with that odd, pleasurable flutter in her loins.

'They say you are very wicked and have run away to escape arrest.'

'Not quite true. A friend has helped me and I want you to join me. I love you, Mariella, more than I've ever loved anyone. I can give you everlasting life,' he insisted, one hand cupping her breast, thumb rolling the nipple that peaked under the lawn nightgown.

'It's true what they say, then. You are a sorcerer. Only God can grant me life eternal,' she protested, struggling to pull away from the pleasure of that intimate caress.

She longed to press against him, the scent of his hair and personal body odour acting like a potent drug. He was gallant, every virgin's dream of a dashing hero, yet she had been reared to scorn the temptations of the flesh, and he put her to the test most sorely.

Whenever he had called, her duenna had been in evidence. She had never been alone with him, but the brush of his lips on the back of her hand in the formal greeting kiss, the opportunity he sometimes took during this to tickle her palm suggestively, had brought about a state of emotional and physical arousal bordering on infatuation.

He was her betrothed, and her heart had broken when they told her he had left Paris, a hunted criminal. Now he was here, in her room, on her bed, and when his mouth captured hers, she closed her eyes, melting and lubricious, welcoming the firm press of his lips.

He explored her gently, doing nothing to frighten her, and her mouth relaxed as she felt the tip of his tongue probing, seeking entry. She could not resist, lying languorously in his arms, and sighing, 'Oh, Dimitri,' into his open mouth.

'Will you come with me?' he murmured, and his hand stole down, drifting over her belly, circling her navel and reaching lower, finding the line of her mons veneris and rubbing persistently.

'You mustn't do that,' she pleaded while the pleasure spiralled. She felt as she did when she touched herself there sometimes, unable to stop but conscience-stricken, convinced that she sinned, her cleft slippery with onanistic emissions.

'Don't you like it?' he whispered, and his lips slid to her throat, kissing the delicate, responsive skin. She could feel goose bumps raising the fine hairs all over her body.

'Too much,' she breathed. 'If we were only married, it would be my duty to indulge such wondrous desire, but we're not and never can be.'

'We can! We can!' he murmured urgently, his breath hot on the blue vein pulsing under the white skin. 'It's so simple, sweetheart. You will feel the smallest nip as I bite you, then a swooning sensation during which you'll attain bliss. I shall drink your blood and, after this, you'll sup off mine.'

'What are you?' she cried, her eyes opening wide as she cringed away from him.

'I'm one of the undead,' he said seriously, his strange green eyes holding sparks like molten steel. 'I'll live for ever, and so can you if you but do as I say. We can go anywhere, do anything, after dark. During the daylight hours we shall sleep, wrapped in each other's arms, then wake refreshed and enjoy a feast of blood before embarking on adventures. The night will be ours, the moon our plaything, the universe our ballroom.'

'You're one of Satan's demons!' she shouted, leaping from the bed. 'You've come to tempt me into sacrificing my soul and being damned to hellfire for all eternity!'

He gave a derisive laugh, his countenance darkening as his mood changed. 'I'm not a demon. I'm a vampire. I want to give you the gift of immortality. Do you love me enough to take it?'

She fell to her knees, hands clasped in supplication, head bowed before the statuette of a blue-veiled Virgin Mary standing in an alcove. 'Save me! Save me!' she cried, then whispered to Dimitri, 'I love you. You'll never know how much, but I can't come with you.'

The statue offered no comfort. She felt hollow inside. Every beat of her heart, each throb of her blood urged her to fly back to his arms, accept the gift and accompany him, be his companion for ever and learn all there was to know about sexual passion and fulfilment.

'I can't... I can't...' Candice whispered with a sob, and Clive's hand clasped hers as he asked anxiously,

'What's the matter?'

She recovered, though still disoriented, Candice in the gondola, but Mariella back in the convent, rushing away from Dimitri, out into the corridor, the stones freezing her bare feet as she screamed for the Mother Superior – yelled for a priest—

'Nothing. It's all right,' Candice managed to smile, but Clive gave her an alarmed look, as if not quite believing her.

The comte had a box in the theatre, the blue, cream and gold decorations of which had made it one of the most beautiful opera houses in the world. Tonight's performance of Verdi's *La Traviata* had attracted a large audience. The foyer was crowded with gentlemen in evening clothes, and ladies whose jewels sparkled under the electric lights.

As Candice linked her arm with Clive and walked towards the red carpeted stairs that led to the stage boxes, she heard Henri say, 'Good evening, Prince Dimitri.'

She turned her head sharply, and the breath lodged in her throat as she saw him standing near a column, distinguished and elegant in faultlessly tailored clothes. A superbly regal aristocrat. No trace of blood or fangs or vulpine eyes.

Have I imagined it all? she thought with paralysing terror. Is it nothing but the fancies of a sick mind? Am I mad?

He looked at her, and she knew it was nothing as simple as insanity.

'Lady Candice,' he said with an ironic bow. 'I missed you when you did not visit the palace again.' The sorrow in his voice caused a throbbing in her soul, the counterpart of her own mourning.

'I was previously engaged, sir,' she replied, thinking how odd were conventions. She wanted to scream and yell, kick and claw him into giving her the answers she craved, while Emma, Clive and Fabian must be just as eager to learn the truth about him, but they kept up the pretence.

'Have you a seat, prince?' Henri asked, straightening his starched cuffs with a flash of diamond-studded links. 'Or would you care to join us in my box?'

Oh, no! Candice prayed.

'Thank you. I'd like that,' Dimitri replied. 'It is one of my favourite operas. I'm very fond of music-dramas, and see them whenever I can.'

Candice was appalled, yet as helpless as her friends to do anything about it. If either of them said, 'Sorry, comte, it's not advisable to encourage him. Prince Dimitri is a vampire,' they'd be laughed at.

As soon as the house lights lowered, Dimitri put a hand on Candice's knee. Her chair was situated between himself and Henri, with Clive, Emma and Fabian on the other side.

He smiled into the darkness as the conductor raised his baton, and the first hushed, poignant notes of the prelude whispered out, played high and sweet on violins.

He listened, already caught up in the music but, at the same time, moving his hand and lifting Candice's skirt, slowly and silently, till his fingers rested on the bare flesh above her garter. He felt her quiver. A glance at her face showed him that she was looking directly at the stage where the curtain had now risen on a party scene. Her coral lips were slightly open, and his phallus pulsed, pressed against his left thigh under his evening trousers.

Tonight he meant to woo her without magic, as a human suitor might do. If only he could somehow prove his love for her. A scheme began to form in his subtle mind. Reading her thoughts he discovered she had been digesting Clive's books and knew of the means by which vampires could be

225

destroyed. He was prepared to take a terrible risk in order to convince her of his devotion. To achieve this he must use the comte, rousing his jealousy and challenging his dominion over her.

Candice did not press her legs together or in any way try to stop his hand from mounting higher. His fingertips passed under the lace hem of her knickers and touched the furry mound and rubbed the curls lightly. She continued to stare at the stage, but her thighs parted and he penetrated further, feeling the slippery wetness of love-juice dewing his fingers.

He parted the succulent petals of her labia and strummed on the tiny rosebud at its heart. She sighed and trembled, then reached into his lap and clutched at the bulge straining his fly buttons as she convulsed suddenly but quietly against his hand.

He wanted to take her to the rear of the box and seat himself on one of the chairs, holding her on his lap, facing the stage. There she would sink down astride his thighs and impale herself on his shaft, then ride it, but very carefully, so no one would guess what they were about.

This was no more than visualisation, yet she took part in it too, as he mentally enjoyed the embrace of her exquisite aperture while he caressed her breasts and clitoris, banishing the impediment of clothing.

During the interval he was at his most polite, strolling to the theatre bar with the comte and his guests and talking gaily of inconsequential things while they occupied little tables and drank wine. He held his glass but did not drink and noticed that Candice avoided his eyes, a hectic flush betraying how much she had been moved by both his physical and mental stimulation of her most secret parts.

He bristled under the suspicious regard of Clive and the almost open dislike of Fabian, and was saddened to see how Emma clung protectively to Candice's arm, her hostile eyes daring him to harm her friend.

His lips felt stiff as he lifted them in a thin smile. What

did they know, these little people? How comprehend the scope and majesty of everything he was offering Candice?

Emma purposefully changed places with him after the intermission and, arms folded over his chest, he sank himself into the opera. Music uplifted him, making him forget he was supernatural. He became absorbed in the sad story of the consumptive heroine and her heart-rending choice between her young lover and the wealth of the old roué who kept her in style. No choice really, as she sacrificed her life when she gave up the young man at the request of his concerned father. Vampire though he was, the death scene affected Dimitri deeply.

'Would you care to come back to my palazzo for a while? The countess will be playing the tables and welcoming others to chance their arm,' the comte said casually, but dipping into his mind, Dimitri could see he was aware of what had taken place earlier between himself and Candice – aware and resentful.

There was a short, thunderous pause during which they looked at each other in unspoken challenge.

'You are too kind,' Dimitri replied suavely. 'But I have a prior engagement. Later, perhaps.'

Somehow, and afterwards Candice could never quite remember the details, Fabian, Clive and Emma had allowed themselves to be lured away by Bianca to try their luck on the roulette wheel in the gaming room. The comte took charge of her, saying,

'I'll look after Candice. She'll be perfectly safe with me,' and steered her in the direction of the gymnasium.

'Such a wonderful opera,' she enthused, a glass of sparkling champagne in one gloved hand. 'I couldn't help crying at the end. So sad... poor Violetta, she so much wanted to live happily with Alfredo.'

'A sentimental story,' he answered with a sneer, then shot her a sharp glance. 'I suppose you believe in love?'

'I'd like to,' she ventured.

'Love or lust? I observed you enjoying the latter tonight. You allowed the prince to fondle your private place,' he cracked out, striding across and glaring down into her face as he commanded, 'On your knees. You misbehaved, and I'm about to punish you for it.'

'I've never agreed to be your slave,' she said as his hand landed on her shoulder and forced her down till her face ground into the carpet, her backside raised helplessly.

'You need mastering,' he muttered, running his hands over those rounded, satin covered hillocks. 'Clive isn't man enough for you. I've been patient, Candice, holding back from taking your virginity, but not tonight. It's time you learnt what it feels like to have a cock in your maiden sheath. But first, that temper of yours must be schooled. You're too self-willed, young lady.'

He dragged her to her feet and she cried out as she saw the flash of steel, but he did no more than take the knife to the back of her gown, slicing through the fastening and the stays beneath, then stripping it from her. The chemise came next, and the ribbon that upheld her knickers. Now she was naked, save for her long gloves, stockings and high-heeled shoes.

Holding her at arm's length, Henri admired her, his hot gaze dwelling on her pointed breasts and the bare mound at the apex of her thighs. 'So beautiful, a perfect English rose,' he said huskily. 'No wonder Prince Dimitri finds you irresistible, but I have already staked my claim.'

'You presume too much, sir, and don't know the truth about the prince,' she began, though her nipples crimped under his regard. 'He isn't like other men.'

Henri gave a bark of laughter. 'No?' he shouted. 'Are you trying to tell me he hasn't a cock and balls? What is he then? A eunuch?'

'He's a vampire,' Candice blurted, fighting the urge to cover her breasts with her arm and her sex with one hand.

Henri roared with laughter, his legs spread, his hands

knuckled on each hip. 'What? Oh, my dear girl, he's taken you in. I know he has a reputation for being strange and sinister, but a vampire? I think not. He is relying on this to intrigue and captivate you. Young girls are sometimes morbidly interested in the conception of death and blood and rape, particularly virgins. A vampire! That's rich! It's high time I beat some sense into you.'

'I'm telling the truth,' she insisted. 'He is not human.'

Henri's face paled and his eyes flashed. 'Be quiet,' he snarled and pulled her over to where the wooden horse stood.

'No, please... don't hurt me,' she pleaded, but inside the dark force took her over, needing pain to bring it to the height of sexual potency. She had been wet when Dimitri roused her, but now she was in full flood.

Henri spread her across the back of the padded steed, head and arms dangling over one side, the angle canting up her pelvis, making her buttocks, especially the under part, open and accessible to the lash. Her hairless labia majora appeared like two segments of juicy fruit squashed between her thighs.

He slipped the restraints over her wrists and ankles, and then with great deliberation took off his jacket. Standing in slim-fitting trousers and black waistcoat, he rolled back his shirtsleeve until his brown and sinewy right arm was bare to above the elbow. Having already selected a thin, wicked-looking cane, he made a trial cut through the air behind Candice.

Her buttocks clenched with remembered pain as the rod whistled. She knew that all too soon it would slice her rump just as fiercely. Bracing herself in the stillness that followed, she was unprepared for the shock when the blow fell. It was as if she had been branded with an iron. Her body jerked at the impact and her fingers grabbed at the leather beneath them. She yelped, then held her breath as surging pain fanned out from the stripe, enveloping her completely.

Henri waited until it reached its zenith and then lifted the cane with even greater enthusiasm and dealt another blow.

This time he aimed lower, a bare inch below the first welt, a matching red stripe marking her white flesh.

Candice screamed at the top of her voice, her face drenched in tears, and yet she felt herself growing limp and yielding, heat flooding her sex as it had each time she was whipped. The sting, the wash of pain, the sense of utter subjection, every one of these feelings aroused her to feverish desire.

The cane thrummed six times, landing on different spots, but sometimes catching those still sore from her last beating. Now her world was limited to her body, its agony and the heat of desire. She slumped over the horse, nearly unconscious, floating in a red haze.

Henri came up behind her and traced over the stripes, parting her bottom crack between the marks. His fingers pressed into her vulva, their access made easy by the copious fluid produced by the kiss of the rod.

'Are you going to be a good girl and obey me?' he asked.

She was too weak to do other than nod. He opened her wider, examining the shaven pudenda, the pink lips and vaginal orifice. When he met the obstruction of her maidenhead she flinched and pulled back.

She heard Henri laugh softly, and then the push of something harder, stronger, thicker than a finger. Helpless to stop him, she knew he was about to smash the last bastion and enter her body.

'No,' she whispered faintly.

'But yes,' he replied, bending close to her, his shirt chafing against her sore back as one hand spread her cheeks and the other held his engorged weapon to her virgin vulva and rocked his hips to force it against the shielding hymen.

'The lady said no,' a voice stated, its deep tone ringing across the room.

Henri's weight was forcibly removed from her. The bonds snapped and she fell to the floor near the bench. Her sight cleared and she looked up to see Dimitri standing there, in black trousers, black boots and a white shirt. He was flexing a rapier between his hands.

'What the hell...?' Henri gasped, hastily buttoning his trousers over his deflated cock.

'Hell indeed,' Dimitri scoffed. 'Are you man enough to fight me for the lady's favours?'

Henri sprang for the rack that contained fencing foils. 'I'd be delighted,' he replied through clenched teeth.

'Not a foil,' Dimitri chided. 'My sword is the real thing. It doesn't have a safety button on the end. I expect nothing less of you, comte.'

'Very well. One moment, if you please,' and with the greatest aplomb and dignity, Henri opened a glass case and lifted out a magnificent, swept-hilt blade fashioned of finest Toledo steel.

'Don't worry about the comte.' With a trick of his mind Dimitri communicated with Candice. 'I shan't use my special powers but fight as I did in the days when a gentleman was esteemed for his skill as a duellist. If his sword spikes my heart and I die, you'll know that I did it to prove my love for you.'

'*En garde,*' he cried aloud, and fell into a fighting stance.

The hard, bright ring of metal meeting metal echoed loudly across the gymnasium. Both men were superb fighters, their feet pounding the cork matting in perfectly controlled motion – backwards and forwards, lunge, parry, riposte.

Candice dragged herself up, leaning heavily against the horse for support, watching those graceful, automatic movements. They looked like dancers in a death ritual. Sweat was running down their faces and dripping blindingly into their eyes. Dimitri's was blood-tinged.

Henri gave an exultant shout, 'First point to me!' as a bright spot of red appeared on Dimitri's white shirt, just beneath the right pectoral.

'*Touché*!' he returned, with a lighting flick of his blade that nicked Henri's cheek.

Enraged, the comte lost a measure of control. The swords

sang, points of fire that darted and blazed as the opponents stamped and attacked, defended and retreated, only to advance again.

'Dimitri, don't,' Candice pleaded, unsure whether she spoke the words or formulated them in her thoughts. 'You mustn't... I don't want you to die.'

'Why?' came the return as Dimitri fought on, gaining advantage, pitting his wits and skill against the comte, keeping out of range of his rapier. He seemed almost indolently relaxed, yet parried every thrust with lightning speed, giving his adversary no chance to pierce his guard again.

Candice struggled with herself, terrified for him. Supposing he really did die, speared by Henri? How could she go on living with no Dimitri to scare and master her, offer her mystical life, and devastate her with passion? He was damned, and there would be little chance of a merciful solution or a place where they might meet again on the other side of the veil.

She wanted to pour out her longing, to tell him what she felt for him, but the words refused to come – the decision so momentous that she hesitated a fraction too long.

It happened so fast that she was unable to see. Dimitri slipped and fell to one knee, his quillon tangling with that of Henri's. Close as lovers, glaring into one another's sweat-streaked faces, they strained to break free.

'Use your strength!' Candice implored, but met a blank.

With a sudden heave, Henri wrenched his sword-guard loose and plunged the blade deep into Dimitri's chest, the tip appearing between his shoulder blades. Skewered on the steel, he arched violently, flinging out his arms, his own sword spinning off into space. In a reflex action Henri withdrew his weapon and bloody foam gushed from Dimitri's mouth. He gave a gurgling cry and crashed to the ground like a felled oak.

'Dimitri!' She found her strength and ran to his side,

almost insane with despair. 'Dimitri, use your magic. Live for me.'

'Why should I?' he whispered, demanding her commitment, his lips bloody, his eyes unfocused.

'Because I love you!' she sobbed. 'I love you and want to be as you are...'

He smiled wanly and then, as she watched in stark fear, faded from sight.

Chapter Twelve

Candice was not surprised to discover that Dimitri had closed
down a part of Henri's brain so that he remembered nothing
of the duel's conclusion.

'It's deuced strange,' he commented later, when he and
Candice entered the gaming room and found Clive. The
others were engaged at the tables, and so it was to him that
he recounted what had happened. 'There I was, beating that
arrogant tyke, Prince Dimitri, and the next moment the rogue
had vanished. Couldn't stomach the fact that he was losing,
I suppose, and did a quick flit out the window.'

'Damned unsporting of him,' Clive commented, though
the colour drained from his face and he stepped closer to
Candice.

She was dazed, her body bruised and stiff from her severe
chastisement, her heart aching because of Dimitri. She was
behaving like an automaton and had answered vaguely when,
after his opponent's abrupt departure, a puzzled Henri asked
her how she had escaped her bonds, 'I don't know. Perhaps
you didn't tie them securely.'

Then she had gathered up her clothes, ruefully examining
the damage.

'Never mind, my dear,' he had said jovially, pleased with
himself for routing his rival. 'I'll buy you more. We'll visit
a couturier and you shall choose what you fancy. Meanwhile,
wear this.'

He had produced a beautiful red silk Japanese kimono,
richly embroidered with birds and chrysanthemums outlined
in gilt thread. He had held it up while she slipped her arms
into the wide, hanging sleeves, and then helped her gird her
waist with a magnificent obi. This kept the robe closed, apart

from the deep V between her breasts. He inserted a finger into this valley and traced over the swell of one breast, stroking the nipple.

'You are one of the loveliest women I've ever seen,' he had said, his eyes darkening with lust. 'If we hadn't been so rudely interrupted I would have possessed you by now, entered your tight, virgin sheath and taken my pleasure of you, the first man to do so. But there's time enough. Spend the night with me and I'll turn you into a woman, with all a woman's passions.'

'No,' she had replied coldly and stared right through him, seeking that other – her dark, proud and sinister lover.

Henri meant less than nothing to her, despite being a handsome, titled gentleman who had just fought a dangerous duel for her favours. He had shrugged at her rejection and wiped the sweat from his face and chest with a towel, shirt stripped off, the thick line of his penis emphasised by his sleekly fitting trousers.

A man many ladies would give their eye-teeth for – but *her* master? Certainly not!

These thoughts buzzed like demented bees in her mind as Clive anxiously questioned Henri, though trying to hide his concern. 'It was the prince, you say? He challenged you?'

Henri nodded, once more the genial host who could not do too much for his guests. 'He did. Appeared out of the blue. I couldn't do other than accept, even though duelling is outlawed. I didn't expect he would fight to the death, but now think it was his intention.'

Is this the moment when Clive will tell Henri that Dimitri isn't human? Candice wondered dully.

As always after an encounter with her supernatural lover, she was knocked off kilter. Her mouth was dry, and it seemed she was surrounded by aliens, not human beings with any connection to herself. But this was followed by such a rush of pain from her welted posterior that she faltered, resting a hand against one of the marble pillars.

235

And where was Dimitri? Had he been wounded beyond healing? Or had he decided that, after all, he couldn't bring himself to be the cause of her damnation?

By tacit agreement she and Clive kept their peace. This was not the time to speak on so strange and macabre a subject. The gaming room was full, Bianca and Henri entertaining on a grand scale again.

Plush-liveried flunkies handed round wine and canapés. Their male attributes were decently covered for the moment, though their uniforms were deliberately cut and styled in a provocative way. This drew attention to broad shoulders and narrow waists, the prominent bulges of large cocks and the muscled curves of tight arses, but the players, obsessed with gambling, took little notice, the gratification of the senses held in abeyance.

There was a certain solemnity about the scene, conversation muted. Everyone at the tables spoke in whispers. The spacious room had been cleared of furniture save for the long tables and chairs reserved for those playing steadily. It was lit by three glittering Venetian glass chandeliers of enormous size and splendour. Modernised, these were now powered by electricity in place of candles.

Decorated by a master craftsman a century before, the walls were covered in hand-painted paper in a delicate pagoda pattern from an era when chinoiserie was in vogue, and the designer had also filled every space on the vast ceiling with harp playing angels, bare-breasted goddess and other classical deities.

Heavy, gilt framed mirrors on each wall added their share of confusion as to what constituted reality. Rather like my mind, Candice thought.

'A fine example of *trompe l'oeil*,' Clive said, as she stared up at the ceiling, wondering if Dimitri might appear from behind one of those billowing, painted clouds. 'A clever optical illusion. See that foot which appears to be hanging down? And what about the chap blowing a trumpet? If you come over here, it looks as if he's taken the instrument from his lips.'

Then he added in a whisper, 'The vampire was with you. Did he touch you? Has he sucked from your veins? Oh, Candice, please be careful. Give him no chance to bewitch you. And what happened to your evening gown? Why are you wearing that strange costume?'

'I spilt wine over my dress,' she lied. 'Henri loaned me this. No, Dimitri hasn't fed on me. Do you intend to tell Henri all you know?'

'Not yet,' he answered and watched her closely. 'Emma says you don't want Dimitri to perish. Is this so?'

'Yes,' she said with a shudder. The thought of him with a stake driven through his chest was anathema to her.

'But he's an abomination!' Clive insisted, trying to keep his voice low and his emotions under control.

'Have you no compassion? He's unhappy and lonely.' Candice knew this sounded quite ridiculous, but could not help defending Dimitri.

'How can you pity him?' he exclaimed with more than a hint of jealousy. 'He's a monster who must be destroyed!'

Weariness drained her. How could she explain – how convince him that Dimitri was not all bad?

'You talk of monsters, but what about them?' she countered, gesturing towards the gamblers. 'Aren't they as monstrous as him, blood-suckers all? Look at the hard-eyed croupiers spinning the ball and raking in piles of money staked and lost by the infatuated players.'

'It's not the same,' he protested, gripping her silk-clad shoulder as if wanting to shake sense into her. 'They're alive... not walking dead.'

'That's as maybe, but what a crew!' she continued, her eyes flashing contemptuously as she pushed him away. 'Selfish old women fawned on by their gigolos, brazen whores who act as decoys, and young ladies accompanied by chaperons who should know better. The men are hardened, cynical and merciless, encouraging the younger ones. Look at them! They're pathetic... all waiting to clutch their winnings or commit suicide if they beggar themselves.'

'I still say this is normal,' he argued. 'Foolhardy perhaps, but forgivable. Dimitri and the princesses are revenants, feeding on the living... horrible night-stalkers who gorge themselves and fall into a deathlike coma when daylight comes. They must be stamped out.'

She could see that further argument was useless. Clive was set on becoming a knight errant embarking on a holy crusade to save her and destroy the vampires who haunted Venice.

'Take me to the hotel,' she said, her body aching and bruised, her spirits at an all time low. 'I've seen enough tonight.'

'You were right, Giacomo,' Flora sighed as she lay in his arms amidst the tangled, semen-stained sheets. 'They went to the palazzo, but it was under a spell. They didn't find the vampires. Oh, yes, that's what they are. Lady Emma has read up about them and told me.'

'I tell my grandmother,' he answered, pulling her over him so that her plump breasts were crushed against his muscular hairy chest. 'And you, *amore*... you stay safe.'

The soft cooing of courting doves parading on the parapet outside his widow, harmonised with faint sounds rising from where the old square dozed in the heat.

Flora propped herself up on her arms and gazed earnestly into his peat-dark eyes. She had never seen anyone so handsome and gloated on his swarthy, sun-browned skin, short straight nose, and pronounced cheekbones.

Her expectations had been limited. Her middle-aged husband, the late Mr Smythe, kind though he was, had never done more than roll on her once a week in their brass double bed, grunt his way to completion and then promptly go to sleep. Flora had brought about her own orgasms by masturbation, and had never thought it would be her lot to have a desirable man who was more than willing to lavish pleasure on her.

She could feel Giacomo's sticky penis hardening again, pressing urgently against her belly. Moving slightly, she opened her thighs, embracing his body, and bringing her wet labial lips into contact with his helm. His strong fingers and thumbs rolled her nipples and, arching her back, she thrust her breasts upwards for more of this treatment, feeling him reach up to clamp his lips on those swollen teats, moving from one to the other.

'Don't fret, Giacomo,' she whispered, leaning over him and relishing that strong, sucking motion, then lowering herself till her mouth was against his, tasting the salt of his sweat, her cheek scraped by his stubbly jaw. 'I'm not taking any risks. Life is too precious now. I think Lord Clive wants to search for the prince again, but Lady Candice is in such a strange mood that he fears to upset her further.'

Giacomo nudged his pelvis upwards, and his cock slipped neatly into her channel. She eased on to it, aware of that marvellous, full-to-bursting feeling occasioned by an erect and lively male appendage. As he penetrated further he brushed against that tender spot high in her vagina, and her clitoris pulsed in response.

He was disinclined to talk, his hands moving across her shoulders and down her back to grip her generous bottom, holding her firm. His eyes were languid with desire, his mouth half open over even white teeth, his breath redolent of garlic.

'Lady Emma says that vampires can't abide that herb you Italians are so fond of. I love the smell. It reminds me of you and that splendid thing of yours,' Flora murmured, though starting to lose the thread of conversation as the insistent pounding of her blood lifted her steadily towards the third climax of the afternoon.

'Don't speak,' Giacomo gasped, clenching his stomach

muscles in order to drive his shaft further into her. 'I keep you safe always. Marry me, Floria. Stay with me. Oh, oh... I can't do without you. That's it, lift yourself then drop down, but slowly. Make it last forever.'

'Marriage! You really want to marry me?' Flora was stunned, lovesick, cock-struck – every hope and dream she had tried to suppress since meeting this virile man rising up and swamping her in waves of delight.

She doubted. He can't mean it. Men are bastards and always let you down. They say anything when they're pumping you. And yet – maybe – just maybe he might be sincere.

'Stop a minute,' she urged and sat up, though remained straddling him, his penis buried to the hilt in her depths. 'Do you mean that, Giacomo?'

'*Si*. I mean it,' he protested, and reached up to cradle her breasts again. 'We do well together, you and me. We love, I think. We move to a bigger apartment and I work... maybe soon have my own fleet of gondolas. You have wide, mother hips. We have many *bambini*. We be so happy, my Floria.'

'Yes, we will,' she sighed, and rocked on him, her eyes slitted in ecstasy.

It could come true. With her nest-egg and business acumen (she hadn't been a grocer's wife for nothing) and Giacomo's brawn and native cunning they might soon establish a little maritime empire.

'That's right,' he murmured. 'No *vampiro*. No dark things. No mad young English lady who embraces evil... just flowers and love and *bambini*.'

His romantic words flamed through her, adding to the physical heat already working like lava in her womb. Flora pumped up and down frantically and, as he cried out at passion's height, so her crisis broke and her vagina convulsed round him as she added her cries to his, swept away by the promise of love.

A day passed, a night and another day. 'He's gone,' Candice said mournfully to Emma, who now knew all about the duel and was as appalled as Clive.

'Good riddance!' she answered sharply, flicking open her fan and whisking it backwards and forwards agitatedly. 'Now perhaps we can get on and enjoy our trip. There's talk of us moving to Florence. The comte has a villa there and has invited us to stay. I'm willing. Are you?'

'I suppose so,' Candice answered listlessly.

Emma glanced at her sharply, unable to shake off the eerie premonition that hung over her like a black cloud.

Candice drooped disconsolately in a basket chair near the terrace balustrade. She was as lacking in energy as Fabian lately, and nothing seemed to spark her interest. They had already dined and were now listening to a band of street musicians entertaining the guests in the garden below, but she was paying them scant heed, seeming abstracted and miles away.

For her own part, Emma found the idea of keeping up acquaintance with Henri and Bianca a thrilling one. Having tasted first-hand the paradox of pain-pleasure, she wanted to pursue it further. No longer a gauche girl, her concepts were changing fast. She might still marry Fabian. Then again, she might break off the engagement. This would mean trouble at home, but who said she intended to return to England yet?

She had recently come into an inheritance from a great-uncle, and was possessed of a heady feeling of independence.

'They say Florence is not to be missed, a vision of fifteenth century architecture,' Clive said, trying to stir Candice's interest. 'Your brother thinks it's a capital notion to go there, don't you, Fabian?'

'Eh? What?' Fabian seemed to be as hag-ridden as Candice, and Emma wondered if he, too, was missing the excitement and danger of vampiric lovers.

'We're speaking of Florence,' she said, with barely

concealed impatience. 'Wake up, Fabian, or I'll become suspicious. Have you been making love with Allegra, Medea or Madelon? I thought you said you'd been keeping watch in his bedroom, Clive?'

'I have, and to my knowledge we've had no visitation,' Clive answered, moistening his lips from a glass of wine and giving Emma an admiring glance.

He was doing that a lot lately, and she was nothing loathe to encourage him, peeking at him under her eyelashes and smiling. He had risen in her estimation since taking on the prince. She knew about him fornicating with the baroness, and her curiosity was aroused. Was his male part bigger than Henri's? Would he spank her? And did he know where her love-button lay or would she have to show him?

Life was filled with promise, offering a fascinating set of alternatives. Why did Candice want to bother with the abnormal when there were so many normal sexual organs to play with? Women's as well as men's. The very air seemed to quiver with pheromones.

It was hard for Candice to get away. Her brother and Emma, to say nothing of Clive and Flora Smythe, kept a guard on her, organising a rota so that she was never on her own.

She was in torment, constantly aware of Dimitri. She kept getting flashes, seeing him lying pale and wounded in some dark and noisome place. No matter how Emma struggled to interest her in clothes, galas, fêtes and the proposed trip to Florence, nothing penetrated the dark depression that held her in thrall.

Then she became cunning. Very well, let them think she had forgotten Dimitri or at least banished him from her mind. She had not realised she was so good an actress until she sprang down the stairs one morning and demanded that they shop, then spend an afternoon at the Lido.

Her ruse worked. After a couple of days of this charade her wardens relaxed their vigilance. She encouraged them by poring over guide books of Florence and, one evening, enjoyed the pleasure of her own company after she had dined.

'Are you sure you'll be all right?' Emma asked, and Candice was not deceived, guessing that she wanted to slip away and keep an assignation with Clive.

'Of course. I'll be going to bed soon,' she answered blithely.

She was not in the least perturbed by her fiancé's unfaithfulness, or bothered because it was her closest friend who was taking part in this deception. She felt detached, as if no longer of their world.

A brilliant full moon hung above the rooftops, shining on the balcony where she stood, clad only in her diaphanous nightgown. The scent of flowers was almost overpowering, and singing drifted up from the lamplit gondolas carrying masqueraders to parties.

It was after midnight when he came, blotting out the moon and her remembrance of anything but him.

'You,' she moaned, waves of light illumining his countenance and streaming through her consciousness.

'I've come for you. Will you go with me?' he asked, and his voice caressed her like the softest silk and made her tingle from the tips of her toes to the crown of her head.

'Yes, Dimitri,' she replied without faltering.

He swept her up, folded her in his wings and flew with her into the night. She was tossed in a vortex of sensation, laved in heat, bathed in cold, colours spinning – rainbows over the sea, aquamarine waters tinged with foam, like waves crested by white horses. She dissolved, and felt her soul rushing through the universal blackness.

She was afraid. Then not. Held fast against his chest, buried in the scented darkness of his wings, she was travelling over the city. Daring to peep down she saw the lights of Venice – the piazzas, the shining ribbon of canals, then the roof of the huge, tumble-down Palazzo Tassinari. They sank lower and the tiles parted mistily to let them through.

Dimitri set her on her feet in a sumptuous, echoing

bedchamber of kingly proportions. 'Did you mean what you said?' he demanded, and his face was stern and cold.

'Yes,' she whispered, trembling with hunger for him.

'You will join me?'

'Yes.'

'Very well, beloved,' he said, gently caressing her hair. 'I promise you the most wonderful experience, superior to orgasm, *le petit mort* in its purest form. After this I will baptise you with my own blood.'

'Yes... yes,' she cried, urging her breasts up to meet his large hands, arching her spine, her throat exposed to his mouth. 'Do it. Do it now.'

'Not quite yet. I've waited so long, and can delay till the first sweet hint of dawn when I can enter you as a physical being. But just for now... I need a taste,' he whispered, and then he was upon her, between her legs, her clothing vanished, his breath cool against her burning face.

She opened her eyes, stared deep into his shining, slanting ones, and reached out and put her arms round him. The wings had disappeared and he was naked, strongly built and muscular, perfect as a Greek statue fashioned in marble, and as cold to touch.

He lifted her, carried her across the room and laid her on the velvet quilt spread over the wide four-poster. The candles in iron, floor-standing girandoles lit the solemn scene. It was as if they were about to take part in a wedding ceremony sealed and sanctified by blood, energy, sexual congress and love.

'I want you to know my history,' he murmured, and pressed his lips into the hollow of her throat, making long, lapping motions with his outstretched tongue.

'You've shown me myself as Mariella,' she gasped, hardly able to speak for the pleasure that darted over her skin as he licked her, the surface of his tongue rasping like a cat's.

'You refused me then, but you won't now,' he raised his head to say, staring down at her with eyes that seemed dispassionate yet brimming with lust.

'Never... we'll never be separated again,' she vowed, a feather-flick of sensation flushing through her body as his teeth nipped at the pink halo of her breast.

'United, entwined, you'll be flesh of my flesh, bone of my bone. Look in the scrying glass,' he commanded.

It appeared in his hand, a convex sphere wherein she saw herself reflected, miniaturised and askew.

His voice deepened, echoed across the years, crossed time and space. He passed a hand over the glass and when she looked again she saw a series of little vignettes. He was a young man in Paris – a medical student, despatched there by his royal father. Handsome, cultured, sought-after, he was a duellist, a gambler, a ladies man. There were orgies with the king's mistress where whips roused the assembly to frantic pleasure and pagan rites were enacted.

They yelled, they danced and beat one another with flails. Virgins crowned with garlands, youths as well as girls, were ceremoniously deflowered, penetrated and sodomised. Tambourines jangled, flutes wailed, drums beat out a tattoo and the waving torches spewed trails of fire.

Dimitri, organising the saturnalia, stuck a large wooden staff into the ground. It was shaped like a phallus, the twin-lobed glans skilfully carved with a rolled-back foreskin, its base rooted in a pair of outsized testicles. The acolytes whirled round it, pressing closer till they ground their bodies against its smoothness, working themselves into an orgasmic frenzy.

Wide-eyed and enthralled, Candice stared as more pictures unfolded. Now Paris was in an uproar, spies everywhere, neighbour betraying neighbour in the general hysteria. The rack, the boot and branding-irons were being used to wring confessions in the torture chambers. Stakes piled with faggots had been erected at the Place de Grève and public executions were taking place. Screams rent the air, and there was the acrid odour of blistering flesh and singed hair as those accused of witchcraft burned to death.

She was aware of Dimitri's hand on the nape of her neck. A tingle flowed through her, across her shoulder blades. The scrying glass hummed, drawing her attention back to it.

'There's Belphegor!' she exclaimed, seeing his elegant, dandyish figure in a small laboratory in Dimitri's Paris house.

'He warned me I was implicated in the witch hunt. He was my saviour,' Dimitri answered softly, his fingers continuing to massage her, pressing the palm of one hand to her cheek. 'If it hadn't been for him I should've been tortured and roasted alive. Instead, I became a vampire. I make no excuses. One could say I took the easy way out. I admit, I was afraid not so much of dying but of the means by which it would come about.'

'I see myself as Mariella, living in a convent. I denied you, shut myself away from life and became a nun.'

'A Bride of Christ. You did much good, mothering orphans, caring for the sick, but ah, you missed so much,' he breathed, and his hand glided down from her face to her eager breast and ribcage, making her quiver as he reached the sensitive dimple of her navel.

Still fascinated by the images in the magic glass, she reached out and took his meaty phallus in her hand, caressing the wet tip. It grew larger, and she continued to slide her palm over the throbbing shaft while she watched the story unfold, saw how he rescued Allegra and Medea, saw the passing of the years. Dimitri's father died and he returned to claim his inheritance, that frowning, grim castle in the mountains that she had already visited.

'The peasants did not suspect you weren't human?' she asked.

He smiled darkly, saying, 'They are serfs who have been loyal to my family for generations. They don't ask questions of their prince. If the villagers find some of their kin weakened or even dead, they do nothing about it. The gypsies know, of course, but they respect the *nosferatu*. I am their liege-lord and they obey me. In any case, I'm hardly ever at home... wandering the world, educating myself, and there is so much to learn. I'll show you wonders you've never dreamed of in the next century and further. And, if you care to travel back in time, I'll take you to Egypt when the pyramids were being built, or England at the construction of Stonehenge.'

His fingertips descended to her inner thighs, and there he paused, saying with a chuckle, 'I like the feel of you depilated mons, but think I'll make your bush grow.'

'You won't disappear again?' she begged, feeling she would go mad if she lost him now.

'I promise,' he vowed, his voice ringing with sincerity.

'Why did you come to me in London?' she asked as he moved down, his lips and tongue skimming over her hip bones. 'I didn't know you existed.'

Taking her ankles in each hand he raised her outstretched legs and began to bite at her heels, soft nips of firm teeth that worked their way down to the backs of her knees and then her thighs.

'Ah, but you did,' he answered, his breath warming her buttocks as he lifted her so that she lay supported by her shoulders, her legs parted as he described sweeping arcs round each cheek. 'Somewhere inside yourself you remembered. Didn't you daydream of a prince on a white charger who would bear you away to his kingdom, where you'd live happy ever after?'

'Girlish fancies,' she gasped, as his tongue crept towards the hidden arse hole, then up to the swollen, juicy folds of her labia and finally touched her clitoris.

'More than that,' he glanced up, his lips silvered by his saliva and her juices. 'You called to me and I came, in the same way that I answered you tonight, even though I was still recovering from the wound inflicted by the comte.'

'I thought you couldn't be harmed,' she said, her voice

breathy as he sucked her bud between his lips, working his tongue-tip over it.

'I allowed myself to be in that situation,' he answered seriously, looking at her from between her legs. 'I wanted to prove my love, risking destruction. Had his rapier speared me to the wall or floor, I shouldn't have been able to escape dissolution. You would have seen me turn to dust before your eyes. Destroyed, as your fiancé would destroy me.'

'Where have you been since then?' she moaned, and a long wailing cry followed her question as he stroked her nubbin dextrously.

'Lying low in a crypt on the island of San Michele,' he replied, adding with a laugh, 'Belphegor found me there and, having recovered his temper, made me drink from him to regain my strength. He's not so bad really, and has now accepted you. My wound quickly healed and I'm whole again.'

'And he won't play any more tricks?'

'No, my darling. He has promised to dance at our wedding celebrations,' he assured her, concentrating on fingering her slippery niche.

'And where will that be?' she cried brokenly, her body shaking and racked with pleasure.

'At my castle. Where else? My followers will come from far and wide. Fellow vampires, witches and warlocks... even those who are mortal but admire us.' He sounded jubilant, as if his wildest dream had come true.

Then he stilled suddenly, an unnatural stillness, his head angled towards the windows. These were tightly shuttered and swathed in heavy curtains. No chink of light could possibly creep through, but he seemed to sense the faintest reddening of the sky and sea that heralded the coming of the sun.

He was like an animal, using animal senses, so lean and male and feral, reminding her of the wolves with whom he claimed to run.

'It is time, and you must bear what is to come. Blows are archaic magic, marks of election and initiation,' he said huskily, and pulled her up, slipping invisible bonds over her wrists and securing her to the foot post, with her face pressed into the curtains.

She had not expected this – but then, when had he ever done anything but surprise her?

Unable to see what he was doing, she heard him step back, and shook with anticipation. What was he about to do? Ravish her nether hole, or her vagina?

For a while he did nothing but run his hands over her back and trace the curves and hollows of her body. She moved and tried to wriggle against him, wanting to contact his flesh, but he held back, though she felt his touch in her most intimate places – inside her core – giving her deep, visceral pleasure.

She cried out in rapture, but he hushed her and carried on with his exploration of every part of her, melting her flesh, muscle and bone, even seeming to bare her very soul.

When he struck her the shock was cataclysmic, the whip a serpent, stinging and biting. Her hips twitched, her knees lifted and she danced in agony. She set her teeth and clasped her tied hands. The nails dug into the palms as he lashed her again. Though she could not see what bound her, the whip was real enough.

She writhed and mewled, then jerked and screamed as the searing agony was crowned by another blow. Her buttocks were only just recovering from Henri's caning, and now they smarted anew, the black whip descending, too fast to follow, driving into her flesh, biting and burrowing, a bright red line left behind each time the lash fell away.

It was Dimitri whipping her – not Henri or Miss Turner. Her master was subjecting her to anguish only to raise her to the pinnacle – his queen-bride who would hold sway, as he did, over the Kingdom of the Undead.

Though she still moaned and bucked and threshed, this

was the turning point of her life. Now she dedicated herself to him, and in so doing found peace.

Dimitri dissolved her bonds and caught her in his arms as she collapsed. He lowered her to the bed and entered her in one swift, numbing thrust. This was real, no phantom penetration, and she yelled as her body expanded to take him, slick-wet and ready, the membrane rupturing with ease.

She had been there before, done this before, but on the astral. This was the first she had been physically invaded by a penis and he took her ferociously, unable to be gentle, too long frustrated, and she gloried in his brutality and need. His superhuman strength, wildness and lust, fired and melted her. She tried to move, but was crushed by his weight as he pounded into her with ravaging intensity.

Ecstasy thundered through her loins as his rough strokes forced her against the bed head, her clitoris throbbing as she pushed her pubis down to meet his cock at every inward stroke. She cried out as his weapon went deeper, opening her as if trying to become a part of her. The air resounded with their savage cries and the slippery, sucking sound of his frenzied invasion of her love channel.

She screamed as she exploded in a violent orgasm that tore her to pieces, and felt the sudden torrent of his icy libation released inside her. She beat at his back with her fists, clawed at the flesh, and then he braced himself on taut arms, staring at her so fixedly that she drowned in his flaming green eyes. With a sigh he sank down, and his teeth fastened in the pulsing vein at her throat.

Candice felt the fractional resistance of skin, then the incision and the hot rush as he drew her life-blood into himself. Swooning, she gave herself up to him utterly, another orgasm bearing her to the peak, sapping the last iota of strength. Her pulse hammered in her ears, the room spun and she was spiralling in a desert wind, riding the dust-devils until he lifted his scarlet-smeared lips from her skin.

'Now,' he commanded, pulling her up till she lay in his arms. 'Now, beloved. Drink of me.'

Candice felt his hand gripping her head firmly. Then he drew his forefinger across his bare chest, the sharp talon slicing into the flesh, a thin red stream welling up.

She was savagely hungry for this nourishment, striving to ingest it, her tongue lapping greedily at the acrid tasting liquid. It burned her mouth, shot like fire into her belly and along her veins. She yelped and rubbed at her lips with the back of her hand, then, unable to resist the frantic thirst, sucked at Dimitri with the avidity of an infant at the breast.

She drank and drank, until at last she lost all conscious awareness.

He watched her body die, tended it with all the care and respect of a mortician. He was weak. She had been thirsty and drained him to the limit. Dawn was almost upon them, that time when he must regain his strength through sleep.

To see someone transform from human to vampire was an awesome spectacle and one to which he had never become hardened.

She suffered, writhed and moaned, her lips curling back from her fangs like a she-wolf's. As the process advanced, he carried her to the bath and laid her in warm water in which he had dissolved a brew of sacred herbs. And, as her body perished, so it voided its waste products and he washed these away till her flesh was fragrant and clean, purified by perfumed oil, musk and myrrh.

When she became quiescent at last, her breathing stilled, he wrapped her in a thick white towel and dried her thoroughly, every inch of skin, each orifice, each strand of her hair receiving his devoted attention. Now she was a corpse, pale and still and cold, as beautiful as a waxen effigy, hair curling luxuriantly about her shoulders, the soft floss regrown on her mound.

Dimitri swaddled her in a black silk shroud, pulled the

curtains round the bed so that it became a catafalque and lay down beside her. Only then did he allow oblivion to overtake him.

Candice knew she had been far, far away, on a long journey. She could remember pain, the vomiting and purging, the dreadful agony as her body underwent the dramatic metamorphosis, her ears ringing with a babble of voices speaking in different tongues, drifting, fading. There had been music, too, like that which she had heard before when with Dimitri.

Then there was a blackness so profound that she knew nothing until awakening to find him beside her, smiling radiantly into her face and coiling one of her springy ringlets round his forefinger.

She was dazzled by the brightness of her vision, everything so much sharper and clearer than when she was mortal. She could hear with extraordinary keenness, each tiny burr of a fly's wing, the slightest stirring of a breeze, the sibilant whisper of cloth, and voices in the markets and squares of Venice. All were exaggerated.

'Don't worry, you'll learn to control this. Welcome to eternal life,' Dimitri said softly, and leaned over to kiss her lips. The feeling was extra sensual, a bolt of excitement darting through her epicentre.

'Is it done?' she exclaimed, rising from the black silk that covered her like a pall. 'Do I look different? Can I see myself?'

'Only in a crystal ball or scrying glass, mirrors won't reflect you now,' he answered, smiling at her eagerness, loving and indulgent. Man or monster, he had attained his heart's desire.

'Let me see,' she demanded, like a child waking up on Christmas morning.

He offered the magic glass in which she had seen his past last night. She gazed at the distorted image of herself – wild-haired, more beautiful than she had ever been – her eyes glittering, her face deathly pale but with flushed cheeks and crimson lips.

'I'm hungry,' she grated, and her teeth flashed, the canines long and sharply pointed.

'It's evening. You've slept all day,' he remarked, watching her with all the delight of a doting lover. 'I'll show you how to choose your victims and feed. I will have to help you, at first. There are several silly legends concerning us, mostly gleaned from unreliable sources. We don't dislike garlic, and some of us have no objection to crosses or things pertaining to the Christian faith. We do sleep in the dark, sometimes in coffins, and we can become all manner of things, particularly mist and dust motes. We can read thoughts and hypnotise humans, other animals, too. You'll learn it all soon.'

'Where are your sisters?' she asked, leaving the bed and trying out her new skills, that lightness of body that enabled her to float to the ceiling and circle the room. 'Everything looks so different from up here,' she shouted, laughing, and landing on his shoulders with her legs wrapped round his neck.

'I'd forgotten all about them,' he cried, one hand on her thigh the other clapped to his brow. 'They're in the cellar. Have been for some days. I was punishing them.'

She slithered down and came to rest behind him, sliding her arms round his waist and running her tongue along the curve of his spine. 'Will you punish me, too?' she murmured seductively, and reached lower to feather her fingers through his pubic bush and weigh his swelling penis in one hand, the other cupping his balls.

'If you need it,' he growled and spun round, his grip strong and menacingly tight.

Now she was on the floor, her legs kicking up around his back as he entered her with aggressive strokes. Gripping her breasts, he drew her closer to him, and then rolled over so that she was on top of him. She clenched her arms round his neck, her fingers digging into the smooth skin. He angled himself beneath her, his cock an upright rod penetrating her so hard that it felt as if he pierced her vitals, heart and brain.

She settled into position and, pressing down on his shoulders, lifted her hips a little, feeling his foreskin slide over the purplish head as her vulva fastened round its tip. She poised there for a second, intensely aware of the spasms of pain and pleasure that shot through her body. Holding herself above him, she sank into the bottomless pits of his eyes.

His face was like that of a tortured saint, expressing his desperation to be enveloped by her heat again, but she rode him gently, taking in the helm, then releasing it – up and down, teasing his glans. He exclaimed impatiently, but she put her hand over his mouth, then fell on him in a single movement that engulfed his weapon. He grunted and bit into her hand as his cock twitched and his cold semen gushed into her.

She released her grip on him, tasting blood as she licked the bite. Conflicting sensations shot through her – the sharp pain in her hand and the freezing inrush of his spunk.

She slithered to her knees away from him, their combined juices smearing his thighs. Dragging herself from the floor, she began to lap thirstily at the creamy ambrosia glistening on his belly before she moved towards his phallus and took it into her mouth.

'Not only me... you should enjoy, too,' he whispered and lifted her so that they lay across one another, his lips to her genitals.

When, once again, they reached a conclusion in which the physical and spiritual were blended, the hunger for nourishment asserted itself and they rose and dressed.

With the theatrical flourish of a magician producing a rabbit from a top-hat, Dimitri flung wide the doors of wardrobes filled with clothes from which Candice could take her pick. Next he showed her how to move around by merely wishing herself to be somewhere. This was a knack not easy to acquire, but when he took her hand in his, she found herself standing in a vault under the palace.

'You bastard! Where've you been?' the princesses screeched, so hideous that Candice did not recognise them at first.

There were chains everywhere and the vampire women tangled in them, their withered bodies crossed by bloodily oozing stripes, their nipples inflamed, their sex lips raw, the juices of their arousal dripping, musky and pungent, to the damp flagstones.

Shadowy figures moved around them making high, keening noises. Hideously formed, their hands slid over the dangling bodies, claws and forked tongues invading cunts and sphincters, winding sexual sensation higher and higher but bringing no relief.

Dimitri stood, spread-legged, before the groaning princesses and said, sternly, 'Has the lesson been severe enough? Do you promise to behave?'

'Yes, yes. Set us free...' they implored.

'I want you to aid Candice. She is one of us now, but will need you to show her how a vampire queen comports herself,' he ordered, striding round them, and flicking over their wasted limbs with a taws which he had snatched from one of his demon henchmen.

'I'll do it. She'll be my precious sister,' whined Allegra, her fiery hair dulled to sullen embers.

'And I. No one knows more about fashion than me,' Madelon promised, a skinny replica of her former golden, dimpled self.

'I will share my wide knowledge of magic with her,' Medea offered, a sunken-eyed hag, with a tangled mane of white hair where her raven locks had once been.

'Let them go, Dimitri. I'm sure we'll become friends,' Candice begged, saddened by their loss of beauty, and disgusted by the weird creatures that gambolled and gibbered as they tormented their prey.

'As a favour to you, darling,' he murmured, kissing her fingers.

In a position of command in the centre of the cellar, he raised both arms wide and chanted a spell to dismiss his hellish assistants. The vault emptied immediately, with only a faint stink left as a reminder that inhabitants of the nether world had been there.

The princesses fell in a tangled heap on the wet stones. They righted themselves and leapt towards Candice, snarling like voracious beasts.

'No!' Dimitri cried, and even she cringed at the steel edge of his voice.

His green eyes darted flames, his face was white with sharply etched lines and his black brows swooped down in a terrible scowl. With a sweeping gesture he hurled the sisters against the wall.

'But we're starving,' Allegra protested, the boldest of the three. 'And haven't the strength to hunt.'

'Take him,' Dimitri answered, and immediately Carl was standing in the cellar.

Snarling and champing their teeth, fighting to be first, the vampires closed round the tall, lean servant, dragging him to the ground. They spread themselves over him like lionesses on a kill, covering his body with bites, while he lay there, eyes closed in blissful acceptance.

They sucked and fed and writhed round him, rubbing themselves to orgasm, then taking his penis in their mouths and drinking of the nectar that fountained from it. With each drop of liquid obtained from Carl, so they began to change until at last they were fully restored to their youth and beauty.

'Ah,' Madelon looked up from the half-conscious man to sigh, 'That's so much better,' and she ran her fingers through her waving mass of white-blonde hair.

'Now we can hunt in earnest,' added Allegra, licking the tip of Carl's helm to obtain the final trickle of semen. 'I'm rejuvenated. Even stronger than I was before. A beautiful youth next, I think. He can fuck me and then I'll drink from his balls.'

'Dear Carl, he's always ready to oblige,' cooed Medea, nipping his foreskin. 'But we've drained him, I fear, and he'll be of no more use tonight. Time to move on.'

They twirled and appeared momentarily attired in flowing robes and glittering gems, then linked arms and disintegrated.

'Now it is our turn,' Dimitri said, smiling into Candice's eyes. 'You have a lot to learn, and the first is how to pass through solid objects. We did it just now because I guided you, but soon you'll do it on your own. It's simply a matter of willing yourself. In time, it will become as natural to you as breathing did in your former existence. But now for feeding. I'll choose the spot, so take my hand and come with me.'

Too quickly for her to register more than a swift blur, they were standing on the quay where the ferries that operated between the islands docked. Dimitri, materialising as a debonair gentleman in evening clothes, complete with opera cloak, walking cane and silk hat, paced the cobbles with Candice on his arm.

She, too, was dressed in the last extreme of fashion, her full taffeta skirt held up fastidiously in one gloved hand, clusters of rubies at her throat, in her hair and banding her wrists, a fur stole slipping with studied negligence from her bare shoulders.

To the casual observer, they looked like a couple of wealthy hedonists seeking sensation in the seamy side of Venice.

The choice was varied, every vice catered for. There were prostitutes of both genders and the shady areas of sexuality between, bars and gambling saloons, brothels, and dens offering the Lotus Land enchantment of opium. Dimitri and

Candice were not the only upper class visitors to this teeming, colourful quarter.

They entered a restaurant and soon Dimitri was stalking their prey, an effete young Englishman and a pretty, well-dressed American girl who were standing at the bar.

'What a balmy night,' he remarked pleasantly, striking up a conversation with them. 'Are you staying in Venice long?'

'A month,' the young man replied, smoothing a hand nervously over his slicked-back brown hair, not quite as sophisticated as he pretended. 'My name's Robert Segar, just finished at university and sent on a tour of Europe by the parents, and this is a friend, Miss Penelope Kerr, from New York. Stunning lass, don't you think? And her daddy's a millionaire.'

Candice could not but admire the way in which Dimitri manipulated the pair. It was like taking sweets from a baby. Within a very short space of time he had spoken to the head waiter, flung a handful of notes on the bar, and swept them off to a private room, where cut glass goblets awaited and a magnum of champagne stood in an ice bucket.

'Are you really a prince?' the toffee-haired New Yorker asked breathlessly, gazing up at him with admiring eyes. 'I've never met a real live prince before.'

'I truly am,' he replied, holding her hand and raising it so that his lips rested briefly against the vein throbbing at her bare wrist. 'Have some wine, Miss Kerr.'

'Thank you, your highness,' she gushed. 'Is that the way I should address you? How grand.'

'Whatever pleases you, my dear,' he answered, using all the charm and persuasion at his command.

'What would really please me is to have you exert power over me, prince,' she stated boldly, a free-speaking, confident young woman. 'I sure would be thrilled if you dominated me a little, maybe spanked my bottom.'

'That can easily be arranged,' he replied, and in an instant had her spread over his knee. He flipped back her skirts, displaying her long legs in black stockings, the white thighs above the lacy tops, and soft silk French knickers.

She squealed in mock protest, but pressed her belly against his lap as he pulled down her crêpe-de-chine drawers and slapped his palm, full force, on her bare behind.

'Oow! Oh!' she cried, and tears sprang into her eyes, but she ground her pubis harder against Dimitri's leg.

'Penelope!' Robert shouted, his eyes bulging at the sight. 'I say, old girl, why didn't you tell me that's what you wanted? I'd have been happy to oblige.'

Dimitri righted the flushed and tearful young lady, and pulled her between his strong thighs, holding her captive. 'I can pleasure you in other ways,' he said, in that low, mesmeric voice. 'Will you submit to me?'

'Oh, yes, prince... whatever you say,' she sighed.

'And you, Candice? Do you behave like this, too? Is it true that you're a lady?' Robert asked, the encounter between Dimitri and Penelope causing mayhem in his crotch.

'I sometimes like him to punish me, and yes, I am a lady,' she answered with an innocent smile, while listening to Dimitri's mental instructions:

'It won't be long, my love. Like lambs to the slaughter, they'll soon be providing us with that vital essence. Watch me. I'll show you what to do, but first, lull him into a sense of false security. Rouse him as I've just roused her. The blood flows more sweetly of they're excited.'

Candice ran her hand lightly over Robert's body, tracing the buttons of his waistcoat, then down across the fastening of his fly. There her fingers met the throb of his cock. From the corner of her eye, she could see Dimitri fondling Penelope's breasts, while she stared at him in fascinated awe, like a rabbit before a snake.

Ultra-sensitive now to the emotions of others, Candice knew the girl's clitoris was swelling, parting the lower, brown haired lips, and Robert was possessed of the driving need to plunge his cock into the cool velvet of Candice's sheath. As she stroked him through the fabric of his trousers she was amused to see the sweat breaking out on his upper lip.

Judging that this had gone far enough, Dimitri made a single pass over their faces, and the couple were inert. He smiled encouragingly at Candice and, using Penelope to demonstrate, leaned over her throat, punctured the artery with his fangs and fed. Her head fell back, she sighed rapturously and fainted in a welter of bliss.

Dimitri raised his head and said, 'Now you,' to Candice.

By this time she was desperately hungry and knew she could not put off the unholy communion any longer. Dimitri guided her mouth to where he had left two small puckered wounds over the vein in Penelope's neck. The sight of them sent lust flooding through Candice and, growling, she fastened her teeth in the same place.

As the life-giving fluid pumped into her mouth, she gasped with a pleasure as intense as orgasm. Reckless joy bounded through her. She was exalted, her satisfaction immense. She had reverted to an animal – hunting – feeding off its prey, a hot tide of jubilation carrying her away.

'Enough,' Dimitri said brusquely, his hard hands pulling her off Penelope. 'We don't want to kill her. Now for Robert.'

He opened him in the same way, and Candice drank greedily at the warm gush of blood. Again Dimitri stopped her before the young man's heart ceased to beat.

'They'll wake with no memory of what has happened, thinking they've had a thrilling, rather risqué adventure when two attractive strangers brought them to ecstasy,' he said, arranging the couple comfortably on the couch, then picking up his cloak and hat.

'I want to feed again,' Candice complained sulkily as the wonderful sensations faded, leaving her with an edge to her appetite.

'Tomorrow,' he whispered and held her tightly. 'We'll go back to the palace and be in our bed at dawn, there to gratify other needs. Though we have forever in which to make love, I want to do it now.'

Who could deny that great dark being his will? Certainly not Candice. He was her Lord of the Universe to worship and obey.

Dimitri had ensured that although Candice had gone, there would be no hue and cry. He had simply used his hypnotic powers. No one missed her. They acted as if she had never existed.

'But I must see them… Emma at least, and tell her that I'm a vampire and with you now and that we're about to leave for Transylvania,' she insisted when they woke the next evening.

'Oh, very well. I couldn't have made them forget you for always anyway. This is not possible,' he conceded, so enchanted with her that he would have given her the sun, moon and stars had he been able.

Candice fed, selecting her victim for herself this time and finding it surprisingly easy, supping with the careless rapture of a lioness who has just pulled down a zebra. Then she wished herself on a visit to her friends.

It was useful to be able to see in the dark, and strange and wondrous were the things she observed as she drifted past the Palazzo Mancini. Fabian was crawling naked at Esmeralda's feet while she dragged him along by a leash attached to a spiked collar, kicking and abusing him, with her other slave, Gaston, in tow.

At the comte's palace, she found Bianca spread out and tied to a whipping-post. With leather straps crossing her breasts and clamps fixed to her nipples, she endured, her fiery hair tumbling across her face, as Henri flogged her and then plunged his fingers into her vagina, using her brutally and forcing her to reach a climax.

At the top of a house in a decaying square she eavesdropped on Flora Smythe and Giacomo wrapped in a close embrace, his penis resting between her legs and partially erect against her glistening vulva. They slept and Candice smiled, reading their dreams of a bright future and giving them her vampire blessing.

She visualised the Hotel Danieli, and was there, seeing Gwenda Turner in a white nightcap with the moon shining full on her upturned face, the rod still clenched in her hand and a servant girl, welts forming on her rump, lying between the ex-chaperon's thighs, her head pillowed on the hairy mound which she had been pleasuring.

As she had half expected, Emma was asleep in bed with Clive sprawled beside her, their attitudes ones of satiety.

'Emma,' she called from outside the window. 'Dear friend, let me in.'

She saw Emma stirring, tossing restlessly from side to side, not even comforted by the feel of Clive's nakedness. She repeated her weird, ululating wail, 'Emma... Emma...'

It echoed, filled the starry vault of heaven above beautiful Venice, but none heard it – only Emma.

'Candice? Is that you?' she asked sleepily, clawing her way to the surface. 'Where have you been? I'd forgotten... I don't know. What's happened?'

'I'll tell you if you ask me in,' Candice whispered, and even the voices of the vampire sisters could not have been more enticing.

'Yes. Of course. The window is open,' said Emma and rose, dragging a flimsy negligée over her nudity.

Her eyes still fogged with dreams, she stared in alarm as Candice floated some three feet off the floor.

'Don't be frightened,' she said, and ran light fingertips over Emma's crimped nipples. 'I'm still me, although I've become as he is.'

Emma goggled and turned pale, reaching behind her, finding the daybed and sinking down on it. 'Candice! You haven't! But how... we were so careful...'

'You can't prevent magic, or stop the course of true love,'

Candice said, her voice as clear and sweet and cold as if carried on the winds from the Alps. 'I was destined to be his, and now we are wed. I've experienced death, and the joy of feeding, but nothing compares to the glory I've known in his arms.'

'What will happen to you now?' Emma said, shaking her head as if still enmeshed in dreams. 'And what are we going to tell your parents?'

'I've thought of that. Fabian must say, and you and Clive back him up, that I eloped with a foreign prince. I shall write now and again, and they are not to worry. I'm happier than I ever thought possible,' Candice said, and flirted her fingers through Emma's hair. 'You're welcome to Clive, if you want him.'

'I'm not sure. I envy you in some ways… you've found freedom,' Emma cried, and clung to those ice-cold, almost translucent hands.

'If ever you're tired of human existence and decide to thrown in your lot with us, then all you have to do is call me and I'll be there,' Candice said earnestly. 'In any case, I'll visit you sometimes. You will have things I can't. The sunshine, the daylight, and children. Vampires don't breed, and I'll miss this. I would have so liked to give Dimitri an heir.'

'And being damned? Doesn't that worry you?' Emma questioned as they sat, curled up together on the couch as they had done so many times in the past.

'No. I've never believed what the church taught us. And if I am damned, which I somehow doubt, then Dimitri will be also, and we'll not be parted.'

'Shall I wake Clive? Do you want to say goodbye to him?'

'No. It's only you I care about.'

Candice kissed Emma's mouth, and whispered, 'Goodbye, and don't forget… if you ever need me… I'll come to you.'

Then she stepped out into the night and Dimitri's arms.

Emma ran to the window. She was not tired now, but her new alertness could not cut through the strangeness that permeated everything.

Looking out, she saw them standing in the air in front of her, that diabolical pair of lovers.

Like cut-out figures, sharply defined, they were attired in garments symbolising travel to a cold country. Dimitri looked savage, untamed and barbaric in baggy red breeches thrust into top boots, his shoulders rendered wider by a wolf-skin coat, a fur hat cocked at an angle on his black hair.

Candice clung to his arm, draped in a swirling purple velvet cloak that mingled with the sky – trimmed with sable, the surface scintillating with gems.

Emma thought she heard a storm brewing, but the moon was full, every pane of glass holding its bright face in miniature. The noise became different – no storm now but the howling of wolves.

She stared and stared, and her fingers gripping the balustrade were colder than the stone itself.

'Candice…' she sobbed. 'Come back.'

They ignored her, turned away, became absorbed in each other and the darkness, and then disappeared, leaving a little glow behind like an extinguished candle flame.

The Instruction of Olivia *by* Geoffrey Allen

Victorian England. A voluptuous vagrant, Olivia, is sentenced to hard labour in the notorious House of Correction. Discipline and punishment are freely administered, and Olivia finds no respite from either the birch or the amorous embraces of the sexually frustrated inmates.

When released, she unwittingly embarks upon a journey that takes her into the dark underworld of London. Although determined to remain pure, Olivia gradually discovers her own desires, and finds resistance increasingly difficult.

But who will be the one to gain access to what has always been denied...

Flame of Revenge *by* Josephine Scott

There is a burning reason behind the Master's directive to his slave to use her candle spells to entrap six very different women, and then to arrange for them all, one at a time, to visit the ordinary looking house in Oxford, where extraordinary passions are aroused and dreams are broken under the influence of pain.

The Switch *by* Zak Jane Keir

Stephanie is a dominant woman with two regular partners and a sex life well under control. However, when she meets mischievous submissive Poppy, who persuades her to change places with her temporarily, and hide out with a biker gang, she has to play the submissive's part – and play it convincingly.

Meanwhile, Poppy is set on causing as much trouble as possible, in the hope of getting the punishment she craves.

Captivation *by* Sarah Fisher

When Alex Sanderson is commissioned to paint a mural on a remote Greek island, everyone is expecting the artist to be a man – not a beautiful English girl called Alexandra. Warned to leave by her mysterious employer's housekeeper, Alex finds herself caught up in a complex game of passion and punishment.

Humiliated and passed from hand to hand, Alex embarks on a dark journey of self discovery – a willing participant in her own Captivation.

Sweet Punishment *by* Amber Jameson

Humility was born to be a slave.

Transported from West Africa to Haiti, she is everything Vicomte de Salace could ever wish for. She is obedient and eager to please, which makes it all the more unacceptable when Henri, his body slave, has the temerity to take her for his own. Punishment for Humility is swift at the cruel hands of Baron Samedi, the voodoo god of Death.

When cane fires later destroy two neighbouring plantations, Humility is offered as a sacrifice to appease Papa Zaca, the god of the fields…

Afghan Bound *by* Henry Morgan

Involved in voluntary medical work abroad, David Harper finds himself caught up in the Afghanistan war. His adventures there bring him into close contact with the cruel torture of prisoners.

Escaping death by inches he finds himself in Iran, where he witnesses captured slaves displayed for pleasure in an Arabian night-club and learns that, properly trained, women can find immense pleasure too.

Returning to England he is introduced to some submissive women, and sells his share in a medical practice to create a training centre. All is going well – until a woman turns the tables on him…

Olivia and the Dulcinites *by* Geoffrey Allen

Abandoning her philandering husband, Olivia enters a world rife with superstition and depravity: the convent of Saint Dulcinea, reminiscent of the Middle Ages, when harsh discipline and torture ensured absolute obedience.

Under the constant supervision of the nuns she is subjected to continual punishment and humiliation. Gradually she learns the true and terrible purpose of their intentions, which are not only for her benefit, but to ensure the survival of the convent.

Olivia is driven to desperate measures, but the nuns are always one step ahead. Perhaps there is no escape from the dark terrors of the Dulcinites...

Belinda: Cruel Passage West *by* Bryan Caine

19 year old Belinda Hopeworth has to find her way, alone and penniless, across the America of the 1850's in search of her uncle, her only salvation after her secure and loving home collapses with the ruin and imprisonment of her family.

Beautiful and cultured, but somewhat naive, Belinda finds that America is a harsh land whose colour, character and erotic cruelty cause her much inner conflict as she falls foul of a variety of villains, deviants and fiends, most of whom are extremely eager to help her on her way – in return for certain favours...

Thunder's Slaves *by* Drusilla Leather

Max Cavendish thinks his brother Jonathan's archaeological expeditions are pointless and boring – until he realises the latest one will give him a chance to get his hands on Jonathan's submissive girlfriend, Justine. Together with a beautiful and sexually inventive American doctor, they are heading for a mysterious island, once a Viking settlement but now dead and forgotten.

Only the island isn't dead, and the warriors who live there have their own plans for Justine. Their attempts to free her from slavery and make an escape will cause all the members of the expedition to confront their darkest sexual desires...

Schooling Sylvia *by* Roxane Beaufort

Miss Sylvia Parnell, a beautiful heiress, leaves Bath and the Academy for Young Gentlewomen for Regency London. There she resides under the guardianship of her aunt, Lady Rowena.

Sylvia's innocence and wilfulness present an irresistible challenge to the worldly Rowena. Correction and punishment are routine in this unconventional household, until Sylvia flees, stumbling naïvely from one frightening adventure to another...

Under Orders *by* Lesley Asquith

Innocent Carol, in debt and striving to promote her depressed husband's success as an artist, is recruited into a secret society by the sadistic Max Alexandrou. Submitting to strict discipline as a means of furthering her husband's career, can she eventually savour the sweet pain/pleasure of humiliation?

Bending to the iron will of others – male and female – Carol must undergo punishing tests and ordeals to discover her own true nature.

Twilight in Berlin *by* Axel Deutsch

To a young woman of twenty, Berlin seems the ideal place to pursue her long cherished career as a model. But it is 1930, and the city is a hotbed of vice and corruption, where pleasure-hungry men and women go to any lengths to satisfy their lustful ambitions.

Ingrid is swallowed up in the dark underworld of the vice trade. In a sinister, twilight world where life is cheap she soon learns the price of staying alive.

Net Asset *by* Jennifer Jane Pope

Jobless Lianne Connolly takes in model Ellen Sanderson as a lodger. Ellen talks her into standing in for a colleague who has fallen ill – but this is no ordinary photo shoot. Lianne meets Nadia Muirhead, the driving force behind a team dedicated to creating the world's most erotic comic-strip, with Lianne and Ellen as the rubber clad heroines-in-distress.

But events take a disastrous turn when Lianne is kidnapped, and finds herself having to recreate her role for the mastermind behind a scheme to bring the comic-strip to the Internet.

However, this time there are two essential differences – no salary and no choices. This time it is for real!

Willow Slave *by* Toya Velvet

Seventeenth Century Japan under the Shogun. Life is lived by strict rules.

Beautiful, submissive Ejimo is sold to a brothel by her penurious father, where her sweet ways and demure manner quickly make her a firm favourite with the clients; rich merchants and Samurai alike. Her beauty is such that it even claims the attention of the Shogun himself.

Tasks are set to test her loyalty, bravery, endurance and sexuality. But as her term of slavery draws to an end will she return to her village, train as a samurai, or agree to become an obedient wife?

Sold into Service *by* Madeleine Tanner

1788. Betty, wilful, beautiful and lusty is taken into service at the manor ostensibly to pay off her violent stepfather's debts, in reality to satisfy the Squire's demand for yet another virgin bride.

Here she undergoes a variety of degrading but delicious sexual practices: voluptuous punishment at the hands of the debauched Squire, the intimate attentions and inquisition of the corrupt priest, and the constant humiliations of a collection of bizarre servants. All are part of the Master's nefarious plan for her ultimate defloration. Should she remain a victim of the Squire's outrageous but compelling proclivities or leave?

With conflicting feelings Betty decides she must flee... but can she escape?

Exciting titles available now from Chimera:

1-901388-20-4   The Instruction of Olivia   *Allen*
1-901388-05-0   Flame of Revenge   *Scott*
1-901388-10-7   The Switch   *Keir*
1-901388-15-8   Captivation   *Fisher*
1-901388-00-X   Sweet Punishment   *Jameson*
1-901388-25-5   Afghan Bound   *Morgan*
1-901388-01-8   Olivia and the Dulcinites   *Allen*
1-901388-02-6   Belinda: Cruel Passage West   *Caine*
1-901388-04-2   Thunder's Slaves   *Leather*
1-901388-06-9   Schooling Sylvia   *Beaufort*
1-901388-07-7   Under Orders   *Asquith*
1-901388-03-4   Twilight in Berlin   *Deutsch*
1-901388-09-3   Net Asset   *Pope*
1-901388-08-5   Willow Slave   *Velvet*
1-901388-12-3   Sold into Service   *Tanner*
1-901388-13-1   All for Her Master   *O'Connor*

Coming soon from Chimera:

1-901388-16-6   Innocent Corinna   *Eden (July '98)*
1-901388-17-4   Out of Control   *Miller (Aug '98)*
1-901388-18-2   Hall of Infamy   *Virosa (Sept '98)*
1-901388-23-9   Latin Submission   *Barton (Sept '98)*

All the above are/will be available at your local bookshop or newsagent, or by post or telephone from: B.B.C.S., P.O. Box 941, Hull, HU1 3VQ. **(24 hour Telephone Credit Card Line: 01482 224626)**.

To order, send: Title, author, ISBN number and price for each book ordered, your full name and address, cheque or postal order payable to B.B.C.S. for the total amount, and allow the following for postage and packing:
UK and BFPO: £1.00 for the first book, and 50p for each additional book to a maximum of £3.50.
Overseas and Eire: £2.00 for the first book, £1.00 for the second and 50p for each additional book.

All titles £4.99 (US$7.95)